GOODNIGHT, TEXAS

it may not have been fair, but if you'll have the right attitude. Instead at being a setback, it'll be a set up for God to do something great in your life.

— Joel Osteen

ALSO BY WILLIAM J. COBB

The Fire Eaters, a novel

The White Tattoo, short stories

GOODNIGHT, TEXAS

William J. Cobb

Unbridled Books

Unbridled Books
Denver, Colorado

Library of Congress Cataloging-in-Publication Data

Cobb, William J. (William James), 1957-
Goodnight, Texas : a novel / William J. Cobb.
p. cm.
Hardcover ISBN-13: 978-1-932961-26-3
Hardcover ISBN-10: 1-932961-26-7
Paperback ISBN: 978-932961-44-7
1. Texas—Social life and customs—Fiction. I. Title.
PS3553.O199G66 2006
813'.54—dc22   2006016143

1   3   5   7   9   10   8   6   4   2

Book design by SH • CV

Originally published as an Unbridled Books hardcover.
First paperback edition, 2007.

For Elizabeth

Global climate change will affect the physical, biological, and biogeochemical characteristics of the oceans and coasts, modifying their ecological structure, their functions, and the goods and services they provide. Fluctuations in fish abundance increasingly are regarded as a biological response to medium-term climate-ocean variations, and not just as a result of over-fishing and other anthropogenic factors. With global warming and sea-level rise, many coastal systems will experience accelerated coastal erosion, elevated sea-surface and ground temperatures, [and] increased levels of inundation and storm flooding.

· CLIMATE CHANGE 2001, INTERGOVERNMENTAL
PANEL ON CLIMATE CHANGE

It is said that animals are presciently aware of impending seismic doom. Catfish jump out of water. Bees mysteriously evacuate their hives. Hens stop laying for no apparent cause. Mice appear dazed and can be caught by hand. Deep-sea fish are found at the ocean surface.

· SIMON WINCHESTER'S KRAKATOA:
THE DAY THE WORLD EXPLODED: AUGUST 27, 1883

He remembered lying on the floor of a cabin, looking up at the famous gunfighter Texas Jack Omohundro, . . . and clearly seeing there wasn't anything anywhere but the two of them, that they were the two parts God had made everything else out of.

He'd said, "Jack, you and I are what everything else is made of."

Texas Jack was working on a bottle of his own. He'd said, "You want the truth? I hate Texas."

And Charley said, "See there? That's just what I'm talking about."

· PETE DEXTER'S DEADWOOD

GOODNIGHT, TEXAS

❧ 1 ☙

THE SEA WAS RISING and into it Goodnight was sinking. Along Red Moon Bay the pink beach houses on stilts loomed
above the lapping water like boxy wooden flamingos. Resort homes
flooded and were abandoned. As the water rose it seemed to hold
nothing but pulsing white jellyfish. The world bloomed with rust
and Goodnight became a fishing village without fish. Every day the
shrimpers left dock and plowed the waves with their nets, bringing
home a harvest of nothing. In the smokeblue aquarium world of the
bars, they drowned and argued.

They went broke slowly, slowly enough to see it happen to each
other and to enjoy it, to enjoy the notice and the watching of it.
They thought about leaving and doing something else for a living,
roughnecking maybe, but the oil rigs were mostly shut down and
weren't hiring.

They considered sinking their boats for the insurance money.
They rubbed their faces dramatically and took a long time to an-

swer if you asked them something, even a simple question like How ya doing? They smoked too many cigarettes, argued, fought, and hid from the wind outside that made the bay waters choppy and frogback green, their boats strain against the moorings in the docks.

That September Gabriel Perez arrived late for work as a hand aboard the *Maria de las Lagrimas.* The bonewhite fifty-footer was at the boat basin in Goodnight, moored in its boatslip under a blue-eyed sky. Laughing gulls floated and jeered above it. The morning wind already furrowed the waves of Red Moon Bay into sliding jade trenches topped with frothy whitecaps. The captain, an Anglo named Douglas, sat on the tailgate of his rusting pickup, sipping coffee from a Styrofoam cup. He had an Abe Lincoln beard, ears like conch shells, and the skin of weathered planks, like a poor man's Ancient Mariner.

Gabriel pulled his El Camino in beside him and got out, held his cigarette in his lips, tucked his rubber boots under one arm, and took the keys from the ignition. He walked up to Captain Douglas, squinting from the smoke drifting into his eyes. Across the street a terrier barked, chasing a sooty cormorant from its perch on a creosote post. A Latina woman in an apron stood a few feet away, tossing french fries to the bird, who caught them in its beak.

Gabriel set down his boots and took the cigarette from his mouth. Sorry about being late, he said. Car wouldn't start.

The captain sipped his black java and squinted back, looking up at Gabriel and into the sun. Save your heartfelt sagas of mechanical failure for some other job, he said, his voice boozer rough. This morning arrives the proverbial pink slip.

Come again?

You heard right the first time. We're officially out of work.

Gabriel cussed, spat. He said it figured. The minute I fucking woke up, he said, I knew this was not my day.

Douglas nodded and sighed, like a drought farmer regarding a tumbleweed. He explained the owner had informed him that morning that he'd decided to sell out, couldn't afford the costs of diesel and their pay with how little they'd been catching. They couldn't compete with the shrimp farms in Brazil, raising them for half the price it cost to catch what few were left in the Gulf.

Fucking Brazilians, said Gabriel.

My sentiments exactly.

Gabriel drop-kicked his rubber boots into the pitted asphalt of the dockside road. He shook his head and walked in a tight circle toward the El Camino and then back. Finally he said, What do we do now?

Douglas believed that to be a good question.

Something else, he said.

Gabriel thought about it for a minute, squinting into the heat-lamp sunlight. They stood silent and stricken. The crawdad smell of Red Moon Bay engulfed them. On the surface of the water near their boatslip, beside the hull of the *Maria de las Lagrimas,* floated a white rubber glove like a severed hand, in a rainbow sheen of diesel, beside a pair of dead minnows.

What do we do now? began Douglas. He smiled like a mortician about to detail the price of caskets. I suggest something that does not involve fish.

ABOUT NOON GABRIEL was back near the docks. He found a place in the mother-of-pearl oyster-shell parking lot of the Black Tooth Café. He'd been drinking for two hours, Tecate with whiskey chasers, but had brushed his teeth to fool the world, down-shift his rage-a-holic transmission into sweet and innocent. In his present blurry condition his movements were like a Tejano gun-slinger, deliberate and pointed.

He checked his face in the rearview to make sure he was com-posed, handsome as ever, teeth straight and white, black hair thick as a brush. He was in his early twenties and perhaps losing that lousy job was the best thing that could happen to him.

When he stepped out, he watched his reflection, liking the way he looked in the window glass of his gold El Camino. Things would work out. He was young. He had potential. Plus he owned a car the color of good tequila. He smoothed back a shock of his hair and straightened his bushy eyebrows, then stood as tall and straight as he could for being a bit on the short side of things.

He headed toward the door and grimaced, noting the license plates of the vehicles filling the lot. Wisconsin. Minnesota. Saskat-chewan. Iowa. The place was full of old Yankee tourists and if there was one thing he hated it was the fucking tourists. Fucking old white tourists. Snowbirds. They were always smiling and friendly. They lived their whole fat lives in good moods. They had pink noses and white hair like lab rats. The only thing they needed now was whiskers and a cage. They discussed the flavor of gumbo like it was the weather or local gossip. Like *I think the gumbo is especially good today, don't you? Just the right amount of shrimp. And the okra! You can't get okra like this in Madison!* It was enough to make you want to jab an oyster knife in a snowbird's gut.

Staring at all the Northern license plates in the parking lot, Gabriel felt like Sitting Bull at the Little Big Horn.

Good moods came easy to these Yankee tourists. They had all

the money they needed and then some. Gabriel spat on the tire of an RV from Michigan as he passed by. Stepping into the Black Tooth, lost in his brain, in his *enojo sombrío,* he calculated a vehicle like that must cost a hundred grand, easy.

Behind the counter stood the owner of the Black Tooth Café, a Russian émigré named Gusef Smurov. He saw the steady demise of Goodnight as an end of this world. But he knew another would arise in its place. Gusef could always recognize the sooty under-feathers of bad times. When the old fisherman Mr. Buzzy had his leg amputated after a catfish wound infection set in, Gusef helped him more than any other person in Goodnight. To cheer him up he said, Yes well think of money you will now save on shoes.

Gabriel walked in and took a place at the counter. He stared at the menu in fake concentration, as if pretending to read the Gospel of Luke and not getting what all the fuss was about. His face took on a resemblance to the bronze statue of a *vaquero.* He wore blue jeans, workboots, and a plain white T-shirt. Around his left wrist was tattooed a bracelet of mesquite thorns, no wider than a pencil. The barbs of the thorns were graceful, blue and sharp.

Gusef asked how he was doing.

Gabriel did not look up from the menu. He said, You want to know the truth?

No. But this you will tell anyway.

The truth is I lost my job. The owner is throwing in the towel on the shrimping business.

Gusef looked out the window and shrugged. Yes well it is not such bad thing. So you fishermen catch no fish. You will have more time to drink. Or stay at home and get much amusement out of shouting obscenities at your wife and gruesome children.

This time Gabriel gave the Russian a sharp look. Not me, he said. I don't have any wife or children.

Perhaps someone is lucky.

Gabriel put down the menu. You think you're a funny man, don't you?

Perhaps you should learn to take joke, Mr. Tough Guy.

Maybe you should tell one, said Gabriel. He looked around the dining room. Is Una here?

She is here but has no time for love talk. She is busy now.

I'll wait, he said.

Before long a pretty girl walked up and put her hand on Gabriel's arm. She was four years out of high school but so small she could have passed for a junior high student. Her hair was blue-black and shimmery, like grackle wings. Her lips the pink of boiled shrimp. She brought Gabriel a glass of iced tea with two lemon wedges. She wore a plain blue dress and flip-flops. She'd lived in Goodnight all her life, but her father was Vietnamese, her mother Mexican. Her name was Una.

She touched Gabriel's cheek and asked him what was the matter.

He told her how he'd been laid off. The injustice of it all. How the *pendejos* could have given him some warning. It wasn't right. I'm not worthless, he said in a loud voice. They treat me like I'm nothing, less than nothing.

Una made a pained face. She said, I'm sorry.

Well so am I, said Gabriel, but it doesn't matter. He started to go on about the coldhearted bastards that owned the shrimpboats, but Una took a step away. She said, I'm kind of swamped.

Okay. Sure. Go.

Don't be like that.

Like what?

Have you been drinking?

Don't start, okay? He directed his attention to the menu. Who's the new guy?

What new guy?

The one in the apron.

Oh. He's just a high school kid. He's not new. He's been here a couple weeks already.

First I've seen of him.

He got kicked out of school.

For what?

He got caught with a knife. In class.

Shit. I did that. You didn't see me getting kicked out.

Well. He did.

What makes him so special?

Gabriel? I'm kind of busy right now?

He reached over and squeezed her hand. Don't worry. I'll be here.

She nodded. I better go. I have orders.

Sure, he said. Don't let me keep you from feeding *las turistas.*

He went back to considering the menu. After a moment he realized she had not even asked what he wanted to eat. A grilled cheese would have been nice.

Beside him at the lunch counter, perched on a stool as pleased as punch, sat a chubby bald man with a white beard, wearing a loud red and yellow Hawaiian shirt, khaki shorts, and sandals. He looked like Santa Claus on vacation. He beamed at Gabriel and said, The gumbo is wonderful today. I don't know how they do it, but really, it's to die for. I give it four stars.

Gabriel looked at the white-haired tourist without smiling. In a low voice he said, If I was you but I knew what was going on in my head? I think I'd just scoot the fuck over and shut the fuck up.

The Santa Claus man quit smiling and moved away.

THROUGH THE ROUND ship's portal window in the door that divided the kitchen from the dining area, Falk Powell stood watching. He'd only been working at the Black Tooth for two weeks, an orphan and seventeen years old. He watched Una bend and wobble in the orbit of the shrimper Gabriel, the tough dude, who in Falk's eyes seemed small and sinewy as a snake. A snake or a monkey. All wiry limbs and veins bulging beneath golden skin, a simian brow. To him Gabriel resembled the other bullies in school, Anglo or Chicano, goons who grew angrier as they grew older, as they realized that with each passing day their backs got closer to the wall.

When Una returned to the kitchen for a dessert order he followed her into the walk-in cooler. She was getting a slice of key lime pie for a customer. They kept the pie in the cooler beside a stack of chilled white plates. Falk pretended to be searching for something, standing near her in the cold air. He picked up a bucket of cherry tomatoes for the salad bar.

Una? Why do they call you that?

It's my name.

But why?

She scooped a slice of the key lime pie onto a plate with a spatula. Maybe because I'm the one.

He considered this. He said, I should have known that.

What?

You being the one.

Standing that close, Falk could smell her perfume. To him it smelled like fabulous Vietnamese flowers and he had never been to Vietnam. When she turned to leave they squeezed close.

I think about you, he said.

She could not help but smile. She felt sorrow for this misfit. His parents dead and gone, living at his cousin's, expelled from school as dangerous. His was a story of misfortune and *mala suerte.* When any soul with eyes could see he was gentle and quiet and only needed to be loved. He should be suckled like a child, pampered with *dulces,* and made to laugh.

With one hand she held the key lime pie carefully away from her body. She put the other hand on his chest, against his white apron smeared with mustard stains. You think about me?

I do.

She stared at his lips. What do you think?

I remember you.

She kept her eyes leveled on his mouth, then stood on tiptoe and lifted her face to his lips. They kissed once and pulled away, then Falk pulled her hips close to his and kissed her again, her mouth opening like a hot flower, the smell of her breath, a taste of sweetness, her lips warm and smooth. To Falk it felt as if he had stooped to enter a tunnel where all the world faded away and there existed only the here and now of her scorching lips, her smooth muscular tongue in his mouth. All his flesh tingled and dimly he was aware of how she held the plate with its slice of key lime pie away from her body, her tiny feet lifted out of her flip-flops, his hands on the small of her back, feeling the swell of her hips through the thin cotton cloth of her blue dress.

When they separated she pushed him away softly, still looking at his lips, whispering that she had to go. She left him there in the walk-in cooler. In this coolness his body still tingled, and he struggled with the surprise of the moment, the before-and-after-ness of it. After a moment he left the walk-in carrying a tray of breaded shrimp.

Gusef stood outside the door, shaking his head. You should not love this girl, he said. This woman. She is good person but that does not matter.

Falk stood there, holding the tray of breaded shrimp in front of his body. He looked up to Gusef and listened to what he said. I was just getting some shrimp, he said.

She is like sun. She will blind you.

Falk simply stood there, blinking, the smell of Una's kisses still with him, a loose smile on his mouth making him appear slightly drunk.

Gusef reached out and tapped his forehead. Wake up, silly boy. You will love her and you will end up dead. And this you will regret from dark hole of wisdom called grave.

As Una moved into the dining room, glancing at the occupied tables to see who was ready for the check and who needed iced-tea glasses refilled and who looked like they wanted her attention, she savored the taste of Falk's kiss on her lips. She would have to lie to Gabriel. She would ridicule Falk as nothing but a boy. A *güero* who didn't know nothing. She would hate these words, the words that would come out of her mouth, a mouth still warm with the taste of the boy's sweet tongue.

A person can be nice. Nice and tender and soft-spoken. He was the opposite of this one, Gabriel, a man and harsh to all but her. She hated and feared lying to him, the lies she felt compelled to tell and, for the moment at least, to believe herself.

For a good two years Una had felt something like love for Gabriel. She knew the stories about him and thought most of them exaggerated. People liked to have a badass around to make them feel high and mighty about themselves. Everybody knew he'd stuck a knife in Pedro Alamogordo's gut, but that was considered by most a positive civic development. Still she knew in her heart and veins that Gabriel was a man upon whom she could not count. Plus he had an anger problem. Whatever feeling Una had that might have been called love was now worn thin and weak, the memory of a good time one night long ago followed by a year of bad ones.

At the counter Gabriel now sat alone. He ate a bowl of gumbo, crumbling a fistful of Saltine crackers into the bowl. He thought about what the tourist had said and didn't get it. Gumbo was gumbo. Shrimp and crab, okra and spices, tomato and basil. There was no mystery. He thought the tourists were full of shit and wanted to turn around and shout at them, tell them they should go back to Minnesota or Manitoba or any of those other cold fucking states that started with an M. Let them know they weren't wanted. That they were out of place.

He held his tongue. Una walked by and he knew she was pissed at him for drinking in the middle of the day, something she hated. The next time she passed he told her he'd be back to pick her up at the end of her shift. She asked where he was going and he said he didn't know. He needed to think.

Gusef watched Gabriel leave and frowned. He saw right through his skin to the darkness of his soul and the clouds in his brain. He told Una she should find somebody new. He said, This angry fisherman, no.

Una told him she needed him to run a credit card for table four.

Gusef seemed swollen with romantic and moral indignation. He will not do, said Gusef. I speak truth. He has two ideas in his head, and it is crowded.

DOWN SHORELINE DRIVE from the Black Tooth Café was the Sea Horse Motel, also owned by Gusef. It was a two-story eggshell stucco beside the green and sluggish Red Moon Bay. Wrought-iron railings and red shingle roof. Cheap enough that when people checked in and signed the old-fashioned register it was like a release form for no complaints. Its claim to stylishness was the fanciful figure of its neon sign—an elaborate sea horse, the name in script above the matching icon with its amber stallion neck and spiny emerald mane. The loopy letters of the neon grapefruit script in the office window usually read Vacancy.

Walter Hamilton—the tourist Gabriel had insulted in the Black Tooth—and his wife were staying at the Sea Horse. They had recently arrived in Goodnight for the fall and winter months. Walter was retired and considered his life one of ease and refinement. He saw no reason for Gabriel to threaten him. For two hours afterward his hands trembled. He drove back to the Sea Horse in his RV that was big enough to accommodate a touring rock band. He told his wife he was going fishing.

I don't care if there's anything in the water but jellyfish and old crab traps, he said. At least I'll be alone.

She watched him leave and wondered what in the world.

Before heading to the pier Walter bought a Dr. Pepper from the motel's vending machine in a breezeway near the office, beside the ice machine. He removed the twelve-ounce can from the machine's low mouth and hid it in his tackle box. Being borderline diabetic he was supposed to avoid unnecessary sugars but he couldn't help himself. Dr. Pepper was just one more thing he was hiding from his wife.

India Hamilton was a righteous woman and did not stand for foolishness. She believed in discipline. Drinking soda pop was not altogether sinful but certainly undisciplined and if she had seen Walter with the can he would have caught the sting of her tongue.

India's hair, like Walter's, was white as snow-goose feathers. Her skin was pale and crinkled, befitting a healthy woman sixty-six years of age. Together India and Walter resembled Mr. and Mrs. Claus and, what's more, they owned a farm in Minnesota that raised Christmas trees.

With the Dr. Pepper hidden in his tackle box, Walter brought India a bucket of ice before he left for the pier. She asked if he was all right.

Your hands are shaking, she said. Have you had your pills?

I've taken my pills.

Then what's wrong?

I don't want to talk about it. I'm going fishing.

She turned back to the newspaper crossword she was doing at the table in the Sea Horse Motel's kitchenette. As he was leaving she said, The fish won't listen.

On the pier Walter Hamilton skewered a dead shrimp on his treble hook and cast into the frothy green waves of Red Moon Bay. He set the Dr. Pepper can on the bleached planking beside him and squinted into the wind. Sunlight reflected off the water in bright spangles. He watched the waves, the fractured glass way they rippled and broke against the barnacle-encrusted black pillars of the piers. Drawn to the smell of sugar, a red wasp flying above the waves landed in the mouth of his Dr. Pepper can, crawled inside, and began to sip.

Walter did not notice this.

He was mesmerized by the breaking waves against the pier pillars, distracted from his anger with Gabriel, how the wave shapes were so geometrical. He saw in these shapes the hand of a gentle and creative God. India had been on a Jesus kick lately. He didn't know what to make of that, but he feared fervent believers. Too much of that, next thing you know you're barricaded behind a bullet-riddled crucifix, daring the feds to come in and get you.

After a moment he remembered his thirst and took a sip from his soda can. As he gulped the wasp inside stung his bottom lip. He felt a piercing jab and flung down the can, swiped at his mouth, swatting the pulpy body of the wasp into the waves. He whined in pain and groaned. His right hand began to shake with palsy.

A couple walking down the pier stopped and asked, Are you okay?

Walter nodded. Something stung me I think.

The man said, Ouch.

The woman grimaced. She noticed Walter's eyes watered and pink. Are you allergic to bee stings? Let me look.

Walter took his hand away and she made a face. Oh, my. It's starting to swell. You should get that checked out, don't you think? You might need a shot or something?

Walter dropped his fishing pole and headed toward the motel, holding his mouth in pain, feeling it begin to swell. He half worried he was being punished by a touchy God who knew his angry thoughts, his faithless doubts.

As he was walking he kept his eyes on the water, his face downcast and shamed from the sting. Near the end of the pier he saw something odd beneath the bubbled froth at the waves' end. He stopped and stared. A new wave's froth obscured it. Then came a clearing in the swells. There. A huge zebra-striped fish was beached in the shadows by the pier pillars, washed in by high tide. The biggest fish he'd ever seen.

In their hotel room, India was still doing her daily crossword puzzle. She was quite good at it, considering it her mental exercise, and was already halfway finished when Walter walked into the room with lips like little inner tubes. His face was red and blotchy. She called the front desk and asked for directions to the nearest hospital. Gusef was there. He offered to drive them, as it would be faster. He liked this old couple who had just arrived and wanted them to stay the season. He owned the RV park behind the motel and told them it would be perfect, a home away from home.

On the way to the clinic Walter told Gusef about the huge fish. He insisted he'd never seen anything like it before, that it was undoubtedly something remarkable. While waiting at the clinic, Gusef called the Black Tooth Café.

THIS WAS NOT the only Goodnight in Texas. Another town called Goodnight stretched wide its dry and wind-chapped lips in a coyote howl on the Llano Estacado of the Panhandle. It was a tiny one-horse town east of Amarillo and north of the windblasted cliffs of Palo Duro Canyon, near the famous JA Ranch, a million-acre spread founded by Colonel Charles Goodnight in the 1880s. Goodnight by the Sea shared this history, although it was a one-time gig. On an early trip rounding up wild longhorns from the Mexican brushland of South Texas and heading toward the Brazos River area, Goodnight and his men had veered east during a spate of torturously hot weather to hug the coastline, where the wind off the Gulf and the summer rains kept the air cooler.

The land was flat and easy from the saddle. The shadows of turkey vultures marked the herds trail as the birds circled in the cloudy sky or caught the updrafts and floated ahead of the scudding thunderheads. Coyotes skittered at the edges of the herd, occasionally chased away by the bigger wolves. Mosquitoes in the swamps sucked the blood from man and steer. The small town starting to form at the edge of Red Moon Bay grabbed the name of Goodnight, hoping to lure the cowboys back to the coast, for the business. But it didn't work. Only the name stuck.

Because of the duplicate names, the coastal town was officially Goodnight by the Sea, the seat of Mustang County. Mustang Island and the glitz and hubbub of Corpus Christi lay to the south. Texas being as huge and lanky as it is, Goodnight by the Sea was a good six hundred miles south of Goodnight in the Plains, so there wasn't much confusion over directions.

The people of Goodnight had lived with the blessings of the sea for many years, for generations. They had grown used to it. They had grown complacent. When the fishing and the shrimping declined, they reasoned it was just bad luck. A lull. A year or two of sea drought. These things come in cycles. That was what they told each other. Next year would be payday. The big kahuna. The drunk-with-money stroll on Easy Street. If they didn't go broke and toothless in the waiting. If their boats weren't repossessed. If the puffy pinkfaced vampires at the bank didn't get their grubby mitts on them, things would work themselves out. They always did.

But this was the year the light of Goodnight was fading. The planet was overheating. In summer the sea turned warm as mustang blood. Rain fell in torrents as if this sunny, windy coast of Texas were the Congo or Borneo. Ditches filled with an algae-green mix of brackish rain and swamp water. Alligators crawled through backyards, beneath rusting swing sets and barracuda wind kites, slept in the shadows of boat trailers. The deep green St. Augustine grass of the lawns grew so fast you could almost see it, feel it squirming beneath your feet like sand crabs. Oleanders bloomed pink and lush as mutated sea anemones. At night people couldn't sleep from the ungodly chorus of croaking frogs.

The sweetheart Gulf of Mexico turned mythical and suspicious. Bottle-nosed dolphins beached themselves on the oyster-shell shores of Tin Can Point and Humosa Bay. Dead loggerhead turtles washed ashore like huge sand dollars. Huge swarms of mosquitoes filled the sky in gray clouds, and some of Goodnight's oldest died from West Nile.

Gusef realized a giant fish beached near the Sea Horse could be useful. He decided to call Falk Powell, the high school kid he'd hired a couple weeks before, at the café. Falk was a teenager who would take pictures of people when they weren't looking, wandering the aisles of Wal-Mart, say, or filling a tank at the Speed-n-Go. People shouted and threatened to kick his ass from one end of town to the next, but that didn't make him stop.

Falk dried his hands on his smudged apron and answered the ringing phone. Leon the badmood bartender, whose ex-wife was known for wishing death and ruin upon him, advised Falk that if anyone asked, he wasn't there.

The dim interior of the clapboard seaside café glowed in slow-motion gloom. Beer signs cast green shadows on the walls decorated with mounted trophy marlin and swordfish. At a table nearby Una was folding napkins, sitting as straight as if she were playing an invisible piano. In the soft light of afternoon she was so beautiful one could imagine she must have broken many hearts, men turned into fish and left to swim sadly beneath the pier lights, hoping to catch a glimpse of her.

On the phone Gusef said, These pathetic stinking fisherman are joke. They cannot catch own dick with both hands. You show them. You take your camera and get photo.

Falk said okay, he would check it out. He hung up the phone, got his camera bag from beneath a kitchen table, and told Una the scoop. Why don't you come along? he asked.

Una arranged the silverware to fold another napkin. I'm supposed to wait here for Gabriel. He should be by soon.

Oh, come on, said Falk. What are you, his servant?

No.

Well then.

You shouldn't say that.

I did.

You shouldn't.

Come with me. It won't be the same without you.

Una finished rolling the silverware, tucking the white cloth dinner napkin just so.

Okay, she said. I guess. If we hurry.

This was after lunch, when things were slow. Only Mr. Buzzy lurked mumbling and burping in the bar, so Leon said he'd hold down the fort. He believed whatever washed ashore couldn't be good. He expected a calamity nothing less than an asteroid or comet.

The doom patrol is heading our way, he said. I got a nose for these things. You find anything washed up there'll be trouble. Those parks and wildlife sumbitches are going to be looking for somebody to blame, and it ain't gonna be me.

Falk and Una walked to the end of the dock, hopped onto the sand beyond the concrete bulkhead, followed the shore. Falk led the way, pushed along by the buffeting wind like a boozy sailor. He was tallish, stooped and gangly, like a young Jimmy Stewart.

He carried his old Nikon with black-and-white film and stopped to take a shot of Una standing under a pier, striped with pillar shadows, her hair wild in the wind, her face moody. The sky was lumpy and mottled gray, the color of stingray bellies. Above them hovered a pair of black buzzards, canting into the wind, gliding, circling back. They flew so low you could see their wrinkled red faces, like winos awakened by barking dogs.

The stiff wind buffeted Falk's white apron, blew Una's black hair in her face, filled their skin and ears with the whirling sound, the smell of salty catfish breath. Una made a slight motion, a muffled hiccup. Her hand to her chest.

Ooh, she said. Enchilada burp. When she saw Falk point the camera again she shook her head no, put her hands over her face. Don't you dare, she said. I look awful.

Are you kidding? You couldn't look awful if you tried.

Oh, hush.

I mean it, he said.

What do you know? You're a boy.

Falk squinted into the wind, his camera lowered. He turned around to look at Una, walking backward. They left two trails of footprints in the sand. Hers were like the brush strokes of a master artist. His were wide and ungainly, like the prints of snorkel flippers. He said, It's not always about glamour shots.

They found the sea monster stranded halfway up the fine white oyster-shell fragments of the shore. From a dozen yards away it didn't look like much of anything. A curdled raft of cinnamon-speckled sea foam floated against it, making the form beneath the surface appear like a black-and-white fishing skiff sunk in the shallows.

Up close it came into focus. It swelled into an improbable mass of enormous wide-mouthed fish. Big as an elongated VW Beetle, its scales striped with a black-and-white zigzag pattern, enormous black jelly eyes distended and swollen, ragged tail fin the size of a small whale's. The wide mouth spanned the entire width of its body, some three to four feet, and had decayed into a bleached white strip, as if the enormous fish had coated its lips with zinc oxide.

Falk shot photographs low angle and above, walked out along

the Sea Horse fishing pier for a bay-water view. Maybe this is what's eating all the shrimp, he said.

Una stooped, tucked her skirt against the backs of her knees, looked into its mouth. O dear God, she said. There's something inside. Something with legs.

Falk moved near, set his camera on the shore. With a piece of driftwood he pried the white-lipped mouth open wider and peered into the shadowy grotto of its gullet.

At first he thought he was seeing a drowned girl. Skeins and swirls of hay-colored hair streamed out of the great fish's throat. He saw pale skin and what he thought was an ear or an open mouth. Only by bending closer did he realize what was there.

The hell, he said. It's a horse. A small one. Like a colt or a Shetland pony I guess.

In the fish's throat the small horse's head faced nose first, its mane swirling forward, one hoof protruding aslant.

Una turned away. She said she couldn't look at that. Why did she come down there? What was she thinking? It was horrible, what it was, and there was nothing they could do. I'm leaving, she said. I better get back before Gabriel shows up.

No, said Falk. Please? Just stay a minute? The excitement of it made his voice spike and quaver, struggling to be heard over the wind. See? Everything for a reason. If I was in school I wouldn't be here to see this.

You'd maybe be learning something.

Ha. That's a good one. He returned to the shore and leaned in for a close-up of the zebra-striped scales, the ridiculous white-lipped mouth.

You shouldn't be proud, said Una. Being kicked out of school. It's a mistake.

Did I say proud? Put your hand right here. I need something for scale.

I won't touch it.

Who's asking you to? I just want you close. Is that a sin?

She was smiling then, looking out at the waves, the bleached bones of the pier, sea creature in foreground, rocking in the pulse beat of tide. You, she said.

The bay shoreline was speckled white and gray, deep with tiny pieces of broken oyster and scallop shells. Fine bits of shell covered the flayed skin of the fish. Flies buzzed around its enormous, distended eyes. It smelled gamy. Falk and Una had to pinch their nostrils shut and gulp the air like beached groupers. He guessed the colt had come from the mustang herd on Isla Pelicano, the shelter island across Red Moon Bay. A mustang colt that had somehow drowned. When the huge fish tried to scavenge it, the body became lodged in its throat and killed it.

It was probably desperate because it couldn't find anything else to eat, said Falk.

I told my cousin Dat the fishing around here is done for, said Una. They should rename it Desolation Bay.

Falk squatted close to the colossal fish and focused on the drowned colt, one dark eye visible in the shadows of the fish's throat. The sun was off angle for good light, but he squatted to take another photo anyway. The wind died for a moment. Without the rush and tumble of air in their ears, the sound of the lapping waves seemed amplified. A mosquito lit on Falk's hand as he was focusing the camera.

Don't move, said Una. She leaned close and swatted the back of his hand, leaving a smear of blood. Oh, it got you.

Falk wiped his hand on the back of his jeans and went back to taking pictures.

You should have that checked out, said Una.

In the last week alone several people in the area had been hospitalized with West Nile virus. Two had died the month before.

Falk scratched the bite and frowned, a puzzled monkey face crossing his pink cheeks, his pale blond fuzz of hair. It'd take more than a mosquito to kill me.

Una reached down and rubbed Falk's hair. You think? I don't know. Sometimes I wonder if we're the next to go.

Falk laughed. What a morbid thing to say.

She touched the tip of one stiff spiny zebra fin with the toe of her shoe. It's true, isn't it?

Well, I mean, go as in split town or go as in float belly-up?

I don't know. You make the call.

Falk reached up and squeezed her hand. Myself, I thought we'd be elected something. Prom king and queen. Most likely to appear on the cover of *Coastal Living*. That kind of thing.

Una squinted at the fish, then turned her face away, letting the wind blow her hair into her eyes. Falk couldn't see the look she was wearing.

Maybe we should, she said.

FALK AND UNA returned to the Black Tooth, heading into the wind now, a gush of ocean spray dampening their faces. It was early fall or what passed for it in that part of Texas, warm, but they were used to it. The light was still flat and bright, the sky a water-color blue, as of a swimming pool at a motor court. There was a hurricane in the Atlantic again. Mustang County officials had ordered an evacuation in July when one had come close, but it had swerved and hit landfall south of Galveston, so the whole thing seemed a dud. This new one was two thousand miles away and beyond their worry radar. The live oaks along the sandy hills the other side of Shoreline Drive leaned away from Red Moon Bay, bent and shaped by the constant wind off the water, saltgrass waving knee high at their trunks. The sky full of gulls and terns, sandpipers and plovers pecking the shore.

For a moment Una held Falk's hand, then smiled and let go, the warm Gulf air making them sweat on contact. She warned him about Gabriel. He could drive up any minute now.

Like I care, said Falk.

You should, she said. He could hurt you.

Falk shrugged. So could you. He gave her a look. Plus, I been hurt before.

Back inside the Black Tooth, the café's fishnet-festooned bar was dark, Leon the bartender smoking a cigarette and moody behind the counter, the only customer Mr. Buzzy, the old one-legged black man leaning back from the table like a windblown oak, only the breeze warping him came from bottles.

Mr. Buzzy said he knew he shouldn't be drinking this early in the day. But it was too late to stop now. Hell, I been doing it so long I can't remember when I started. No point in getting downmouth now is there? What good is that?

His nose was purple-black, broken-veined, and shaped not unlike the saddest, smallest bell pepper. His hands shook when he spoke. Falk wanted to hold them to make them stop, but that was something you just didn't do. He couldn't imagine actually touching such wrinkled claws.

What Mr. Buzzy loved and what Mr. Buzzy knew how to do was to fish. He knew where to find the flounder, in the shallows, in the salt flats at night, perched in a skiff, an open-face saltwater reel under his thumb, a limber rod casting its thin shadow in the moonlight, tinged with gold where the Coleman lantern cast its glow.

He never spoke about children, wife or brother or sister, but everyone imagined his family must be miles away and dead most likely. All he had in the world was the brew he loved to drink and the fish he caught.

He gestured for Falk to come close.

You oughtn't be out in public like that, said Mr. Buzzy. Wearing an apron like that. Like an old wartneck woman makin' biscuit gravy. People start thinkin' things. He spoke in a husky voice that descended into a phlegmy laugh.

Falk grinned and considered his food-besmudged apron. Right, you got a point. But, I mean, I can't stop people from thinking, he said. If they commence to talking, you let me know.

I will do that, said Mr. Buzzy.

Falk asked if he needed another beer. Mr. Buzzy closed his eyes and said, Like a hound needs howlin' lessons.

Tell me somethin', he added. What you and that sugar-tush waitress gal doin' walkin' outside? Now don't lie to me. He winked and waved his cane gently, like he expected a story not necessarily factual or accurate.

Falk explained about the enormous dead fish. How huge it was. How it had a white colt in its maw, probably drowned from the mustang herd on Isla Pelicano. What a strange and fabulous thing. The black eyes staring from beneath the green water's lightspangled surface, the clownwhite lip skin peeling away.

That's not a good thing, said Mr. Buzzy. No sir. Where is that fish? I need to see this with my own two eyes.

A quarter-mile down shore. Beside the Sea Horse fishing pier.

That's too far, said Mr. Buzzy. He held up his stump, the empty sheath of his old khakis pinned back, his leg severed above the knee, the squat thigh muscular and unnatural looking through the faded tan cloth. How the hell am I supposed to get there with this thing? Tell me that.

Falk rubbed his nose and made a noncommittal sympathetic don't-I-know-it-and-then-some face like he had no answer to a question such as that but he understood why it might be asked. He suggested perhaps a ride could be arranged.

Mr. Buzzy shook his head like he'd had enough, maybe too much. It's gettin' to be where a man can't move from one place to the next without some advance plannin' and strategizin'. Ain't that the hell.

Falk asked Leon if they had a shovel out back or somewhere.

Why's that?

Falk said it just didn't seem right, letting the fish wash up on the shore like that. You know it would end up buzzed by flies, baked by sun, stinking to high heaven. Least he could do would be to plant it in the dark.

Mr. Buzzy nodded Amen and said, A horse be washin' up dead in the mouth of a fish, now that's a foretellin'. Bad things a-comin'.

Maybe if we bury it nothing bad will happen, said Falk.

What? said Leon. Are you stoned or just plain foolish? It's worth money. Call the Smithsonian. D.C. White pages. They'll know.

Mr. Buzzy frowned. Don't tell those parks and wildlife bastards. Bloodsuckers. This is hush-hush, is what it is.

Falk absentmindedly started untying his apron strings. I need some better shots anyway. First I'll take another roll or two. About sunset. The golden hour.

Leon fished a pack of cigarettes from his front pocket. I'll help. We split the profits, fifty-fifty, *capisce?* You sell that to the AP wire service for money. I got a brother-in-law who works there. I'll call and set up a meeting. Get some big bucks before the weekend.

You think?

A giant fish with a horse in its craw? I know.

Mr. Buzzy waved his cane in the air. Before they started spending all this money made off a big dead fish, could somebody head next door to the Speed-n-Go and get him a pack of smokes?

I'd do it my own self, he said, but at most I be half a man. His trembling barnacled hands, like the flippers of a hoary sea turtle, nudged a cluster of coins and bills on the table top.

Falk took the cash and stepped outside, his mind filled with the idea of big money and the lazy swirl of Una's black hair, the bloom of her oleander-petal lips. In the sky above him floated laughing gulls like white paper kites.

2

AFTER WORK Falk and Leon drove a Purple Monster tow truck down Shoreline Drive to where the colossal zebrafish was beached near the Sea Horse Motel's fishing pier. The tow truck had orange flames painted on the front fenders licking to the back, a metal ramp on the rear that lowered, trucker tramp mud-flaps, and a winch to haul the monster out of its seaweed coffin in Red Moon Bay.

By then it was dusk. The road was a chain of beached whale's backs, barnacled with gravel and bumpy with potholes. The live oaks leaned away from the wind coming off Red Moon Bay, the palm fronds swayed and rustled. Leon pulled onto the shoulder, between the road and the shore. The smell of beached dead thing was so strong it radiated like heat waves off hot asphalt. In that light, dimming to gray fuzz surrounding the black silhouettes of the pier against the sky, the world was spectral and diminished.

The tide had receded, leaving most of the creature in the sand.

The stinky colossus sloshed in the shallows like a beached gigantic tropical fish. The moon was low in the eastern sky above Red Moon Bay, catching a pink glow from the sunset, like lunar blush. Falk grimaced at the smell. He dropped the tailgate and pulled on work gloves. Cars sped by on Shoreline, and one honked in complaint, the tow truck straddling one lane.

Falk and Leon walked around the fish for a few minutes, then stopped and cooked up a scheme. Inside the truck's cab they found a painting drop cloth, a sheet of clear plastic splotched with droplets of white latex wall paint. Falk unfolded it on the shore, beside the huge fish, as Leon maneuvered the winch hook into position. The wind turned the corners of the dropcloth back, so he weighed the ends down with shells.

Falk looked at the smelly tangle with reluctance. He figured it was worth something. To someone.

Leon said, If anyone asks, I had nothing to do with this.

While they were arranging the plastic drop cloth the Mustang County sheriff's patrol car pulled onto the shoulder of Shoreline Drive.

Oh fuck me, hissed Leon.

THE SHERIFF BEHIND the wheel trained his swivel spotlight on the fish and upon Leon and Falk, crouching there like thieves of the sea. They straightened in this spotlight beam and held their hands up to block the glare, seemed to be saluting.

Sheriff John Littledog uncoiled his magnificent form from the car and approached in no great hurry, his boots crunching the oyster-shell grit between shoulder and shoreline, his radio crackling in the background. He was quarter-blood Kiowa, the tallest man in Mustang County, and wore a black eyepatch over his left eye.

He'd lost the eye over a woman. It was one thing known by most every citizen in Mustang County.

He had a face you got a good look at it you knew he'd seen some good and bad times, enough to weary of steering the mistaken back to the path of righteousness. He'd been a high school basketball star years ago and still got credit for that.

Sheriff Littledog's tallness in the headlights cast a wicked shadow. He stopped near the fish, took off his hat, and rubbed his grizzled gray head. His six-feet-seven-inch frame was not without a certain grace. People told him he could have been in the movies but he frankly didn't give a shit. He put his hat back in place and said, The fuck is this?

Leon stepped forward and shook the sheriff's hand. One bigass fish is what I'd say.

Falk only nodded, crouched down, and tugged at the tarp. When he'd been caught with a knife in school, he'd been arrested and charged with carrying a weapon on school grounds to teach him a lesson. It worked. After spending an afternoon in the sheriff's jail, he didn't want anything more to do with him.

Leon spoke up. The gist of it. Big fish beached and a curious thing it was.

Sheriff nodded. That is a fact. What kind is it?

Leon shrugged. Beats me. None I ever seen or heard tell of.

Ain't that the hell. Sheriff Littledog walked around it, squatted low to get a close-up view. With the spotlight behind him his tallness cast a long shadow over the waves of Red Moon Bay.

That Oscar Martinez's truck you're driving?

Leon said yes, it was. He'd let Gusef borrow it, and Gusef had given them the keys.

Must be a special occasion, said Sheriff Littledog. Martinez treats that truck like his woman. Sheriff Littledog grinned. Or maybe his *muchacho*.

Leon said they had quite a find. He showed Littledog the horse's head wedged in its throat, the blond mane and hoof.

Well I'll be goddamned on a Sunday, said the sheriff. He shook his head. Whatever this is, it ain't right.

Can I claim it? asked Falk.

Claim what?

The fish.

Sheriff Littledog put his hands on his hips. An odd gesture, almost girlish, one hip cocked to the side. Never heard of a boy claiming a dead fish washed in on the tide before. But whatever. No skin off my ass.

You don't need it for evidence?

Evidence of what?

I don't know. The horse in its mouth?

You mean I should fingerprint the fish?

You tell me.

What we got here looks like a swallowing to me. Last I checked that ain't a crime rightly in the books.

He told them to turn their hazard lights on so some drunken fool didn't hit them while they were pulled over on the shoulder. Martinez would beat them bloody if they so much as scratched his truck. But as far as them claiming a dead fish, it was fine with him.

Leon said, Won't be stinking up the Sea Horse now will it?

You be doing the county a service, said the sheriff. With that he walked off and gave them a lazy wave. He made a U-turn on Shore-line and headed back toward town. It wasn't till the sheriff was gone that Falk noticed how fast and hard his heart was beating.

They tied a rope around the tail of the beached fish and managed to use the winch to haul it out of the water. When they got the thing scooted onto the tarp it appeared somewhat smaller. By then moon-light spangled the bay surface and lapped in silver ghost tongues at their feet. They folded the drop cloth over the fish and tied it on both ends. It was wet and slimy and smelled horrible. They wrestled one end onto the hydraulic tongue and heaved, grunted, lifted the other slumped, soggy end, and pushed it into position. Leon loosed the steel cable of the winch and wrapped it around the middle of the fish where the crushed fins created a small dent in its belly, then fas-tened the hook at the end of the cable to make fast a large loop.

They raised the hydraulic tongue and hauled in the winch cable until the giant fish sat in the middle of the flatbed of the tow truck. There it resembled an enormous bloated zebra wrapped in plastic.

They drove to Falk's aunt's house. He was living there now, his parents killed in a bridge collapse the summer before. In the back-yard was an old plastic kiddy pool that had been hauled out of a house somewhere and left behind the garage where it collected rain. No one ever used it. In the shadows of a security light mounted on the garage, Falk dumped the pool on its side, stepped back as the rainwater whooshed into the sandy yard thinly covered with grass, then realized it was too small.

He went to look for his uncle.

The backyard was Uncle Ed's territory. He was a thin, bald man, somewhat vague and underwhelmed by the routine of his life.

The fishermen of Goodnight said Falk's uncle had once been a hellraiser, forearms big as Popeye's, that in his day Uncle Ed had hauled enough shrimp out of the Gulf of Mexico to feed half of San Antonio. But his day was over. An accident had seen to that: He'd been filling his bay shrimpboat at the dockside pump on Rattlesnake Point when something had gone wrong. The pump nozzle slipped out of the tank and failed to shut off, gushing diesel across the deck and catching fire from a spark.

Now the roughs called him a gimp, good for nothing more than hauling crab traps out of Humosa Bay. A bottom-feeder of bottom-feeders. Falk stood up for him when he could, but that wasn't often. Goodnight was a town that could be mean if you listened to the wrong people.

Three squares of yellow light cast their glow on the cement outside the windowed garage door. Inside Ed was mending a wire crab trap. Falk told him what had happened and asked if it was okay if he parked it in the garage for the night.

They walked to the back end of the tow truck. The white legs of the small pony were just visible in the bluish glow of the backyard security lights. Ed leaned against the tow truck, staring at the hooves dangling out. He picked up a stick and poked at it. He shook his head. Well I be dog.

Ed dropped the stick and brushed his hands on his pants. By God it does smell don't it? Maybe you ought not to let Vicky see it. Get rid of it soon. If she sees it, she'll raise hell. I know that sure as shootin'.

Falk and Leon drove back to the Black Tooth. Gusef was eating dinner at a booth in the front room, near which a trophy marlin was mounted on the wall. He said, Where is sea monster? Tell me coyotes will not eat only fish in sea for dinner.

Falk assured him it was safe and sound. He suggested Gusef should have it stuffed and mounted, make it a roadside attraction. You can put up billboards for it on Highway 35, drum up some business.

Gusef nodded. Maybe we make money off big ugly thing. Maybe godforsaken bays are filled with it. I will show lazy worthless drunken fishermen what they cannot catch. That will make them feel good I am sure. And myself become Mr. Popular. Perhaps they vote me mayor. He took a sip of his drink. Or toss me in water with anchor for necklace.

I'm thinking more like a curiosity thing.

Gusef made a shrewd face. Yes well I should display it in Black Tooth. I will mount it above front door for all to see.

Falk rubbed the fuzz of his sunbleached hair. I was thinking something like that. Maybe after some negotiations though.

Gusef stared at Falk. He asked, What?

I was thinking of making some money off it. That's all.

Gusef nodded. He said, Well okay. You are not stupid. I could pay you.

All right.

Not very much. It is not Spanish galleon.

Well, said Falk. We could work something out.

Gusef smiled. We could.

GUSEF PROWLED GOODNIGHT after closing, thinking about the fish, what he could do with it, trying to weary himself in the dark. He drove his woebegone Cadillac down Shoreline to Pelican Way, past the darkened yards of one-story beach bungalows, beneath the yellow glow of front porch bugbulbs and utility pole-mounted security lights whose bright bluewhite beams cast wild and spastic shadows as they cut the tangled maze of windblown and mosshung live oak branches. He stopped at the Speed-n-Go for gas, filled his tank beneath the hum of mercury-vapor lights, somnambulist seagulls gliding by like memories of his divorced wife and children.

Gusef walked heavily and vodkafuzzed to the cashier, waited in line behind a grizzled shrimper who knew his name. The man turned to him like a shipwrecked fisherman just off the life raft, snaggletoothed and windburnt, and indicated his purchases with one wave of a knifescarred hand, baring a what-the-hell smile.

Chocolate milk, wine, and cigarettes. He winked and stretched forth his turtled neck. It's gonna be a good night.

Gusef nodded. Yes well one is for belly, one is for hole what is in heart, and one to call forth demons of memory.

The man clapped Gusef's shoulder and said, Goddamnit, yes. Hank Williams couldn't have said it better. He waved the sack of wine, milk, and cigarettes as he faded through the automatic glass doors.

Gusef walked to his car and settled into the seat once again. Part homeless wanderer, part feudal baron in exile. He drove past the junkyard across Highway 35, with its rusting cars amidst a thicket of palmetto and swampgrass. Insect smears cluttered his windshield and he cursed himself for not washing it at the convenience store. He circled back around to the Sea Horse.

The parking lot was quiet, but the door to Room 17 was open, a rectangle of light spilling out onto the rusted Nissan parked before it. Gusef stood outside his Cadillac and watched the open door, lit a cigarette, let loose a blue cloud from his mouth. In the office he found one of his employees, Billy Wright, about to eat a bowl of coconut sherbet.

The bossman cometh, said Billy.

Gusef adjusted the stack of magazines on the lobby coffee table. Yes well someone must make sure you do not sleep at desk. Guests do not like to see drool on counter. Or perhaps if I did not visit you would inject heroin with lowlife friends in bathroom.

I wouldn't do that, said Billy. He put a spoonful of sherbet in his mouth and savored it. We'd at least find an empty room to do it on the sneaky side o' things.

A clamor outside brought them to the windows facing the inner parking lot. Gusef opened the door and peered out, the bell above him jingling. They could hear a man shouting something unintelligible. Stomping. Slamming a door. He appeared in the doorframe of Room 17 and stepped to the rear of the Nissan parked there, its trunk lid popped open. He removed a cardboard box and lugged it inside, grunting. Gusef and Billy could hear him now. His loud voice shouting, MAYBE JUST MAYBE IF YOU DIDN'T WATCH THE GODDAMN TV SO MUCH YOU MIGHT KNOW WHAT I'M TALKING ABOUT.

Billy leaned close to Gusef. That's Crawford again, his habit of wife yellin'. He says he's an oilfield technician? Well, I'm a drummer for ZZ Top. I say he's a coyote if you catch my drift.

Gusef rubbed one eye into which his cigarette smoke had drifted. I do not like this loudmouth. His woman she deserves better.

Yes, she is a sad one, said Billy. Never trust a man who slaps his wife around, that's what I say. And this woman? If she was a flower, she'd be a black-eyed Susan.

Many things I regret, said Gusef. Letting him move here is one of these things.

Why not give him the boot?

Gusef shrugged. Where would she go?

They stood silent for a moment, listening to the loud voices, the sound of the wind rustling the palm trees along the parking lot, popping the American flag above the pool, its grommets tinging against the metal pole. A sign on the door read, AMERICAN OWNED.

Billy walked back to his place at the counter, wriggled onto the stool. In front of him was the bowl of sherbet.

Have you tasted this? he asked Gusef. Coconut sherbet. It's Leon's idea we should start serving this with every meal at the Black Tooth. Add some class.

Gusef stood in the doorway, silent.

Billy took a dainty sip from his spoon. Frowned. If you ask me, tastes like suntan lotion.

Gusef flicked his cigarette butt into the parking lot and nodded. Well yes perhaps this is good thing. If fatso tourist falls asleep by pool with mouth open, tongue does not get sunburn.

FALK RETURNED to his aunt's house to get some sleep. There he shared a room with his cousin Leesha. Her real name was Alicia Ann, but she thought the double name too hick, and Alicia too dowdy and dweebish. Leesha was the only person who knew that in bed at night Falk prayed. It was her doing. When Falk's mother and stepfather died the year before, Leesha's mother took him in. Aunt Vicky had mixed feelings about this move. She had a problem child of her own and no spare bedroom. Leesha, who slept alone in the smallest room, on the bottom of a bunk bed, wasn't surprised when he showed up. She knew her mother was a softie, with a weak spot for the orphaned teen.

Aunt Vicky made Falk move in right after the funeral. He said he could live on his own just fine, but she wouldn't have it. She claimed she'd brought him into her house to keep him from going completely wrong. That evening they were all in the living room, cluttered and cramped, newspapers and remote controls on the coffee table, videos atop the TV, shoes on the shagcarpeted floor. Falk held a duffel bag of his clothes.

She asked him, You and Leesha can share a room, can't you?

He nodded, his eyes looking away. I don't want to be any trouble.

Don't worry about that, said Aunt Vicky. It's no trouble at all.

You better not toss and turn in your sleep, said Leesha. You do and I'll end up smothering you with a pillow.

I don't think I do.

She smiled at him. I'm just kidding. I wouldn't smother you. I'd probably shoot you. She pointed her hand at him like it was a gun, shooting, making firing noises with her lips.

Alicia Ann? Let him be.

I told you not to call me that.

It's your name, girl. That's what you get called when you misbehave. Aunt Vicky gave Falk a wink. Okay then, she added. That's what we'll do. Now, honey, why don't you go unpack your things. There's towels in the pantry if you want to take a shower. Leesha, you come help with dinner.

Looking again at Falk, who was lugging his duffel down the hallway, Aunt Vicky said, Listen. I'm trusting you two to behave, sharing a room like this. You keep your hands to yourself, you hear?

Leesha said, Mom! That's disgusting.

Falk tried to smile, seeing the looks on their faces.

I remember being seventeen, said Aunt Vicky. She shook her head. Any funny stuff and you'll be sleeping outside with the dogs.

Leesha pushed her mother's back and said, Everyone's not a pervert. Like you.

The first night atop the bunk bed in Leesha's room, Falk could barely move. He had never slept so close to a girl before. Leesha was fifteen then and pretty, pale-skinned, with a black teardrop beauty mark below her left eye. Her hair was dyed the color of sunflowers, coffee-dark at the roots, parted on the side. She pinned it in place with barrettes the shape of dragonflies, and highlighted her eyes with dark mascara and blue eyeshadow. He could barely breathe around her. That first night he changed into pajamas in the bathroom they shared, and when he returned she was already wearing a floppy T-shirt. He climbed the short ladder to his top bunk and said goodnight.

I'm not going to sleep yet, she said. I'm studying for a Spanish test, *y yo estoy nada.*

Falk heard Leesha turning the pages of her Spanish book below him and could smell her scent of soap and girl's perfume.

I am nothing? he asked.

Oops. I meant, *yo sé nada.* I know nothing.

I know that.

Oh, great. Now I got a Spanish critic hovering above me.

I'll be quiet, he said.

When she sneezed, he added, Bless you.

After a while she said, This is hopeless. I'm going to blow this, big time. And you know what? *No es importante.* She turned off the light and turned in her bunk below him, wiggling the bed.

They were both quiet. He could tell from her breathing that she was awake. Sleep tight, she said faintly.

You too.

After a while she said, What are you thinking up there? You're still as a corpse.

Nothing.

I bet.

I'm trying not to bother you.

I can barely see your feet, she said. Your heels look like globs. They're so big! You're freaky.

Don't look, he said.

Do you miss her?

The darkened room was a purple color, as of a deep plush velvet curtain, a fold into which they had stumbled. Who?

Aunt Cynthia. Your mother.

He took a long time to respond. The wait for his reply was as if he were walking around the shore of a pond. Finally he said, Yes. His voice was faint and brittle. Leesha heard him and her eyes swelled, staring open-lashed at the metal grid of wires and springs above her, atop which lay her orphaned cousin.

You should pray for her soul, she said.

I do.

You do?

Yes.

Show me.

Leesha heard the bedsprings squeak, the frame creak as Falk moved above her, until his face hung upside down in the purple darkness of the room, staring at her, his straight hair hanging down like fringe. He said, You don't show something like that. It's private.

She looked him right in the eyes like she had nothing to hide or fear. His hair was funny, hanging down like that. She said, I don't believe you.

That's your problem.

Prove it, then. Get down on your knees and pray for your mother's soul.

She knew she shouldn't be saying that but she didn't care. She wanted to talk to him in the dark and it was the only thing that came to her mind. She always said what was on her mind.

His head disappeared, the bed creaked, settled. Finally he said, You can trust me.

I can.

You can.

Okay then. Sleep tight.

Later he let her see him pray. His hands together and everything. She loved him for that. She didn't know any other boy in Goodnight who prayed with feeling. Plus she liked the way he carried his camera everywhere he went, his odd photos of people and the abandoned buildings around Goodnight.

For a cousin, she could do worse.

. . .

Now, a year later, on the night that Falk and Leon pulled the enormous zebrafish from the bay, he prayed for his mother's soul, and that some good would come of the discovery of the fish. He told Leesha about the giant thing, about taking photographs of it, how Leon said they'd be worth something, maybe the Associated Press wire service would buy them. They were in the bunk bed, the lights off, talking as they had grown accustomed to do each night.

She said she'd bet money he was going to become a big-time photographer for *National Geographic* or *Time* magazine. I can tell, she said. I just know it.

Wishful thinking, he said.

You wait, she said. I just hope you'll remember me when you're rich and famous.

He laughed. After a minute he said, I doubt I'll ever be forgetting you. But just in case, you should let me take your picture.

Now?

No. Sometime.

Why would you want to do that?

Because I want to. Because you have an interesting face.

She was silent below him. Finally she said, in almost a whisper, What a nice thing to say.

It's true.

Okay then. But I might cross my eyes. Stick out my tongue.

I'll do it sometime when you're not looking.

You better not take one when I look stupid.

Don't worry. You'll be natural. You never look stupid.

I don't know about that. Make me look like Uma Thurman or Nicole Kidman. Someone glamorous and elegant.

You'll look like you, he said. Only natural. No poses.

She was silent. Falk's brain was buzzing. He lay wide awake, staring into the purpled darkness. After a while he could tell she had fallen asleep from the sound of her breathing. He could smell her soap, her musky teenaged-girl perfume. Into the dark he said, I'll take a picture of you. And you'll be beautiful in it. When you're not looking, he whispered. You won't even notice.

AT THE CANOE CLUB on Cuerna Larga Road, the sign above the door read, A Nice Place for Nice People. Still you watched your purse or your wallet. Also painted on the outside was the legend: Beer. Wine. Set-Ups. In better days the rough-hewn building had been a barn for a herd of Santa Gertrudis cattle nervous from rattlesnakes nipping their hooves.

Now the floor was mottled gray concrete, cracked and treacherous, spotty with bloodstains at the end of a spirited evening. The ceiling was lofty and black with fruit bats. From the exposed rafters dangled fishing nets and tackle, Clorox bottles used as crabtrap markers. The club's name came from an entire canoe poised above the crowd, athwart the rafter beams, beside it a jumbled collection of wooden oars.

When Una and Gabriel first arrived they waited at the door for the bouncer to check their IDs. Gabriel said, Come on, dude. We're getting to be practically regulars here.

The bouncer was wide as an ice machine and had a crumpled, dome-shaped shaved head. Rimples of fat creased his neck. He nodded them in, saying, We don't technically have regulars. All our patrons here are what you might call irregulars.

Hours later the air was blue with smoke and you couldn't hear yourself think. It had reached the time of night when all the good people were home in bed and those left standing in line at the bar wondered what mistakes had led them to this point in their lives. When and if they wondered at all.

Una sat in a booth and arranged before herself, on the sticky tabletop, a zoo of colored plastic animals. Across from her Gabriel ranted. It wasn't fair he'd lost his job. The world was going to shit. All the white assholes were ruining everything, the money grubbers. You be a cracker tourist you might as well be a vampire, he said. We should call them *las blancas vampiras*.

He leaned over the table. His face melted. His cheeks drizzled down as if he were a wax figurine in a museum on fire. *Turista, vampira,* he said. Same difference. *Lo mismo.* You suck the lifeblood out of other healthy people and turn them greedy and lifeless, except what they need instead of blood is money. Something to sell. A beach towel or an inflatable raft or a kite or a bottle of tequila. A margarita or their souls. All the same. All for sale to *las turistas.*

Una ignored him. She arranged her plastic animals. She was proud of them. Blue lions with curled tails. Orange long-necked giraffes. A red rhinoceros with a horn so sharp she wanted to poke Gabriel in the eye just to make him squeal. Pink elephants with S-shaped trunks. But she was missing something. She frowned. She needed a green monkey for her collection. *Un chango verde. Da me lo.* Just like your mother, squawking Spanglish.

She wondered who'd said that.

She had had too much to drink she did not feel good at all she

45

should go home. She watched a tray full of drinks float by and on an elaborate daiquiri glass sipped a lime green monkey. She watched it float by and after a moment realized that was exactly what she needed what the fuck! She knew what she would do. She would find out who was drinking that. She would ask them pretty please can I have your monkey? That was a good idea. She nodded. She would ask sweetly. It worked every time. A pretty girl who asks sweetly always gets what she wants.

Across the table from her Gabriel sulked. He looked at her and said, What?

He faded in and out of focus. What what? asked Una. She stared at him as if he were a museum exhibit, a caveman in a natural history diorama: *El Pescador Último*. He was so handsome and such a fucker. A handsome fucker. Where did that monkey go?

What did you say? asked Gabriel.

Me? Una turned and stared behind her, then shook her head. I don't know. She shouted to be heard over the tumult of the bar.

A waitress walked through the crowd calling out in a singsong voice, Last call for alcohol!

I don't think I said anything. What do you think I said?

Gabriel hunched over the table. You said something.

No I didn't.

I saw you.

You saw me say something? she shouted.

I saw you, Gabriel insisted. You nodded.

Una waved him away with one hand, as if he were nothing more than a horsefly at the beach. You don't know what you're talking about. She got up from the table, her legs wobbly. Before she left the booth she leaned across and hissed in Gabriel's face, You're a handsome fucker, you know that? But you don't know shit.

Gabriel frowned. Don't talk like that, baby. That's not you.

I'm sorry, said Una. I think I need another drink. She stood up as if to head for the bar.

Maybe you've had enough, said Gabriel.

She looked at him for a moment. She said, And maybe I haven't.

Una.

What? I'm not doing anything. Wait. Wait a second. I'll be right back. I have to go find that monkey.

Gabriel said something she didn't hear clearly.

What? Una leaned closer. What was that?

Save the last dance for me, he said. Gabriel wasn't smiling. His words smelled of a veiled threat, a command to be followed.

Una leaned away from him, took a gulp from her margarita. That's not what I thought you said.

What did you think I said?

She set her glass down sloppily, almost tipped over the table. I thought you said Save the lap dance for me. She laughed. Get it? Her eyes went big. My monkey! Where's my monkey! I have to find that monkey!

She lurched into the crowd. A funhouse world undulated beneath her on the Tilt-a-Whirl floor. She tripped and stumbled. A lunk with long sideburns picked her up and when he did she wrapped her arms around his neck and held him tight, clasping his neck as if it were the neck of a pony while riding bareback. Pony! she giggled.

He laughed. I think someone's had too much to drink, he said.

A girl at their table pointed her beer bottle at Una. I know her. She works at the Black Tooth. She's all right.

Una peered over the guy's shoulder at the strange faces bobbing around the table. Do you have a green monkey? she asked. I need a green monkey.

What about the pony? asked the guy holding her.

Forget pony. I need my monkey. I saw it come this way? She nodded and closed her eyes as if she would fall asleep, curled against this stranger's neck. I need it, she said. For my zoo.

Una cuddled closer to his neck. Pony, she whispered. She was dimly aware one of his hands was cupping her butt cheeks to hold her weight. It felt good. He was as solid as a tree. She heard Gabriel's voice say, Get your hands off her.

The clamor of the crowded bar dimmed for a moment. People nearby turned to stare and grin, some stepping back a bit in case things got ugly.

Off who? asked her savior.

Off her. Off my girlfriend.

This your girlfriend? I don't see any sign on her.

Pony, said Una aloud. Pony pony pony pony pony.

She doesn't need a sign.

I don't know about this. The drunken guy holding Una turned to the table of people he was with. What do y'all think?

The girl who knew Una looked at Gabriel and said, I think he's had too much to drink, too. What we got here is a pair of drinking problems.

The whole table laughed. It was the same-old-same-old, a couple of drunks having a spat.

Then Gabriel reached out and swiped the drink glasses and beer bottles off the table. Glass shattered, ashtrays fell into girls' laps, and one guy stumbled backward and fell on his ass in the confusion. Others jumped back and shouted.

From her angle propped against her savior's neck, Una could see a girl who said, Now there's no call for that.

Her savior said, The man is out of fucking control.

Gabriel took hold of Una's wrist and started pulling her away. She felt the tugging and her arm stretched. A voice called, King? King, goddamnit. Goddamnit, King. Put the girl down and let these people alone. They got more troubles than we do. So let's just stand aside and pretend this never happened. You're going to get us thrown out, is what you're going to do.

I'm not doing anything, said King. It's closing anyway.

Una found herself back on her feet. Gabriel pulled her beside him and marched them through the crowd, people staring. In her ear he said, I'm going to get that big motherfucker if it's the last thing I do.

Una tried to catch her breath. She told Gabriel to slow down.

I'm going to get that motherfucker, he said again.

Honey? Don't. Really. I was just—

You were just what? he hissed. You were just going to leave me in a bar in the middle of fucking—

If you'd let me finish! she shouted. I just wanted a monkey for my zoo. If you wouldn't always, I mean, slow down!

Una saw faces whirling by her in the crowd. Rubberneckers at a car wreck. She tugged her wrist and twisted her hand. Would you let go?

Gabriel hit the exit door with a sharp smack of his open palm and they stumbled into the parking lot, the light above them blinding their eyes, Una still fighting his grasp.

Get in the car, he said. Get in the car or I'm just going to leave you here, okay?

The humid air made Una want to wipe her face. She yanked her hand and said, Let me go! Would you let me go?

The heavyweight bouncer, Mr. Ice Machine, morphed out of the shadows and jabbed a wide hand in Gabriel's chest. He looked like the kind of guy who would bite the head off a duck if he was dared to. He punched Gabriel with his open hand and said, Let the woman go, okay?

When Gabriel released her wrist Una stumbled into a car and banged her knee. Ow! she cried. She leaned over to rub the burning sharp pain. Oh, God, she said. She put one hand to her forehead. I don't feel so good.

Behind her Gabriel swung at the bouncer but missed. He swiveled into a glossy black pickup truck and hit his head, then got back up. The bouncer smacked him openhanded on the top of his head, as if he were a giant bug. Gabriel got to his feet and swung again, but the bouncer stepped back and Gabriel's hand smashed into the pickup's wide side mirror, breaking the glass.

He winced, holding his right hand, and crumpled into the parking lot. Oh fuck, he said. Fucking shit.

Una crouched against the front fender of a car a few feet away. A wave of nausea crested and she puked onto the oyster-shell parking lot. After that her stomach felt empty, but she continued retching. She felt like she couldn't breathe. She wheezed, trying to catch her breath through the mucus in her throat. One of the girls from the table showed up holding a green plastic monkey. She looked at the bouncer. I saved this for her, said the girl. I'm sorry. We didn't mean anything.

The bouncer pulled Una's hair out of her face. He said, Just get it all out, darlin'. Get that poison out.

People piled out of the bar, closing time. A guy in a crumpled cowboy hat walked up, laughing, until he stopped beside the glossy black pickup. What the fuck? Look at this. He neared his mirror, propped from the front right fender on metal struts like a piece of farm machinery. It was smashed and broken.

Now I don't like this one bit, he said. Who the fuck broke my mirror? He saw Gabriel in the shadows, mumbling. Yo, little drunk dude? Tell me you didn't just smash my mirror? Tell me that and everything's going to be hunky-dory.

Fuck you, said Gabriel. You probably looked into it is what you did.

The cowboy lifted his hat off his head, sighed, and put it back in place, his shadow in the bright light above the entrance going tall, then shrinking into the parking lot and casting a pool of darkness. He stepped forward and neared Gabriel, who was still hunched against the back fender of the glossy pickup. He said, I guess I'm not as pretty as you.

You were born ugly, said Gabriel. And you'll fucking die ugly, too.

Someone walking by laughed and said, Someone's beggin' for an ass-kickin'.

The cowboy turned to people walking by, said, I'm a reasonable man, is the truth. But this piece-of-shit taco eater, he broke my window.

Beside the building stood a yellow plastic mop bucket full of dirty brown water, a mop sloshed in it, a wringer mechanism on the lip of the bucket. The cowboy picked up the mop, a huge dripping filthy thing like a Rastafarian hairdo, and walked back to his truck.

As Gabriel got to his feet the cowboy swung the heavy wet threads of the huge mop across his face, slapping him broadside with it. People groaned. Someone laughed.

Stinking mop water splashed all over Gabriel. He grabbed the mop head and jerked it out of the cowboy's hand, then slipped on the wet asphalt and fell again.

As he started to get up the cowboy kicked Gabriel in the shoulder and knocked him against one great knobby-treaded tire. Hey, shithead! You know what your problem is? He kicked him again. You got to learn to keep your mouth shut, little shit! He kicked into the shadows again, his boot crunching against something. Gabriel scrabbled under the pickup like a spider.

Una stood upright. She was panting, trying to get her breath. Leave him alone! she screamed. He's drunk! Can't you see that!

The cowboy backed off, looked around at everyone, lifted his hat off his head again and replaced it. He raised his eyebrows at Una. Well of course he's drunk, china doll. Hell. We all drunk. He laughed. That's no excuse for anything.

Around him people climbed into their cars and trucks, slammed doors, started engines, turned on radios. We all of us drunk, the cowboy shouted into the humid wind. He shook his head. Don't change a damn thing.

On the drive home Gabriel winced every time he shifted gears with his right hand. He stank of the filthy mop water and his face was disfigured with anger.

Una sat slumped and nauseated. I'm sorry, she said. I'm sorry. I'm sorry I'm sorry I'm sorry. I didn't mean anything. I didn't mean to cause any trouble. I was only looking for a monkey. You're the one who overreacted. If you would have just—

Why don't you shut the fuck up? Can't you shut your fucking mouth? Is that so hard?

Don't tell me to shut up.

I'll tell you what I feel like telling you. Gabriel fished a cigarette out of the pack in his front pocket, his hands shaking. He punched in the cigarette lighter.

Una said, Those guys were assholes. We're never going there again.

Gabriel refused to look at her. He put the glowing orange tip of the lighter to his cigarette and mashed it too hard, crumpled a kink in his smoke.

Una reached across and stroked his wet hair. Baby? Come on. Baby?

Don't call me baby, he hissed. He brushed mop water off his forehead and wiped it on his pants. How could you do this to me?

Una turned away. Staring out the window, she watched the waves in the moonlight. I said I was sorry and you didn't listen. You act like I was flirting with him. All I was trying to do was—

You're drunk and disgusting. You think a man wants a drunken woman hanging all over strangers in a bar? Is that what you think?

I hate when you smoke. That's what's disgusting, if you want to know the truth.

Gabriel turned to glare at Una. She slouched in her seat, her head leaning out the window.

Are you going to be sick? If you're going to fucking puke you better tell me to stop because if you get it on the side of my car I'm going to—

Gabriel pulled his El Camino onto the oyster-shell shoulder of Shoreline Drive. With the car suddenly stopped the air off Red

Moon Bay reeked of salt and fish. A car's passing headlights glared into the front seat and shone upon Gabriel and Una, their faces wooden and harsh. It seemed as if they had paused for a moment, unsure of which direction to go next, at a turning point, a fork in the straight road along the ocean.

Una rubbed her face and sighed. You know what? I'm not sorry. You think I did it to you? You're pathetic. *No hice nada.* You did it to yourself.

You were the one hanging on that *pendejo,* said Gabriel. That's what started all this.

I'm sick of this. It happens every time. You know that? I never have any fun.

You were hanging—

Maybe I should.

Should what?

I don't need this.

Should what?

Una got out of the car, stumbling on the uneven shoulder of the road. Leave, she said. Just leave, okay?

Don't push me, Una. Don't fucking push me.

Go home. I don't need you.

Gabriel watched as she stumbled down the shoulder of Shoreline Drive, illuminated in the headlights, her small body like a young girl's, something forlorn and heartbroken in the way she moved alone on the road in the night. For a moment he considered running her over, just to put the both of them out of their misery.

He gunned it and drove off, the El Camino tires burning rubber on the rough asphalt, leaving Una in a cloud of burnt tire smoke and exhaust.

3

GABRIEL WOKE in a disembodied fuzz. He felt as if he were lying at the bottom of the sea. He stared at the ceiling and for a time saw rippling water reflections in a queasy, dappled pattern, like drips from melting fish scales. When his eyes finally came into focus he recognized his bedroom ceiling, decorated with pointed splotches of spackle. His bones felt as if they were pinned by an enormous gravity, as if the planet had grown bigger during the night and he had somehow shrunk. His ears rang like he had dived to an incredible depth. His head pounded with each beat of his tequila-soaked pulse. His mouth was spiny and parched as cactus.

At his kitchen sink, he drank a jar of water and was still thirsty. His eyes felt scorched and swollen. It hurt to blink. His skull steamed and bubbled. The aftertaste of fuckup coated his tongue like poolhall chalk.

As he stood there, he watched a scorpion scurry across the floor.

Its barbed tail curled upright and poised to sting, pincers clicking like tiny castanets. Gabriel resisted the impulse to grab a shoe and squash it.

He feared what would happen if he killed a scorpion. He believed in a bestial mysticism. That if he swatted a wasp, another wasp would sting him. If he hit a dog with his car, another dog would bite him. Biblical retribution applied to the world and all things in it.

He wasn't sure about plants.

He took four aspirin and considered swallowing the remainder of the bottle. He watched the chestnut-colored body of the scorpion swagger across the linoleum to disappear in the shadows beneath the cupboards. Before it disappeared it turned to look at him, its pincers turning with its head, like the horns of a bull. It seemed to be daring Gabriel to come after him. The moment unwound on the kitchen floor like a miniature bullfight.

Gabriel vowed he would never drink again.

He vowed that by day's end he would have a job.

His right hand was swollen, the knuckles split and guilty. Whenever he moved it sharp pains made him wince. When images from the end of the night surfaced in his mind, like wicked fish, he closed his eyes and tried to focus: a parking-lot scuffle. The mop head filth slimy against his face. Una screaming. Driving home, covered in the stink of humiliation. Una sick and resentful and hating him. Watching her walk away in the headlights, half wanting to run her down and be done with it.

Beyond that, a sea of squid-ink night.

He drove to the Speed-n-Go and bought a copy of the *Goodnight Gazette.* He considered this local rag best used for birdcage linings or as a soaking pad for muddy boots, but he was unemployed now and needed direction. The cover story mentioned some enormous fish discovered near the Sea Horse Motel, but he was still having difficulty focusing his vision, so he flipped through to the back pages.

He was glad he had somehow managed to avoid waking up in jail. He drank a twenty-ounce cup of coffee and read the want ads, sitting at the tables that passed for a deli in the convenience store. The Pakistani clerk gave him a dirty look but what could he do. It's a free country but nothing is free. One of the want ads was from the Mustang County Independent School District. Gabriel called from the pay phone. They asked if he could come by that afternoon.

He would need a job-interview outfit.

An hour later he parked among the palms on Iglesia Street, walked up to knock on his cousin Oscar's door. He was a Martinez, Gabriel's mother's side of the family, come up from Mexico, and known as something of a *bato loco*. He did a little of this and that. He ran a shop that was part taxidermist, part tow-truck business. Gabriel heard he sold some weed on the side. They weren't close.

The last time Gabriel had seen Oscar had been at the funeral for Tía Rosa. Everyone had said how similar they were, the same height, the same size, like brothers. Gabriel thought this insulting. Oscar had a nervous problem with his face muscles. He constantly blinked with both eyes. People called him El Guiñador. He was a freak, and Gabriel didn't like the comparison to a spaz. Plus Oscar was beefy.

As Gabriel stood on the porch, he sniffed the air for his cousin. He seemed to be out. Grackles squawked in the oleanders near his front porch. Oscar's truck wasn't in the drive. After knocking and waiting for a good five minutes, Gabriel walked around to the back door. Locked. High grass and banana-tree leaves rustled in the wind. The sky above tangled with power lines.

Shadowing the back door a huge magnolia tree held out its wide, waxy, deep-green leaves like some primordial swamp creature asking for a handout. Gabriel put his nose to the window and listened for movement. A magnolia leaf fell with a large plop. He glanced behind him to see what it was. Oscar's jungly yard gave him the creeps. The bark on the palms was huge and shaggy, like flakes of elephant skin.

He cupped his hands to the back window and peered through his reflection on the glass. Inside was a clean kitchen table. Gabriel wondered if Oscar was gay, *un maricon:* He was so neat. It made a body wonder. You wouldn't think a taxidermist would be *tan limpio.* Gabriel looked around the patio and found a giant conch shell, big pink lips, the sound of the ocean against your ear. He tapped it against the windowpane closest to the door handle. Nothing happened. He tapped harder. He punched and the glass shattered.

He listened for a dog. The house was quiet but for the purr of air conditioning, and smelled clean. Gabriel figured it might technically be breaking and entering, but if it was *su familia,* they'd never press charges. In Oscar's bedroom he shuffled through the closet and found the dark sport coat Oscar had worn to the funeral, a white shirt, and a necktie. Oscar was like that. He was freaky looking. With his blinking and a round brown beer belly, he dressed like Mr. Pretty to go out to bars? You never heard about him complaining about his woman? *Probablemente un maricon.* A greasy flamingo with a big belly, good for stuffing birds and fish caught by rich crackers with nothing better to do.

Gabriel dressed in Oscar's bedroom, checked himself in the mirror, turned on the TV. He went to the kitchen and drank a glass of milk. Oscar had cable, so Gabriel watched the weather channel. Talk of storms in the Atlantic. Too far away to care. They tracked them all the way to Africa now. He stared at himself in the mirror some more. He checked his watch and saw it was time to go.

On the drive to the job interview, he remembered his miserable school years. He'd done his time in Corpus, so the locals didn't know him. That was good. That way none of the smug bastard teachers would recognize him, the ones who thought they knew everything but push came to shove they didn't know shit. *Pendejos.*

Now that he thought about it, he was warming to this job.

He was going to like taking *los niños* for a ride.

DRESSED IN THE navy-blue sport coat with brass anchor-and-rope-bedecked buttons on its sleeves he walked into the Mustang County High School administration building annex. Behind his sunglasses he checked out the sweet Jesus booties on the teenaged honeys and tried to appear totally sober, no monkey business. His cousin Oscar was bigger than he and the sport coat was outsized, its sleeves loose around his wrists. Gabriel did not realize how much he resembled a somewhat seedy ship's first mate about to appear at the inquisition for a sinking.

At the desk of the front office he waited for a moment while a pair of giggling girls fussed over a parent's consent form for a field trip. He smiled when they glanced his way. They left and the male secretary, *otra maricon en escuela*, asked, Can I help you?

Gabriel said something the secretary couldn't hear.

Could you repeat that, please? said the secretary, then looked away as a phone began to ring on an empty desk behind him.

I'm here for the driver's ed instructor job, said Gabriel.

The secretary led Gabriel to the counselor's office. He said, Take a seat. Mr. Hinajosa will be with you in a minute.

Gabriel's mouth was so dry when he tried to answer, he made no sound. He nodded as the secretary turned and stepped away. Left alone, he tried to breathe deeply and get his shit together. His hands were sweating and felt like a pair of slimy gafftop catfish. He wiped his good left hand on Oscar's fancy dress slacks. His other hand, swollen and discolored, he held away from his body so it wouldn't touch anything, thumb up and fingers out straight.

It looked like he was offering the Invisible Man a handshake.

The high school smelled of dust, ammonia-mopped tile floors, chalk, and teenaged-girl perfume. It reminded him of the years of bullshit he'd endured, sullen and quiet, sitting in the back of all his classes waiting for the end of every hour. Waiting for the time when the bullshit teachers and the bullshit principal would mean nothing more to him than a 7-Eleven geek in a wimpy jacket asking for his ID to buy a six-pack. Sure, I got it right here, Chump.

The counselor hustled into the room late and immediately reached out to shake Gabriel's swollen right hand, which caused him to wince and grit his teeth in pain.

Oh, I'm sorry, said the counselor. Are you okay?

Gabriel nodded, trying to recover from the spasm. No problem, said Gabriel. He held up the swollen knuckles as if offering them for evidence. I just jammed it yesterday while working on a transmission. Think I might of broke something.

It looks terrible! said the counselor. Have you been to the doctor?

Gabriel shook his head. Don't believe in doctors. He considered his right hand, swollen and held in the air above the desk. The skin was discolored a deep purple in a mottled pattern beneath the knuckles. Wouldn't mind some painkillers though, he added, wincing.

The counselor told him he should see a doctor then, whether he believed in them or not. Mr. Hinajosa was a pockmarked Latino with gray hair. To Gabriel he looked soft as an old woman in line at the post office. Hinajosa said he was sorry for making him wait. Yes, they needed a driving instructor. What were his credentials?

I know how to drive like nobody's business, said Gabriel. For three years I was a trucker and got a commercial license to prove it. Plus my daddy was killed by a drunk driver two years ago north of Laredo. And I been on a crusade ever since to teach people don't drink and drive. I figure this way I'll reach a bigger audience.

Gabriel added this last detail as psychological motivation. He figured this counselor fart would relate to it.

Actually his father was an auto mechanic in Corpus and the two of them had not spoken in some five years since Gabriel had graduated from high school. Last powwow they'd had George Perez had told his son Gabriel if he didn't quit staring at himself in the mirror and making tough faces he was going to end up doing five to ten in the Convict Hotel.

Gabriel replied, Well fuck you too, and walked out.

Don't let the door hit you in the ass, said Papa.

You'll see where I end up, goddamnit, shouted Gabriel. And it's going to be on top, I grant you that.

The pay is not as good as I'd like to offer, said Counselor Hinajosa. But school budgets, well, you know how the taxpayers are. For now we can start you at eight dollars an hour, part time. We could also use another bus driver. He smiled and raised his gray eyebrows over his pocky face in a silly-ass expression.

Gabriel nodded. I don't know, he said. He took out a cigarette and fished in his coat pocket for a lighter. I got a couple other gigs lined up.

I'm sorry, but there's no smoking in this building. The counselor smiled weakly. The whole school. Inside and out.

Oh, yeah. I hear you. He started to put the cigarette behind his ear, then stopped, kept it in his hand. He thought that might look wrong somehow. Sure, he said. *No problema.*

I'm sorry, said the counselor. It's rules.

Rules is rules, said Gabriel. Made to be broken. Just don't get caught. He laughed awkwardly.

The counselor said, Well, you know, with kids. A good example and all that.

Gabriel placed the cigarette on the counselor's desk as if it were a gun he were handing over in a Tombstone saloon circa 1883.

So. This bus driving. Sure. I might be interested. How many hours we talking?

After they shook hands and Gabriel left the office, Hinajosa groaned. He shook his fingers to loosen the squashed bones and dry the nervous perspiration left by Gabriel. He opened the top drawer of his desk and removed a prescription bottle, shook a pill into his palm. Swallowing a Xanax, he tried not to imagine the harm that could be wrought, what could go wrong with Perez. That boy had more than a screw loose. *Es un mal bicho.* He shouldn't be hired, he should be studied. Those sideburns. That tattoo. Oh well. You can't change the world. He wouldn't do, but he must. The county needed another driver, and Hinajosa didn't have the time or energy to keep looking.

He checked how many Xanax were left in the bottle, how many refills he had. He was going to need more of these, that was for sure.

Una's Mother Cooked a breakfast of *huevos con chorizo* that morning, spicy with sausage and eggs and cheese and brown eddies of grease. She said Una needed to put on weight. You never eat my *comida* and look at you. Like a little girl with worms. Where is the meat on your bones? *Tienes huesos de aire.* You look like a ghost. Men do not want ghosts, this thing I know. A man wants a woman. Not some spook who floats above the sea. *Hombres no quieren a una alma flaca.* A skinny ghost. That's what you are.

In the small, yellow-curtained kitchen of their double-wide trailer, she put before Una a heavy white plate with chipped edges, decorated with blue flowers, a legacy from her marriage years ago to a Vietnamese sailor who'd drowned at sea. Each morning Una ate off these plates. Usually she ignored them.

This morning she wondered about her father. He was famous among her relatives as only a small dead man. A small dead fish-eater Una's mother had once loved and had been foolish enough to marry. God had punished her for this, they said, by drawing him down into the sea. God cast his bones among the seashells and jellyfish, said her grandmother, her *abuelita*. God scattered your father's bones among conches and scallops. Marry a *güero* and the same thing will happen to you.

This morning her plate was filled with scrambled eggs with sausage and tortillas slathered with butter. *Tome*, said Una's mother. I will not let you leave this house until your belly is full. Then perhaps you will grow. Then perhaps you will have more in your belly than food.

Una rolled her eyes and poked at the plate. You're insane, she said. *Mama loca*. Men like me fine as it is and actually I don't need any man or anything in my belly other than food. I can live on air just fine. You want me to be another fat girl? *Otra gorda?* No way.

She took a bite from a tortilla and chewed slowly. The mark her teeth made could have been the nibble of a wren or a sparrow. I know what I need, she said. I need money. I need a car.

I can get you a car, silly. Take mine. It runs.

It's a piece of junk. I don't want a junker. I want a nice car.

What about that boyfriend of yours? He probably doesn't want you anymore, you so skinny. Marry him and make him get you a nice car. A big one so I can ride in the back.

That's the last thing I need, said Una.

Her mother stood at the kitchen sink, her back to the table. She didn't turn around but said, A big white four-door sedan, so I can ride in the back like Miss Daisy and tell you where to go. She laughed as she rinsed the dishes.

Una made a face and hissed as if she were a cat spying a dog. To Una her mother looked comical, like a Mexican munchkin. She wore a frilly yellow apron tied at the back. Wisps of gray streaked her long hair the color of *mole,* its ropy braid hanging down her back like an object in a *relicario,* one devoted to souls who suffered too much work for too many hours of their lives. Her legs were wide, her ankles puffy.

Una watched her and struggled to banish her feelings of bitterness and scorn, glaring at this woman who ruled her life with authority. This woman who appeared to Una nothing more than a life-sized troll doll, all wide stumpy figure and wide face full of kindness and anger and worry. This woman who loved her so much it hurt her, Una, to think of it, to recognize it. The weight and the duty of it. This woman she also loved so much it hurt. This woman she loved but did not want to become.

She knew her problem was not a failure of desire but a failure to recognize the right man to love, *el deseo propio.*

As her mother continued to urge her to eat and make herself more desirable to men, Una slipped away unnoticed. She faded out of the room like the skinny ghost *mama loca* accused her of becoming. She walked out the back door of the trailer, taking care to open it quietly, pushing it into place and holding it firmly until she let the tongue click into the groove of the doorjamb.

Outside the morning was green and warm already, blue sky and humid, the grass wet with dew. She looked in all directions to make sure she was alone. The rear of the trailer faced only the wooden fence and a strip of overgrown St. Augustine grass, lush and tall. Behind the wooden fence someone mowed the neighbor's yard. The cut-grass smell tanged the air and the vibrating sound filled Una's ears. It made her feel even more enclosed than she was.

A trio of large banana trees grew at the back of the trailer house, near the fence, and between them Una crept on her hands and knees until she was completely hidden in the shadows beneath the trailer house. Here was a space less than three feet high beneath the body of the trailer frame. Here she kept the tips she made from working at the Black Tooth Café. She was afraid to put the money into any bank. She feared the IRS would steal it from her. She declared nothing but her minimum wage for taxes, with Gusef's consent. He'd told her not to put it in the bank, that there would be a paper trail of exactly how much she had. That they would then take it from her.

Part of Una believed if she lost it, she would be cursed forever.

All her life she'd had no money. She felt somehow cursed in a financial way because riches that came easily to many other people in Goodnight—people with weekend vacation homes, a Mercedes or Lexus in the driveway, yachts in the boat basin—never seemed to come her way. She held on to her tip money like a beautiful spirit with black hair and long red fingernails guarding a hoard of gold, although hers was green-paper currency tucked away in a special metal file box beneath this trailer house.

In this shadow world beneath the trailer she crept to a narrow place between the tires so small she figured only her arm would fit into it. She reached and pulled out the metal file box she used as a bank. She unlocked the small padlock that fastened it and quickly jammed her earnings from the night before inside. She did not count the money. She liked to see it increase in leaps and bounds.

She was gone only a few minutes. When she returned her mother said, You should put your money in the bank, like normal people. You call me crazy? *Eres la 'jita loca.* What if someone sees you? What if they steal it in the middle of the night?

What if you mind your own business? said Una.

Her mother shook her head. God must be punishing me. He gives me a daughter who does not eat. A daughter who is nothing more than a skinny ghost, no bigger than a pinto bean. A daughter that only the white ghosts of Goodnight would want to touch. A daughter who will leave me alone and wretched for the rest of my life as soon as she buys her fancy car.

Hush, said Una. I have to get dressed for work.

On her walk to the Black Tooth Café, Una wept. She wept for having so little money, for her poor mother, for her drowned father. She felt ugly because she was poor. She remembered how her mother's relatives would sometimes kid about her father being a coward, and how ashamed she was of this, their coldheartedness. Her father had fled to the U.S. from a village in Vietnam called Ha Vang, or Yellow River. Una's Uncle Alonzo had never much liked his sister's husband, and nicknamed him Yellow Belly. When he first disappeared some of the family had thought he'd run off again, and told each other, Rosa should have known this would happen, marrying a yellow belly.

Later, when his shrimpboat was discovered sunk, they would still say that, behind her mother's back, but would add, That's not funny.

Gabriel had actually once worked for her father, and at first that shared connection had bound her to Gabriel. Now she was sick of it. She told herself she would never ride in Gabriel's car again. Remembering the night before, she fumed. Shame coated her like the salt spray from Red Moon Bay that filled her grackle-black hair and long eyelashes. The wind pinned the fabric of her plain cotton dress against her small figure.

Walter and India Hamilton passed her on Shoreline Drive. They didn't recognize her as their sometimes waitress. They thought it strange for such a young girl to be walking down the road like that. Why isn't that little girl in school? asked India.

Walter didn't know and didn't want to meddle. These people lived by their own rules and he did not want a thing to do with it.

Una walked on, trying to pull herself together. She followed the shaded columns of palms along Shoreline Drive. She seemed to float. Her black hair filled with wind and flapped behind her like a pirate's flag.

At one point a carload of stupid teenaged boys passed her. They hooted and howled and whistled. Hey, gorgeous! You need a ride? She did not respond, did not shoot the finger or scowl. She pretended they did not exist and that she was walking along the bayside of a different world empty of people or disgust.

She saw the beautiful blond girls from her old high school drive by, saw them turn to stare. Their fathers were doctors or lawyers or investment bankers or real estate people. They spent their lives laughing and looking in the mirror, these girls with nose jobs and breast implants and straight white teeth that cost thousands and thousands of dollars. They thought nothing of their vacations to San Francisco or Hawaii.

Una walked on, the wind pinning her dress to her legs, her tears clotting and drying in her eyelashes. She breathed the smell of car and truck exhaust, heard the throttle and roar of delivery trucks trundling past, the deep-throated rattle of motorcycles and their riders' looks, smelled trashfish on the sandy shore the other side of

Shoreline Drive. She floated past lush yards of deep green St. Augustine grass with palm trees and wind socks with dogs barking and wagging tails when she slowed to pet them.

By the time she arrived at the Black Tooth, her hair was wild and tangled, her eyes pink and fevered.

Gusef asked, What is matter?

She started to speak and stopped, shook her head. She stood in the glow of one of the Black Tooth's many aquariums and looped her apron over her neck, tied the strings about her waist, and stared straight ahead.

The usual, she said. My life sucks. So what else is new?

AUNT VICKY WANTED to know what was stinking up her garage. She shook Falk awake by grabbing one foot sticking out from the blankets of his top bunk. She told him to get out of bed. She said, You've got some explaining to do, mister.

One thing Falk liked about having been expelled from school was not having to get up early. He was not the early bird. He squinted at Aunt Vicky from his pillow. Go away, he said.

You get up. You sleep too much as it is. A boy your age should be up at the crack of dawn.

Leesha was in the bathroom putting on her makeup. Aunt Vicky watched him, frowning. She said, Come on, hurry up. She watched him climb out of bed wearing only his underwear, and she watched as he turned his back to her and pulled on his jeans. She wore her real estate saleswoman outfit, crisp and frilly, with smoky pantyhose and the scent of perfume.

Why aren't you wearing pj's? She watched his skinny white

body, his thin shoulders, his pale hair a trail of fuzz at the back of his neck. Did you hear me?

I don't like them, he said.

She shouldn't see what I just saw.

Falk blushed. Don't look then.

Don't give me lip, said Aunt Vicky. It's my house, she added. She looked at herself in the mirror of Leesha's vanity dresser, then reached out to straighten a gag postcard wedged between the mirror glass and wooden frame. It showed a horse-sized jackrabbit with antelope antlers. A jackelope. Falk's mother had sent Leesha this postcard two years ago on a trip to El Paso. It was something she did, sending her niece postcards when she went on a trip, something Leesha liked.

Aunt Vicky watched Falk in the mirror. You sleep here in Leesha's room I told you to wear pj's.

She doesn't care.

I do.

I don't walk around in my underwear, you know.

You're saying just forget it is what you're saying?

Come on. Does it matter?

Do me a favor? Don't argue.

Falk pulled on his T-shirt and straightened it. Tell you what. I'll get one of those deep-sea diving suits. You know the kind? I've seen them in old movies, with John Wayne and a giant squid.

You're not funny.

I'll wear that to bed. Every night. I promise. He grinned. Helmet too.

Aunt Vicky smacked him lightly on the back of the head. Enough with the sass.

I thought you liked sass?

Not this morning.

She marched Falk outside. He shuffled barefoot, his blond hair sticking up goofy, like a blue jay's crest. The morning was cloudy and windy, the air soft and damp. They walked around the corner of the house on the flagstone pathway to the detached garage, where the purple flame-fendered tow truck filled the space of the open door, the enormous fish looking flattened and saggy in the shadows. The garage was a combination carport and tool shed, big enough for Uncle Ed to work on cars. It had only one mobile garage door, and the tow truck blocked Aunt Vicky's Subaru.

Why is there a gigantic fish parked in my garage? she asked.

Falk rubbed his head and scrunched up his nose at the smell. Mercy, he said. That's rank.

I asked you a question.

Why is it in the garage? he echoed. Falk shifted on his bare feet in the oyster-shell drive. Because otherwise the dogs might get it?

Dogs? Aunt Vicky made a face. She was an attractive woman just turned forty, smile wrinkles on the side of her face. She was famous in the real estate world of Goodnight for handling vacation homes. For getting what she wanted. One way or the other. She said, We don't have any dogs.

Falk squinted his eyes at her. Neighborhood dogs? Coyotes?

Coyotes? Are you insane? Look at this. What is this?

Ropy purple tubes hung off the side of the tow truck, trailing out of the zebrafish's belly.

Falk shrugged. Intestines, I guess.

Guts. You mean guts.

Okay. You win. Guts. Now are you happy?

That's disgusting. Aunt Vicky stalked around the garage, the frills of her pink blouse flaring. It's not enough that I get up every morning to slave away my life and come home every night to cook dinner for every man woman and child that lives here, I have to face this in the morning.

Falk smiled at her, made motions of playing an air violin.

I'm not laughing, she said.

Lighten up, okay? I'll get rid of it, said Falk. I'll move it right now and you'll never have to see that fish again.

You better. Aunt Vicky stepped close and tousled his hair. Or I'm going to beat you, she said.

You would not. He grinned. Would you?

Try me.

FALK DROVE to the Black Tooth Café, enjoying the massive feel of the tow truck, the giant fish visible in his rearview mirror. He parked in front. He didn't want anyone driving by to snap a picture, but he didn't plan to be long. If he could get an exclusive on this, it might be worth something, like Leon said. Within minutes a swarm of flies descended upon the fish, and the smell made customers gasp and cover their mouths when they exited the café and had to walk past it. People stopped their cars in the middle of the road and stared. What the hell is that? shouted someone.

When a traffic snarl developed, Sheriff John Littledog cruised by slowly, flashing his lights and sirens briefly. The parking lot of the Black Tooth filled and people pulled over onto the oyster-shell shoulders of Shoreline Drive. Before long a crowd of snowbirds gathered, awed and gabby. Gusef stood beside the tow truck and told everyone how he would mount the fish on his roof, how he had captured it from the ocean's depths.

He gesticulated and urged people to admire it, beaming and half besotted, a mad barker of the dying bays.

I fought stinking bloody monster for two days I did, he said. My hands blister and mangle like bleeding stumps of meat. Salt encrusts my eyes they sting and swell shut but still I hang on. My ass is sore my hemorrhoids aching but still I sit in chair at back of boat and pull on fishing pole as if dragging up God himself from depths of sea. My cowardfish friends tell me, Give up, Gusef! This is madness! It will kill you!

But did I let go? Did I whine bitch and moan like old woman with curly black man hairs on her chin eating bowl of borscht in leaking hovel? Did I whimper like local shrimper good-for-nothings who cannot find their ass with both hands? No! I hang on and shout at cursed creature. You think you're tough, I shout, you do not know Gusef Smurov. You think you're tough old fish well yes so I am tougher. I am toughest! I don't care how many Puerto Ricans you swallowed whole give me your best shot I take it and spit back at you!

And finally it gave up ghost. When we towed it in you see we could not get it in net it's too big of course we towed it alongside boat and when we reached dock two thousand pounds it weighed! I shit you not! It break scale I tell you. In half it snapped it like breadstick.

Someone in the crowd asked how they knew it weighed two thousand pounds if the scale broke. Gusef waved away the naysayer, saying it probably weighed more in fact. But that was what the scale recorded before it exploded like the head of a teenager who abuses himself too much.

Yes well we pry mouth of monster fish open and guess what was inside. You see horse but there was more I tell you. He looked around at his trembling white-haired audience. You must guess. Guess, you fools!

A pair of water skis? asked one old customer.

A television? asked another.

A set of *Encyclopedia Britannicas?*

No no no. What inside I find is angel! Gusef's eyes grew moist and dreamy. An angel I find. With white wings and lovely woman's face. And breasts! Heaving bosoms like Sophia Loren!

Some in the crowd snorted at this point, shook their heads.

Laugh, my fine idiots! Pope's truth I tell you! Angel it was, beautiful buxom sea angel. She crawled out of pile of stinking fish guts, wiped clear her eyes and scraped clean her wings—Here he pantomimed cleaning off fish guts and slime from his face and arms—and before I could ask single question she coughed twice and flew, like enormous white wood stork, and last I saw she faded into sky over Red Moon Bay, heading for Isla Pelicano. Still coughing, like perhaps she smoke too many cigarettes while in belly of great Leviathan.

At the close of his story Gusef stood there grinning, beaming at the crowd of snowbirds and nodding his head, insisting it was the gospel truth. Let Lord smite me down where I stand if word of this is false!

Falk tugged his elbow, spoke low so only Gusef could hear. That's a clever story and all, but shouldn't I be moving along with this thing? I don't want every yokel taking a picture. Plus it's starting to rot, you know?

Yes yes yes, said Gusef. We must hurry. You go now to man who stuffs fish and I send Leon to pick you up. He will expect you. Pay no attention to him. He is crazy but he is master fish stuffer.

A MEMORY of Una's kisses hypnotized Falk as he drove through the Gulf coast wasteland of Goodnight's back roads. His eyes stared straight ahead as if looking at a screen of green and windy nothing. He remembered the electric feel of her warm breath mingling with his when he leaned close to her to kiss and she lingered there with her lips open, the smell of her skin in his eyelashes, his ears and hair. It was enough to make him do something stupid. To risk his life.

It was a good twenty miles to the taxidermist's. The sky darkened and lightning flickered in the west. Falk passed the weedy junkyard with rusted husks of Chevrolets and Buicks guarded by a pack of lanky German shepherds. He passed the Repo Outlet Mall with its 30 percent off Failure and Despair discount. He passed the minigolf course where the poor of Goodnight and teenaged kids on dates swung their dinky putters at windmills and dinosaurs. Beside the Y Not Putt? was the XXX Adult Video Megamart with its guilty smirk and parking in rear.

He passed Bamboo Willy's, with its beer-garden volleyball court where no one ever played. He passed the DNA testing service billboard famous around town. It featured a baby the size of a sperm whale and the caption "Who's my Daddy?"

Falk had seen it all before and today none of it mattered.

He smelled Una's kisses on his lips. Not like the kiss of death that Gusef warned him they could be, but like the kiss of a life worth living, a life that made him forget having no mother or father or sister or brother. A life salty and luscious, heady with exotic spice and the smooth unfolding pink petals of her lips, the muscular needy squirm of her tongue. He smelled her plaintive pulse of sorrow and desire and stubborn belief that all would not end in bloodshed and disgust. What he smelled whispered that there was hope after all. That was what he smelled as he drove through a rainstorm on a windswept coast with a gigantic unheard-of fish on the flatbed of a tow truck behind him.

After Bamboo Willy's he entered a depopulated zone where everything decrepit and falling apart seemed to have come to die. Even the telephone poles leaned crookedly from having been battered by tropical storms and seemed for all the world like black crucifixes awaiting their martyrs. Trailer houses with walls torn off exposed the pink cotton-candy insulation inside.

He passed a prairie of mesquite trees, sorrowful and droopy, covered with sharp thorns like stingray barbs. In the weirdness of the mesquite thicket the world seemed charged. The sky filled with black and red insects that copulated in flight. They filled the air above the back roads and hissed as their conjoined bodies splattered against the tow truck's windshield. After a few miles they covered the windshield so thickly it resembled the splattered, cratered surface of the moon.

The entire landscape seemed forlorn and abandoned. Shredded strips of tire tread from tractor-trailer rig blowouts curled and wizened on the pocked asphalt. Oil-field pumping stations rocked rhythmically like gigantic roadrunners. Country folks' yards collected rusted cars with weeds reaching to their broken windows taped with plastic.

Since he'd left the Black Tooth the sky had turned blue and curdled. It began to rain. Huge drops pocked the windshield with sharp splats. Falk switched on the wipers. At first all they did was smear the juices of the many bugs across the glass.

The air filled with rippling silvery curtains. A hazy sheen of mist rose above the road. As the rain kept falling the windshield cleared, but Falk was still glad when he arrived at the taxidermist's.

Martinez hailed from the state of Tamaulipas in Mexico. He had mounted the tarpon and sailfish Gusef had caught and placed for show in the Black Tooth Café. He was known as the best around, maybe a bit eccentric. When Falk pulled up with the giant zebrafish in the flatbed of the tow truck, Martinez was standing beside it as soon as he opened the door. He seemed to have arisen from the sand itself. He whistled through his teeth and said, *Esta hecho una lástima.* That is one big motherfucking fish you got there, surfer dude.

Martinez was Gabriel Perez's cousin, the one who did not yet know his house had been broken into, his sport coat lifted. The one who had a problem with his eye muscles that caused him to blink compulsively. He walked the length of the flatbed, checking out the fish, blinking repeatedly, with both eyes.

Este pez is before the time of men and dogs, he said. *Es prehistórico.* It must have been at the bottom of the ocean. Where even the sunlight cannot swim so deep. Where even light turns back and swims toward the surface. That is from where comes this monster fish.

Makes sense to me, said Falk. I mean, it's one big fish. You don't see that at Siesta World now do you?

Martinez stalked around the tow truck, blinking. What do you know, surfer dude? You don't know shit.

Falk stood for a moment silent, watching the blinking Martinez appraise the fish. The rain beaded like mercury in Martinez's glossy black hair. Droplets dribbled down his forehead and cheeks until he wiped them clean.

Did I hurt your feelings, surfer? Martinez slapped his back. If your face grows any longer my dogs will start howling.

You don't have to be insulting about it. I mean, I'm just here to drop off the fish. Gusef said he talked to you, right?

Tell me this. What does it mean?

What?

Fish with a horse in its mouth? *Diga me.* What does it mean?

The rain was falling harder now. Falk held an old newspaper over his head to keep dry. Hell if I know, he said.

Martinez's hair was dripping wet and his T-shirt soaked dark. He didn't seem to notice or care about the rain. It means something, he said.

Nothing good I would guess.

Martinez laughed, flashing bright white teeth. He looked straight at Falk for a moment, both eyes blinking. Why you? Why is it you with this great fish? A little surfer dude with a great fish?

Well. I found it. Kind of. A tourist saw it, then told Gusef. He sent me to look at it. I took the pictures. I got a camera.

Oh, I get it. Martinez nodded, blinking. The right place, the right time. The Soviet is using you, too, I bet. Somehow.

I'm going to make some money off it too. You watch me.

Martinez leaned close to stare at the zebra stripes of the great fish. Now you got me scared, he said. A white boy with money is a

dangerous thing. Next thing I see you running for *el presidente.*
Kissing hands, shaking babies. *Por qué no?* He laughed.

Falk moved away from him. Are we finished here? I got things
to do.

You're a busy boy.

Falk pointed at the truck. You want me to back this up somewhere?

Don't get mad, surfer. Just fuckin' with you.

I'm supposed to get back to work. Leon's going to be by in a
minute to pick me up.

Yeah, we're all impressed.

Martinez directed him to a bay in his garage. He wheeled around
an enormous fiberglass tub on a dolly. It was wide and white and
smelled of bleach. Martinez said he used it for the big Gulf fish, tarpon and sailfish mainly. A shark now and then. Never anything
this big.

Shit, he said. If it breaks this thing, you tell the Soviet he's paying for a new one, okay?

I'll tell him your bathtub broke is what I'll tell him, Falk mumbled.

Qué?

Okay, sure. I'll tell him.

Falk lowered the tailgate of the tow truck to a thirty-degree angle, the end positioned over the plastic tub. They got behind the fish
on the flatbed and pushed. With the rain the flatbed was wet and
slick, the fish impossible to get a hold on.

Jesus and Maria, said Martinez. This mother stinks.

When at first he and Falk pushed the slimy body, it barely
budged. They pushed until their faces turned purple and both

grunted. Their feet slipped on the flatbed. Martinez cussed and told Falk he had an idea. He got a long metal galvanized pipe from the garage and slipped it under a hollow where the zebrafish pectoral fin bent beneath the weight of the body. Then he lifted and Falk pushed. They inched the giant fish forward until it began to slide down the ramp.

When they were finished, slime coated Falk's clothes. He smelled horrible.

You stink bad, surfer boy. You're going to have to burn those.

Thanks for pointing that out.

That's okay. Martinez grinned. I won't charge extra.

Falk smelled his hands and made a face.

Wait. You better wash up. The Soviet won't let you in his café.

He took Falk through his cluttered and dusty office area to a rust-spotted metal sink in the restroom. As Falk dried his hands he looked around. A display of hardware and auto-parts calendars covered the tin shed walls, half-naked buxom girls straddling motorcycles or holding monkey wrenches like they were bottles of shampoo or Tupperware. The whole wall covered with breasts and legs and big blond hair, Daisy Duke ragged cutoff hot pants, lipstick and smiles, like a *relicario* of tits and ass.

Falk stared at them and was half ashamed to do so. He wondered whose sisters or daughters they were. He realized it didn't matter. Still it bothered him. He told himself they were just pictures. He didn't think of photographs as holy but he did see in them a sneaky power. He wondered what it would be like to photograph a beautiful naked woman. He could do it. He never had. But he would.

Martinez walked up, carrying a battery. He set it down on the floor, breathing hard.

A dusty transistor radio hung from a nail by one foggy window. It was tuned to a country-music station, and a voice crooned, "Drop-kick me Jesus through the goalposts of life." Martinez nodded toward it and said, Don't you just love that hillbilly shit?

Falk said he wondered where the hell Leon was.

Go then. You're too cool for the hillbilly tunes aren't you? But you like my girls?

Falk shrugged. Sure.

No, you don't. You're probably a *joto*. *Es posible.* I hear *maricons* can get married now? Maybe you'll get married then?

I'm no *maricon.*

That's what you say, surfer dude. You look? I don't know. Iffy? You know what I mean? Martinez stepped close to Falk. He cupped Falk's face with one puffy hand. He was grinning. Iffy? Maybe just a little?

Falk twisted his face out of Martinez's hand. Go fuck yourself.

Martinez laughed, blinking and breathing hard. *Sí,* that's how you look to me. A little iffy.

Falk walked toward the road and away from Martinez. He watched for Leon's pickup. Yeah, well. You're a charmer, you know that?

A few minutes later Leon pulled into the driveway, a beer in his free hand. As Falk climbed into the cab, Martinez wanted to know if they wanted him to save the fish meat. Maybe they would eat it? Maybe serve it in the Black Tooth? He said he would if they didn't.

It's a little gamy but that's no crime, he said. That great fish make good fixin's I bet.

You're joking, right?

He blinked and smiled like a Latino Buddha. *Vaya te. Voy a llamarte cuando es listo.*

.   .   .

THAT DAY GOODNIGHT'S fleet of shrimpers left dock as usual, bitter, hopeful, and dogged. The sky clouded blueblack and scudded thickly by afternoon, rain drifting off the warm water of the Gulf. The wind picked up. The boats tossed in the gray swells and dragged their nets halfheartedly. The men watched the seabirds, lightning in the distance. Dark-plumed storm petrels flew low over the dunes and bay when they should have been out at sea. Brown pelicans hovered over the waves but did not dive. Not enough fish in the water to catch.

Even the weather was wrong for September. The bay water felt thick and slimy, too warm for the season, ripe for storms.

Dolphins continued to wash up dead on the shores of Red Moon Bay and Isla Pelicano, the uninhabited barrier island that stood between Goodnight and the Gulf. The fish and game scientists studied their corpses and had some theories. The papers said an algae bloom was to blame. The scientists were betting on a bacteria that attacked the dolphins' respiratory systems, like an aquatic lung fungus.

The locals said simply, Things are fucked up.

The parks and wildlife people considered closing the shrimping season in the bays. The locals greeted this warning with groans and resignation. They weren't catching enough to pay the costs of their diesel and the repair of the nets anyway. Although the Black Tooth's customers assumed the seafood was caught locally and therefore fresh, it was hardly top-secret info that Gusef bought the jumbo shrimp frozen from Ecuador and Peru. Or Brazilian shrimp farms. Even if the waters of South Texas became completely barren, it seemed there was theoretically no shortage of shrimp in the world.

But South Texas wasn't the only once fertile part of the ocean being fished to death. Even the Grand Banks of Newfoundland were played thin.

Not many were paying him any mind, but in the back of the Black Tooth Mr. Buzzy was talking. To whoever would or would not listen. The old man said years ago the fishing around here had been as different as night and day. He remembered a hogleg trout he'd caught thirty years back. At first he'd thought it was a baby tiger shark. When he opened it up he'd found a Delaware license plate in its belly. A bit rusty and dented, but you could read the letters clearly—BR 549, I shit you not.

Nowadays you'd be lucky to catch a gafftop catfish a pound, pound and a half if the gods were smiling on you and most likely they ain't. Course his wade-fishing days were over since the rot got his leg and now he was nothing more than an Otis Redding ripoff, just sittin' by the dock of the bay, all day long, maybe not half the man he used to be, more like a quarter or a third on a good day.

Mr. Buzzy said the problem was people grabbin' too much and not using any common sense about what to keep and when to give it a rest. Back in the day he saw men catch twice as much shrimp with half as much work and leave plenty for the next season. Not anymore. The boats were bigger, the nets were wider. It was more like a goddamn corporation.

The fishermen sitting nearby agreed.

The ex-captain of the *Maria de las Lagrimas* stroked his Abe Lincoln beard and nodded grimly. You ask me, this is the end of something. I mean, really. I need a goddamn new line of work.

His friend nodded. If you're backin' out of the parkin' lot, I'm already there.

I'm not kidding, goddamnit, said Captain Douglas. Jesus. Anything must be better than this.

His friend looked pained. You think you're the only one hurtin'? Should of seen the look my wife give me this morning on my way out. He grimaced. Look like death eatin' a cracker. So join the club, *hombre*.

Captain Douglas bought a round.

To drowning our sorrows, he said, raising his glass in toast. They all took a drink, even the rummies and rednoses at the end of the bar.

The other fisherman raised his glass for another toast. To hell with fish! They can kiss my ass!

THE CAFÉ WAS swamped for an hour around noon. Falk returned to work after Gusef let him take a shower and change clothes in an empty room of the Sea Horse. He asked if he could work a double-shift that evening. He told Gusef he wanted all the money he could get.

Billy the assistant cook was loopy and hungover, there to help out during the lunch rush. He was an ex–merchant marine who claimed to be suffering from post-traumatic stress disorder. A few years before he'd been aboard an oceangoing tug that had sunk, leaving him adrift in a life raft for three days. Or at least that was what he'd told the feds to get his disability checks. He wore a ponytail and had a grizzled face, his arms a mess of homemade tattoos.

Shouldn't you be paying attention to those fries in the basket? asked Falk.

Yeah yeah yeah, Billy said. They ain't going nowhere. I just seen some things, you know. Like, you ever see a high school girl vomiting blueberries? It's awesome. Truly a thing of beauty. Saw that last night. Or, like, have you ever seen a pregnant woman getting married, wearing an oversized white wedding gown and a black velvet sombrero? Or one of those videos of self-mutilation people? You know. The ones who cut off their body parts for kicks? Have you? I bet you haven't, have you?

Falk said, No, you got me there, I haven't seen that either. But most importantly it looks like we're out of oysters so could you get back in the walk-in, bring a tray of the ones already breaded?

Afterward Falk felt bad for snapping at Billy, who was harmless enough, but it was hard to keep on top of things when the orders kept coming fast and furious. Billy didn't know when enough was enough. The Black Tooth was full of snowbirds just arrived. They loved the gumbo and that particular day were out in full force, spreading oleo on Saltine crackers or just crumbling them up directly into those bowls full of funky Cajun fish stew. You had to keep on your toes. Being a cook was a low-paying, thankless job, but still, Falk wasn't about to blow it off. If he was going to cook he was going to be good at it, and if he had to crack the whip on Billy the Space Case, and him a good ten years older, so be it.

About three o'clock the place was dead. On a back table in the Black Tooth's dining room Falk spread out a collection of his bird photos, brilliant close-ups of crested caracara, roseate spoonbills, American avocets, wood storks, and oystercatchers. Many of them had been taken in the windswept desolation of the abandoned brokendream back roads of Goodnight. Una said she thought they were just beautiful. She thought he should take more of them. Maybe he could become a wildlife photographer? He could get a website and sell his photos on the Internet.

Falk rubbed his nose and frowned at the photographs. They were pretty, yes, and he loved the grace and mystery of birds. But there was something hackneyed and syrupy about them as well, something that reminded him of the idealized drawings of quarter horses and appaloosas that girls filled their notebooks with in the fifth grade. They made for good postcards but was that good enough? That not many people cared one way or the other, and would decorate their homes with glossy reproductions of showy birds such as loons or Canada geese or wood ducks landing on autumn ponds, only made the issue thornier.

His favorite photos were those of houses dilapidated and collapsing, a scenery of decay and active ruin. What he envisioned was a photography that celebrated the beauty of decay, of things falling apart, of what happens to the world after the boom, after the gold rush, after the bubble burst, a vision of sublimity in rot. This he told Una.

Not to be a buzzcrusher or anything, she said, but I don't really see the point in these abandoned-building shots of yours. What's so fascinating about old worn-out things? I don't get it.

I don't know, said Falk. Pretty birds? I might as well be doing postcards of teen beauties in slinky bikinis. I might as well shoot furniture for Sunday newspaper advertisements.

You don't have to go that far.

He wanted to believe that it was all about the moment. When the light was on the subject. The golden light of sunset, the bluetones of dawn, the whitish cast of fog on the nightwaters. The halo of glow around fishing pier lights.

Una pointed to the photo of a collapsing house. I mean, it's all about failure, isn't it? How things are crumbled and rotten? Who wants to hear about that? It's a sad story. You really want to devote your life to sadness?

Not all the time.

Maybe you should listen to me sometime. Maybe you'd learn something.

Falk considered that he was learning something from Una, but he wasn't sure what. What it felt like to want what you couldn't have? Which was an important thing to know?

Una returned from taking her orders and sat down to do the dinner prep, rolling silverware and sweeping the back dining room. Falk lingered for a moment staring at her, until she told him to stop.

Quit staring at me like that, she said. You're giving me the creeps.

I can't help it, he said. I like to watch you. Is that so bad?

Una kept rolling the silverware and for a minute seemed not to be paying any attention to him, until she said, When I think about you, you know what I think?

Falk shrugged.

She shook her head. I think boy. I think high school dropout.

I'm not a dropout. I got kicked out. There's a difference.

Why'd you have a knife in school anyway? How dumb can you get?

Everybody has them. I just should have hidden it better. It's that stupid zero-tolerance thing that got me.

But why'd you have it in the first place?

You went to that school, didn't you? There's a lot of creeps.

She kept rolling the silverware, putting a dinner fork, salad fork, butter knife, and spoon on a cloth napkin, then rolling it and tucking one corner back inside the flap, the whole thing making a tidy, tight bundle.

And I'm not a boy, said Falk. Or a dropout.

I'm just telling you what I think.

You don't know anything about me.

Una nodded. Exactly my point.

Falk asked if she was feeling better now.

What makes you think I wasn't feeling good?

Gusef told me you were upset when you came in today.

After a moment she sighed. If you have to know, it's over between me and Gabriel. I've had it. I'm never going to ride in his car again.

Falk didn't know what to say at first. Finally he whispered, That's good.

No, it isn't. Now I don't have a ride. I have to walk everywhere. It's humiliating.

If I had a car I'd let you drive it.

She rolled her eyes. If you had a car it would be a piece of junk. Like everyone else I know. That's not what I want. I want something nice, you know what I mean? Something that looks good and smells good. Something sleek. Pretty.

Cars are nothing special, said Falk. What I'd like to own is a boat.

Una said he wanted to be just like Gusef, who had recently bought a weather-beaten yacht called the *Crazy Jane*. It was an old wooden cabin cruiser that had sat too long in the marina. The hull was crusted over with barnacles, making it slow and heavy.

Boats have romance, said Falk.

What do you know? said Una. You're a child. I'm an adult. And for an adult, without a fine car you are less than nothing.

Cars are just lumps of metal to get you from one place to the next, he said. Look at Gusef. It's better to have an old junker. You should get one of those.

Never, she said. Una frowned and shook her head. I will own a car when I can buy the best. An Acura. Maybe. Or the best Toyota. Top of the line.

That's nothing but materialism. Status displays. It won't make you more important.

You're foolish, she said. You don't own one. You just borrow Gusef's leavings.

I know what's important in life. And it's not cars.

Stop your silliness. I can't listen to this.

She walked away. Falk called out, It's good for you. Walking to work. Keeps you strong.

She put one hand in the air behind her, fingers flapping to the thumb, making a yackety-yack-yack motion.

When she returned to the kitchen to pick up an order Falk told Una, What about this? I'll buy you a car. Would that make you happy?

No, you won't, said Una.

I will too. I promise. I swear on a stack of Bibles. He smiled.

Since when have you ever seen a stack of Bibles?

No matter, he said. It's a metaphor. You know. Just a thing you say to mean something else.

I know what a metaphor is, said Una. I'm not stupid.

THE CBS AFFILIATE in Corpus Christi sent a news crew in a white van. It had a satellite dish on its roof and blue and red lettering on the side that read, ACTION NEWS: LIVE, LOCAL, LATE-BREAKING! The reporter was a short, glossy man named Dale Pope. He shook everyone's hand and asked who saw what.

Mr. Buzzy waved his cane at the artificial man and asked, You any relation to Rome?

Dale Pope smiled, bright and wide, as if advertising his dental work. Come again?

The Rome pope. That's what I'm sayin'. He you brother? Mr. Buzzy looked at Una and winked.

No. Not hardly. Dale Pope laughed. He turned away from Mr. Buzzy and beamed the light of his bright smile on Una. So where's the big fish?

Gusef declared the fish to be held in an undisclosed location. They had big plans for it, and it would be unveiled when the time was right.

Dale Pope's smile dimmed. You mean to tell me there's no fish?

Fish is hidden, said Gusef. Like God.

Dale Pope groaned and talked to his assistants. They could be overheard saying something to the effect of Goodnight being a hicksville goose chase. But before they left, Dale Pope asked to interview the discoverers. Falk took off his apron and emerged from the kitchen. When they were introduced Falk recognized Pope from Channel 7 and thought the news man looked exactly like he did on TV, only wider.

Una still seemed a little shaky. Her eyes were pink and dreamy. I don't really know anything about it.

Dale Pope insisted she be part of the on-camera report.

No, really, she said. I don't know anything. Falk's the expert. He's the hero.

I am not, he said.

Dale Pope looked at Falk, then at Una. He smiled like a beauty contest emcee. You don't want to waste my time, do you? You were with him when he took the photos, weren't you?

I was standing there.

Please?

Okay.

They went on camera in front of the café, in the parking lot, for a few moments, but cars driving on Shoreline made too much background noise. Dale Pope then ushered everyone around to the back of the place, facing Red Moon Bay. He interviewed Falk and Una standing in front of the boat basin, where shrimpboats floated in their moors, their booms and rigs like tangled seagoing cranes against the sky. Drunken shrimpers in rumpled clothing and rubber boots, who had caught nothing or close to it, stood behind Falk and the reporter. They stared into the cameras as if suspicious of their intent. Some waved to unseen audiences.

Una looked uncomfortable, as if she were being forced to cooperate by a ruthless dictator with a bald head and large mustache who kept breathing on her with a mouth reeking of garlic. She didn't know what to do with her hands. She brushed her hair out of her face and squinted into the low gray clouds.

Dale Pope asked her what she thought of the great fish that had swallowed a horse.

It smelled, she said. It was gooey and smelled. I thought, Some sea monster. She smiled then. It's like that with everything, isn't it?

Dale Pope blinked and smiled and nodded. That's one way to look at it.

It is, said Una.

The reporter then asked Falk what he thought when he saw the horse in the fish's mouth.

I was, you know, I mean, excited? I was thinking that's, that's something, really. I mean, a horse? In its throat? It's, you know, it's a rare thing. I've never heard, never really, I mean, of one of those. You know. Washing up on the Gulf Coast?

Dale Pope turned to Una.

What would you think if you saw something like that in the water while you were swimming? he asked.

I'd be nervous. She laughed. I'd freak! I'd swim faster.

The reporter smiled with all his teeth. I bet we all would, he said. Staring into the camera he added, Back to you, Jerry.

Off camera, the TV man relaxed and shook hands with everyone who had participated and some who had not. Una stared as he thanked them heartily in a voice too loud for the occasion. He slapped a mosquito on his neck.

Uh-oh, said Una.

He turned to look at her, his grin fading into uncertainty. Uh-oh what?

She grimaced. Oh, you know, she said. West Nile.

He scratched the bite. Really? That's a problem here?

Falk shrugged. Well, it's been, you know, we've had some, well, not many really.

People have died, said Una. Don't you watch the news? I'd keep an eye on that. If I were you.

After the news van left Gusef suggested, Perhaps I call it Swallowed Angel Café, yes? No. That would be too confusing. Black Tooth is fine. Is disgusting, I know. This I like. Disgusting things are good for soul. If ever I step inside Red Lobster, please shoot me dead and hang my rotting body from lights on fishing pier until it drops into sea.

At the end of the shift Falk was back in the kitchen, sitting on the stainless-steel counter reading the newspaper, killing time. Billy was yacking about having a date with some convenience-store woman later that week and how he was going all out for this one, getting his hair cut tomorrow and everything, when Una came back and made herself comfortable in the waitperson's station on the other side of the kitchen counter. She took off her half apron and counted her tips. When Billy paused for a second she said, And what about you, Falk?

He shrugged. That's a good question.

Una smiled. Choices, choices.

Falk gave her a look. She met it full and threw it back at him. Well, me, I can't take the suspense, she said. She told them she was leaving, and it was their loss.

Falk undid the white strings of his long cook's apron. Yeah, it's been lovely, really, but all good things must end.

After she walked out, Billy was grinning. He said, So what's this with you and Una?

Nothing. We're just friends, is all.

Billy nodded, grinning even bigger. Uh-huh. You just better watch your ass, *amigo*.

GABRIEL WASN'T A LOCAL, although his mother had been raised in Goodnight and he'd lived there long enough to develop a reputation. He'd rammed a boat against one of the piers when he was drunk, trawling too close to shore for shrimp that weren't there. He was famous for stabbing Pedro Alamogordo. Pedro was a local thug whom everyone was afraid of, so afterward Gabriel had been something of a scary hero.

And the town expected trouble over that, payback in blood, but before it could happen, Pedro burned his house down in a meth lab screwup, with himself in it. After that unhappy ending, most of Gabriel's later pranks were excused by his temper or his drinking. He would beat up people and then tell them, Sorry, man, I was plastered and I don't remember a thing.

He didn't think about love too much. When he did, he considered it something of a pain, like a toothache or a weakness in your bones. And Gabriel didn't believe in weakness. He believed in strength, and he often told himself, Strength Is Virtue or Virtue In Strength. He couldn't decide which he liked better as a personal motto. Though to say Gabriel didn't think about love too much might imply him to be a not particularly reflective man. That would be far from the truth.

Gabriel had a tendency to brood. His thoughts tended to get stuck in a rut. Or a ditch, like his mind was a truck high-centered with its tires spinning in the mud. Gabriel realized this was not a good thing. But what can you do? You are who you are. He didn't believe in changing to suit other people. He tended to brood over how he had been wronged and how to get payback. All of those notions somehow circled like storm clouds around the eye of the hurricane that was Ramona Delgado-Vu, otherwise known as Una, the drop-dead beauty. After touching her he had never been the same.

Four years ago, a summer day in the shrimping season, a sky so blue and bright it hurt to open the door with a hangover, set the light to jumping out at you, set your teeth on edge just to step outside. He'd signed on with a Vietnamese shrimper named Dat Vu to fish for a few days, cull the catch, run the winch on the nets, see if they got along and make it a regular gig.

When he stepped aboard the *Smokin' Susie,* there was the girl. He frowned and stifled the urge to just spit. He didn't like the idea of sightseers and that was what females aboard usually meant. She was a skinny thing in a baseball cap and long black ponytail talking softly to what he quickly figured must be Viet-Papa.

Shrimpboats smell not so faintly of old dead fish and shrimp baked by sun and stewed by warm Gulf wind, but when he squeezed past Daddy's Girl in the small wheelhouse she smelled like honey pie. She made him forget the pain pounding in his head, the blinding sun, the rocking boat chugging out of the boat basin, a swarm of gulls yacking it up and filling the sky above with black and white feathers, yellow splayed feet, and laughing beaks, sending flickering pulse shadows below as he worked the net to make sure it would drop right. He did his best to ignore her and tell himself she was the boss's daughter: Off limits. No dice.

But later there she was in blue-jean overalls and baseball cap, skin a pure cinnamon color that made you want to touch it, to see if it was real and not Maybellined. She looked sweet and goodhearted, shy and bored. Like she was ready for a change in her life, something besides a stinking shrimpboat.

Hey, he said, you ever get hungry?

She said, Sometimes. She smiled. Moved away from him like she knew what he wanted.

Well, okay, then, he said.

It was a year before he saw her naked in the moonlight. Not until after her father died.

It was worth the wait.

The house where Gabriel lived had been ramshackle and beaten even when it was new. Now it was old, collapsing quietly, mouse-infested and messy with clothes thrown every which where and beer cans scattered near a plastic trash bin in the kitchen. He rented from an old woman who was frightened of him. Sometimes he paid on time and sometimes he didn't. When he didn't, she called and asked, Please.

It was five miles out of town on 881, near the western limit of Humosa Bay, on a half-acre lot of live oaks and palm trees, a patchy stretch of sandy soil. The front yard was an automobile cemetery. In it sat the hulks of Fords and Chevys like radiation-mutated beetles grown giant and sluggish, gently rusting in the sun, their wheels lavished by rattlesnake grass, and more often than not a trio of turkey buzzards floated overhead as if waiting for the inevitable to happen.

In the fields surrounding the house a middling herd of white-faced cattle lazy and thoughtful stood or moved slowly to chew one thing or another. Visible through the oaks and palms, they ranged wherever they chose, sometimes lapping rain water collected in a sawed-off fifty-five-gallon drum once used as a barbecue pit and now mainly as a water trough.

Wearing jeans and no shirt Gabriel walked barefoot into the kitchen and stared out the window at the tequilagold El Camino parked before the rusting junkyard. The idea of living in the car occurred to him in a moment of whimsy. He mused that it wouldn't be so bad, actually, if he got a shell and put in a makeshift bed of some sort to tour the countryside in a pipe dream. He could leave Goodnight in an instant, get in the car and never look back.

He opened the refrigerator door and scratched his gut. Inside were two cans of Tecate left in a plastic six-pack ring, a quart bottle half full of Gatorade, and not much else. A stick of butter, a carton of eggs, expired milk. He took out the eggs and reached up with his foot to touch the power button on the old TV sitting on the Formica counter across from the dinette set at which he ate his meals. He cracked an egg into a cast-iron skillet and watched it sizzle. The skillet smoked, the smell of it making his stomach tighten.

With the TV babbling in the background he heard the name of Goodnight by the Sea and the anchorman Jerry Tillinglass promising a remarkable find from the ocean depths, reported by their roving Eyewitness News chief Dale Pope. He flipped the eggs and was waiting for the yolk to harden the way he liked when he heard Una's voice talking to the reporter, a voice that moved his lungs a half inch to the right and made him catch his breath.

As he watched he saw the wormy cook Falk Powell, the punk who couldn't carry a blade to school for a little protection without ending up the boy martyr, standing next to Una. Gabriel knew the look he gave her.

Gabriel stared at the TV screen and said, The motherfucker.

IT WAS AFTER midnight by the time Falk finished mopping the kitchen floor, the long room filled with bright fluorescent light shining on the stainless-steel counters, copper-bottomed saucepans and skillets hanging from metal racks above the four ovens, the smell of ammonia in the air. He took off his apron and went to the dining room, where Una was vacuuming. Gusef drank ice-cold vodka at the bar. When he saw Falk he motioned him to take a seat beside him, and called to Una to stop and join them.

He poured shots of vodka for both of them. Here, he said. Drink. Is good for you. Put smile on mug.

Falk gulped his down, scrunched up his face.

Una pushed hers away. No, thanks, she said. I think you're having enough for all of us.

Gusef nodded. Okay. This will be my last. He sipped the liquid with elaborate care, then replaced the shot glass on the counter. My last one forever. He grimaced. Yes?

You putting money on that? asked Falk.

Gusef grinned. He told Una, I give you ride home.

To Falk he said, I have something you must see.

What about me? asked Una. Don't I get to come?

Not this night. This not for your eyes.

What's the secret?

We are going to Hubba Hubba Club in boondocks, okay? Boys' night out. We watch titties jiggle and we grin. We put five dollars in their panties and this makes us happy. You understand?

You're disgusting.

Gusef laughed. With you I share this disgust. And more.

In the dented Cadillac, Gusef ranted. He pounded on the dash and insisted his life had been one great mistake. Too much drinking. Not enough women. He laughed. He said, I should have been stunt driver. He aimed the Cadillac at a roadside mailbox whose flag was a wooden duck.

Gusef! cried Una.

He swerved away at the last minute, then wobbled in the road. I'm okay, he said. Okay. Okay. Okay.

When they pulled in to drop her off, Una looked at Gusef and said, You need to get home. You too, she told Falk.

Do not worry, said Gusef. We are not children.

Driving away he turned to Falk and said, We do not go to Corpus. I have something else you to see.

Goodnight was asleep. Cloaked with a velvety blueblack darkness, the moon above like a half-licked butterscotch candy. Gusef steered the rumbling brokenmufflered Cadillac back onto Shoreline Drive, keeping their destination a secret.

The glows of mercury vapor lights snaked their bands of yellowish hue across the dashboard, their chests, their faces, the backseat, the rear windshield. A great blue heron passed through the penumbra of streetlights while seagulls glided over the shoreline beside the road.

At the Sea Horse they turned in and parked at the back. Gusef killed the engine and held a finger to his lips. Falk nodded. Crossing the asphalt parking lot, they passed through a breezeway between the units, and there, in the hum and glow of the Pepsi and candy machines, Gusef stopped. You want make some extra money? he asked.

You bet. Much as I can get.

You spend all your time working. It is waste of youth.

What else am I going to do? asked Falk. Got no school to study for.

This is good then. Soon you will be rich stinking bastard!

Gusef told him he needed a new man to take care of the Sea Horse's lawn. This fucking shithole is going to hell in basket, he

said. I fired useless drooling lawnmower man last week because he
loaf too much. Yes well now look at it. The mosquitoes fuck in the
monkey grass and this not good for business. He grinned. Mosquitoes bite and kill the guests with virus, that is not good thing. Dead
guests pay nothing, you know?

I'll start tomorrow, said Falk.

Good. Now come with me. I show you something.

They crept behind the hotel's back unit, a jungled mass of banana
trees, oleanders, high grass. Gusef pointed out what a mess it was,
how this needed to be mown first and pronto. Each room had its
own small back patio. In the darkness, these appeared as only small
squares of light in the dark pattern of the high grass. Once inside the
thicket of banana trees and oleanders they followed a dim path. Falk
could hardly see a thing, but Gusef seemed to know the way. After
a short distance they stopped. Gusef held one finger to his lips. Do
not make noise, he whispered.

The darkness was so thick Falk felt as if he were falling into it. A
sensory deprivation feeling, as if floating unsecured to the land itself. They stood quietly until they heard a soft trilling sound. A
night bird called once, paused, called again.

Do you hear owl? asked Gusef.

I hear something, said Falk.

This is screech owl, said Gusef. *Otus asio.* I find this last week
and love sound. Listen. It is like little feathered horse. You mow
here, you hear sound each night.

After a long pause it hooted again, an indefinite beat, rapid at
first, then slowing and dying out, mournful and soft. Falk thought
the sound reminded him of an oboe or clarinet, but was not sure
which.

They stared at the back patios of the motel. One window filled with light cast its glow onto the high grass, and there Falk saw a woman brushing her teeth at a bathroom sink. She had her hair pinned up and wore a pink terrycloth robe. Gusef paused at the edge of light and put a hand on Falk's shoulder.

This woman, she is sad thing, whispered Gusef. He shook his head and closed his eyes as if some pain kinked the guts of his belly. She has worthless husband. He does not deserve life. Or her. But he is very loud and I want nothing to do with him.

Falk watched her, spellbound. He didn't know what to say. At one point she turned toward the window. From their skulking place in the dark yard, Falk and Gusef saw her sad and momentary face, her skin pale and eyes dark, wisps of bleached hair loosened from bobby pins, now hanging to her cheeks and shoulders, an expression of misfortune shaping her mouth, the way she held her head.

I want you watch her, keep eye on her. Her worthless husband is ugly and vicious man. Dangerous man. You understand?

Falk nodded. Okay, I get it, he whispered. The woman reminded Falk of his mother. Her hair had once been dyed the same color as this woman's. They shared a similar expression of forbearance. Yet his mother stubbornly refused to play the victim. She believed in work, not navel gazing.

This Puritan forebears work myth he accepted, and like so many others in Goodnight, lost himself in mindless toil, the frying of fish, the cutting of grass, until he surfaced breathing shallowly in the jungled motel's back reaches as the woman began to undress, Gusef vodka drunk beside him and weaving, saying, This we do not see. Come now. Do not look. Close your eyes now. Go.

4

THE HIGH SCHOOL KIDS saw him standing outside. At the front of the bus, before the bulbous orange hood with its shiny grille, walking around the black-striped sides, ignoring the curious teenaged faces in the slatted windows, the clatter as they lowered the top halves to stick their heads out and stare.

His right hand was in a cast to the wrist, the thumb and fingers free. He scratched his neck with it in a way that made him seem as if he knew he was being watched. He walked on like he didn't give a shit what they thought, squatted down to check the oversized blackwalls. Smoking a cigarette, squinting up at the sky. Dark muscle clouds flexed above, looked like rain coming off the Gulf. He wore a plaid Western shirt, blue jeans, and boots. One of the sophomores walking by said, Howdy. The look he got shut him up right quick.

Gabriel's thick hair and movie-star thug looks made the girls pause in chewing gum and half sneer, half smile his direction, turn to say something sassy to their friends, look back again.

Bobby Jarvis the smartass said, Who's he? The world's most obvious kidnapper?

He said it softly. The laughs he got were nervous and furtive.

Gabriel tossed the butt into the gutter. When he stepped aboard the bus it was as if a badass priest had entered a mufflered tabernacle. He took a seat and grabbed the gearshift big as an upside-down golf club. The quiet hush of students in shock. He said nothing to them. As if born to it and accepting the role with a mixture of resignation, disdain, and bravado, he shifted and gassed and muscled the loud engine down the route like a hood at the wheel of an ungainly hot rod.

It began to rain, thunder rolling from the low clouds. A flash of lightning made the kids squeal. Gabriel switched on the wipers. The slapping of the blades back and forth seemed unnaturally loud.

At the first stop he said, Watch your step. He even smiled. The two sisters getting off paused at the door and said, *Thank you* together like twins though they weren't. He paused before he pulled away, watching to see that they weren't going to throw themselves beneath the wheels and give him a bad rap on his debut, watching raindrops seep into their dresses and dampen the cloth, making it cling to their underthings, the wind in their hair.

Each shift of gears and crank of the door handle defined the muscles and tendons in his right arm. The mesquite-thorn tattoo made them all agog, the students who were cowed in his presence and invented for him a criminal past before he even finished the first route. They talked and laughed, but more tamely than usual. The boys were careful not to stand out.

Gabriel rode above it all, wearing an ain't-this-the-hell smirk. He perched in the green Naugahyde driver's seat like a disgruntled god, hands callused from years of handling shrimp nets and winches, accustomed to snatching eels and crabs from squirming hauls on deck, now touching loosely and with complete authority the steering wheel of the amber-with-black-striping Bluebird No. 37. He didn't yell at them. He didn't point or threaten. He didn't need to.

When the boldest of them learned Gabriel would be teaching some of the Saturday driver's ed classes, he asked, If we give you twenty bucks will you pass us, no problem?

Gabriel shrugged and said, Make it sixty, you got a deal.

They couldn't tell if he was kidding or not.

THAT WEEKEND he spent his first day as a driver's ed instructor. He parked his El Camino and strode across the Mustang County independent school district parking lot smoking a cigarette and sporting the brain-pulsing headache and cottonmouth of a hangover. His hair was combed back in thick waves and he wore a white T-shirt, denim jacket, blue jeans, and boots. He took a seat behind the wheel of the Ford Taurus with its Student Driver sign upon the roof and started the engine. He drove to the back door of the gym—where three students stood waiting, two girls and a boy—and pulled up carefully and smoothly. He got out and walked up to them, twirling the car keys on his right index finger like a six-shooter.

Hello, ladies, he said.

They said, Hi. The male, a chubby boy named Jason, who was usually in trouble, made a face. I'm not a lady.

Gabriel grinned. I'll be the judge of that.

The girls giggled.

So you want to learn to drive do you?

One of them nodded.

Why?

The dark-haired one with a wide face said, Then we can go wherever we want. We won't have to be asking for any rides anymore. I hate that.

My mother wants me to run errands for her, said the other girl, a pale girl with a nice face and big eyes. Boy is she in for a surprise.

Gabriel scratched his neck and nodded, then tossed his cigarette. Not having a car must suck, right? He narrowed his eyes. I can't remember when I couldn't drive wherever I wanted to. Nobody breathing down my neck. Must be hell.

Are you a real instructor? asked Jason. Do you have a degree or something?

The girls laughed.

Gabriel smiled at them and shook his head. I'll just ignore Curious George today, if that's all right with you two.

It was fine with them. One scowled at Jason. You're kidding, right? You don't need a special degree to teach someone how to drive, stupid. You just need to know how to do it. I bet he's good at it, aren't you?

The other said, He drives the bus. He must be. You need a special license for that, don't you?

He shrugged. You do. Not that I give a shit.

Jason said, He don't look like no teacher to me.

Get used to it, sweetheart. Gabriel opened the car door and told them to get in, instructing Jason that he'd best get in back and keep his yap shut if he knew what was good for him. Once they were inside he gave the pale girl in the front seat a wink and added that school was now in session.

Do what I say, he added, and you'll be free in no time.

He taught them to put their hands at ten and two o'clock on the steering wheel. Don't grip it too tight, he added. It's easier to move your hands in a turn if you keep them open, curled like this, see? Hold it like a baby. Firm but you're not choking it to death, right?

The dark-haired girl in the back seat scooched forward to listen. You drive number 37, don't you? I've heard about you. They say nobody gives you no shit on that bus. It used to be a wild one and now it's halfway human. I wish I could ride your bus. We've got Mrs. Roheburn and she's always yelling at us to sit down and shut up. It doesn't do no good. We call her Mrs. Rugburn.

You must be the quiet one in your family, is what I'm guessing.

The pale girl laughed. He got you, didn't he?

The girl in the back pouted. She said, Just trying to make conversation.

Gabriel almost smiled. He looked at the dark one in the mirror. She was watching him with a hurt expression, chewing gum.

I didn't get anyone, he said. What's your name?

Debbie.

Okay, Debbie. You just pay attention, that's all.

Okay. I was just trying to be friendly.

I know that. He glanced at the girl sitting beside him in the front seat, passenger side. Her dyed yellow hair was parted on the side, pinned in place with dragonfly barrettes. A beauty mark on her cheek. He liked that. A sundress with thin straps that left her white freckled skin uncovered, blue veins like little rivers in her chest, white bra straps. He could smell the woman in her. And she looked like she knew some secrets. Had some too. Or would.

No harm in being friendly, now, is there? he said.

The girl smirked. I guess.

You guess, he said.

What happened to your hand? she asked.

This? He held up his cast like it was show and tell. *Es nada.* Broke a couple bones the other day. Driveshaft crushed it.

Does it hurt?

He shrugged. Only when I move. He turned the cast right and left. No big deal. Just pain, is all.

What's your name again? he asked.

Alicia Ann Day. People call me Leesha.

He gave her a slow look. Okay, Leesha. Forget the hand. What you need to do now is listen. And I mean listen. To what I say. Think you can handle that?

You don't have to get huffy, she said.

He waited.

Okay okay, she added. I'm listening now?

He started out with the basics. The turn-signal indicator, the lights, the difference between a left turn and a right, swinging wide a little bit on the right so you don't clip the curb.

He talked as he drove. He effected an instructional manner, as if he were being taped for a video.

So in a minute you're going to get behind the wheel, he said. And we'll see what you can do, right? But there's something I want to get straight first.

He stopped and gave Leesha a look that made her tingle. Ten years ago, he said, my father was driving home from pouring concrete in Sinton, coming home on the back road. He was minding his own business. Didn't have no life insurance or anything, a law-abiding man, not expecting anything to go wrong. My sister Maria and my brother Tony at home. My mother too. And then some redneck full of Wild Turkey and Miller Lite slammed into him head-on.

He softened a moment for Leesha, gave Debbie and Jason in the back each a look.

He said, So my father? Hit head-on? He was decapitated. Head torn clear off. They found it in the field, gulls pickin' out the eyeballs.

Ouch, said Jason.

Debbie hit him.

You think that's funny?

Jason glared out the window. I didn't say it was funny. It must have hurt.

Shit. I doubt that. He probably didn't feel a thing. Gabriel thumped his chest with his index finger, twice. I'm the one it hurt. He was my father and he's dead now. My sister's an orphan and since that happened, since she has no daddy, she's gone bad. Last I heard she was strung out in Matamoros.

I'm sorry, said Leesha. She sounded like she wanted to hug him.

Me too, said Debbie.

Gabriel shrugged. Them's the breaks. So I'm going to teach you how to drive now, and if you ever drive drunk, I'll hunt you down and hurt you, you got that, sass mouth? he asked, staring in the rearview.

Jason scowled. I didn't say anything.

Must be learning then.

. . .

HE DROVE DOWN Karankawa Road to the public tennis courts on Farm-to-Market 881. They had a big parking lot, the asphalt bleached an elephant-hide gray by the sun, chunks of black tar near potholes here and there, weeds growing up. The sky above was swampy dark. When they stopped it began to rain hard.

Let's do it, said Gabriel, telling Leesha she'd be the first to take a crack at the wonderful world of self-transportation. Always walk around the back of the car, he said, in case some maniac gets behind the wheel while you're outside and tries to run you down. When they passed each other she was smiling, the rain spattering off the trunk of the Taurus, the smell of swamp gas and asphalt sharp in the air.

Behind the wheel, Leesha took a long time scooting the seat forward to reach the pedals. She couldn't find the lever to unlock the seat position. Gabriel said, It's important to get comfortable from the get-go. He leaned forward and reached between her knees.

What? Leesha blinked and leaned back, his hair in her face, the brief brush of his touch against her leg.

The handle is down here, he said. Here. Feel it.

He waited until she put her hand over his, the warmth of it.

Okay, she said. I got it. She made a face as she scooched the seat forward. Her hair was wet and bedraggled in her face. She breathed with her mouth open, and before setting the seat in place she touched the lever again and scooted farther back. Goddamnit to hell, she said. She struggled to get it to go forward. Gabriel just watched.

Leesha finally got herself situated.

Can you reach the pedals?

I think so, she said.

You think so? That's not good enough.

Yes.

Yes what?

All right already. Yes, I can reach the pedals. See? She turned her white legs for him to see she had plenty of room, her dimpled knees visible in the shadows of the car.

Well then. Now what do you do?

She rubbed the hair out of her face. She put her hands on the wheel in the ten and two o'clock positions, adjusted the rearview so she could see out it. Then she reached over and turned the key, but the engine was already running. The starter squealed a high-pitched grinding sound.

In the back Jason laughed. You'll be lucky not to kill us all.

Leesha looked in the rearview and said, Shut up, jerkoff.

He'll get his chance, said Gabriel. Don't you worry.

I'm so nervous I can't think straight. Look at my hands. She held one hand out to Gabriel. Look how they're trembling.

He reached out and closed his hand around hers. Never mind that, he said. He held on to her. You're going to calm down and you're going to learn how to drive this car like a NASCAR pro. You hear that?

She felt the warmth from his hand flowing into her entire body. Her legs were weak and felt like they were barely touching the pedals. She looked at the windshield, where the raindrops were fat circles getting sliced away by the back-and-forth of the wipers. I do, she said. I will.

Okay then. He released her hand, his fingers lightly trailing against her palm. Let's go.

.   .   .

Una Awoke in the small, boxy room of her trailer home with its low ceiling and flimsy paneled walls. Across from her sat a birdcage that held a pair of red canaries named Fa-lo and Toong. She spoke to the birds for a moment and poured a bit of birdseed into their cup. They squeaked and chirped to her cooing voice, scooting sideways on their swinging wooden perches.

Una hated living in a trailer home and she swallowed this hatred every morning when she showered in the tiny bathroom. When her skin was clean she felt less anger at the smallness of everything and a sense of hope bloomed each day as she felt she grew closer to her goal of escape. Her life would not always be this way. She knew this in her heart. How it would change, or what the circumstances of her new life would be, she was uncertain. But it would change.

That she was a twenty-two-year-old woman still living at home with her mother was never very far from her thoughts. She realized how this would seem to other people. She knew what the world thought of people living in trailer parks and that she was one of them. Her father had insisted theirs was a life of freedom. The trailer home rested on wheels. Any time we want, we drive away, he had said.

He seemed to believe the trailer sales propaganda.

Of course that was all foolishness. He was gone now and it didn't matter. He had bought the trailer home years before and had never taken it anywhere. For all the trailer homes in the world you rarely saw any of them being towed down the road to another location. They were usually plunked in one place and in a short time became weathered and decrepit. Too often they ended up engulfed in roaring blazes or overturned by hurricane winds, their roofs ripped off, rain-soaked belongings later discarded in a soggy heap.

The Bay Breeze Trailer Park, where they lived, was a tropical parking lot of transience. Weeds grew high around the wheels of the trailers. Behind them stood the lush, dark-green tangle of banana trees with huge veined leaves and thick stalks. Palm trees lined the drive and live oaks grew here and there between the lots. A few of the residents were like Una and her mother, long-timers, and tended to have either the most clutter around their trailers or the neatest and most attractive units.

Two of the trailers nearby were rentals for the short-timers. These people were the lowest order of life in the park, and Una did her best to avoid them. The men would stare at her and try to flirt. They parked their junky cars and pickup trucks near her windows.

The night before, late in the most secret part of the dark, she had been awakened by the sound of scufflings and voices and groans.

For a time Una lay there half believing it to be the sound of the ghosts of a couple who had died in that trailer home. The man had caught his wife cheating on him and had killed her and then himself. Sometimes late in the night in the two years since then she had heard noises coming from the trailer, the sounds of arguings and moanings, even though it was empty of living humans.

Recently a shaggy redheaded man whom Una did not trust or wish to speak with had moved in and played rock music too loud and watched TV late into the night so that its flickering blue image leaked out his windows.

Eventually she got up to peek through her curtains. A clamor too vigorous and lubricious for ghosts. There in a parking space of the trailer next door, close to where she slept, the lowlife neighbor was having sex with a much smaller woman, hidden beneath him, in the bed of his pickup truck. Una watched for a moment, then returned to bed. Their sounds stopped after Mr. Driesler across from them turned on his security lights and came out onto his porch in his robe, his dog barking in the driveway, Driesler calling, Stanley! Get back here. Stanley! Stanley!

It took Una a long time to fall asleep.

The next morning, as she dried herself in her cramped bathroom, her eyes were puffy from lack of sleep. With her recent shame at Gabriel's behavior and vow that she was done with him, it was harder than ever to feel confident and full of renewed hope. Hard to slip into the belief that all this would be over someday. As she put on her makeup she heard the pickup truck start up and drive away. She chose a simple blue dress for work, a vintage calf-length dress with brocade on the neckline and sleeves, one of her favorites. She left the house at nine forty-five as always. Only when she opened the door, there was Gabriel leaning against the railing of their small porch, smoking a cigarette.

He looked showered and shaved and well groomed, his shirt tucked in, jeans clean, smiling and handsome. He told Una he missed her. That he'd gotten a job. That he was working for Mustang County now, driving a school bus and teaching kids driver's ed. It wasn't perfect, but it was something. For Gabriel, saying this, he was all but begging on his hands and knees.

It's good to see you, said Una. But I'm leaving for work. I'm going to make some money too.

Una? Come on. Don't be that way.

Don't be what way?

You know what way. I mean, you want me to say I'm sorry, right? Okay then. That's why I'm here. I want to say I'm sorry, said Gabriel. I'm sorry. Okay?

That doesn't change anything.

Una walked down the wooden steps of the porch, bleached gray by the sun and wind, into the lush grass of their tiny yard. Gabriel followed beside her.

So what're you saying? Just forget it, is that what you're saying?

She walked so fast he had to struggle to keep up.

I'm afraid of you, she said. I can't be around someone like that. That's not how I want to live my life. Go pick on someone else. Go screw up someone else's life. You're going to leave mine alone. That's what you're going to do.

I saw you on TV, you know that? Is that your new boyfriend? That lame *chingada?*

She kept walking. I'll call the police, she said.

Oh, come on, Una. Let me give you a ride. Please?

She didn't slow her step or turn to look. He stopped in the road at the entrance of the trailer park.

I still have that tape of you, he said. You want to be on TV so bad I should send that to them.

She didn't turn or waver.

When Gabriel got in his car and drove toward the Black Tooth she was already on the sidewalk beside Shoreline Drive. He slowed near her and pleaded for her to get in the car. Traffic backed up behind him and honked. A flock of seagulls swarmed overhead, as if food was going to be thrown from the windows. Una didn't say a thing. The shadows of the gulls crossed and recrossed the white strip of concrete sidewalk before her, an unfolding and familiar path of trouble and remorse.

WALTER AND INDIA Hamilton had been Methodists all their lives. India considered it a safe and level-headed dogma, no great to-do about worshipping the bones of dubious saints and a minimum of witch-burning. Since she had reached her seventh decade of life her fervor had intensified. Now she thought of Jesus as a kindly and protective big brother, and God as an actual father with whom she would be reunited in Heaven. She smiled to see teenagers walking the beach with T-shirts that read, PROPERTY OF JESUS.

The world was too much of chaos and ugliness. If in your heart you could hold the Baby Jesus, you could see the tenderness in all. It was a matter of kindness. Of compassion. That softened the edges of the world, put it all into perspective. A woman had recently drowned her three children in a bathtub in Houston. If you looked at the waste and suffering of the three children's lives, it was horror. If you considered the children as freed from the hunger of this world into the bliss of another, the pain their mother must have felt and was feeling as she went to trial, it was still horror. But horror mixed with sadness. Forgiveness, even.

India sat on the bleached wooden planking of the pier and watched the mullet swimming beneath the surface of the green bay water. A black skimmer cut a liquid line over the surface, its quick wingbeats keeping it aloft, its orange beak immersed in the water, closing quickly when it caught a silver minnow. The air smelled of salt and fish. The world was full of kindness and mercy. You had to see beyond it. There was feeding and dying, yes. But there was also the liquid beauty, the tang of the living.

And they were among the tang of the living, even if Walter sometimes acted to the contrary. Since the zebrafish had been discovered and its glory snatched from him, Walter had been out of sorts. India had joined the New Testament Church on the southern end of Goodnight. He treated her with scorn for this. In the last week they had barely spoken beyond politeness. It worried her. She loved Walter and wanted to care for him. But the affair of the fish had somehow hurt him, made him too aware of his outsider status here.

They don't respect us, he told her. The people here think we're too old and feeble for anything but to give them money. We don't belong.

What he had not told her was the brazen threat that Gabriel had flung in his face in the Black Tooth Café. They still often went there for lunch. Walter told himself he'd be damned if he'd let some Mexican punk scare him out of town or any restaurant he wanted to visit. But he noticed the looks that the locals gave him, looks that said, Look, there's another fat tourist. Sometimes he felt as if the world had changed when he wasn't looking.

It had become his cross to bear. *We don't belong.*

India had told him, Then perhaps we should leave.

He had not answered.

Because he would not leave out of fear. Besides, where would they go? Where would they belong?

. . .

THE FIRST DAY Falk mowed the shaggy lawns of the Sea Horse, Gusef directed him to the storage room beside the swimming pool and told him, Everything you need is there, now go to work and don't bother me. Falk dragged out the lawn mower, its wheels wobbling, to a place between the shed and the chain-link fence that surrounded the deserted rippling blue waters of the swimming pool. Inside the shadows of the shed again he stumbled and squinted until he found a red five-gallon can of gasoline and a quart of oil capped with a cone of aluminum foil and a small funnel.

When he returned to fill the mower a woman appeared beside the pool, the same one who had been in the window of the bathroom. She had wavy bleached hair and wore a black one-piece bathing suit with a brightly colored towel wrapped about her waist. The beach towel had a bright blue backdrop decorated with the yellow-and-green image of a toucan perched in a banana tree.

Falk fiddled with the lawn mower and tried not to look her way. He sensed she was somehow forbidden and close. She dragged a chaise longue clattering loudly across the pool court. Her eyes were masked by a pair of black sunglasses with huge oval-shaped lenses that made her appear somewhat like a gigantic insect, a wasp woman. Falk could not tell if she noticed him or not, though her face was turned his way. He tried not to look.

He filled the lawn-mower tank with gas and spilled it when he glanced toward the woman, now bending over the aluminum frame of the chaise longue to straighten the toucan beach towel, revealing a glimpse of her tan line and breasts. He walked back to the shed and struggled to remember what he was searching for, until he realized it was the can of oil he'd already placed outside.

He left the shed and blinked once again in the bright sunlight. Doing his utmost to avoid glancing in the direction of the woman by the pool, he squatted beside the mower and added the oil with much care and concentration, as if he were an alchemist trying to obtain just the right mixture of fluids that would magically combine to create the viscous luster of liquid gold. A voice spoke to him, but at first he did not acknowledge it, such was his concentration, plus the thrum and fizzle of blood pulsing in his temples.

He heard the voice again, soft but more clear. He looked up to see the woman in enormous sunglasses leaning against the chain-link fence surrounding the pool and waving to him.

Hello! she said. Excuse me.

Yes?

Could I ask you to do me a favor?

The woman's voice was so faint Falk could not understand what she was saying. He stepped closer. He said, I'm sorry. I didn't catch what you said?

A favor? Could you do me one?

Falk nodded. Yes. I hope so.

You're getting ready to mow the grass here, aren't you?

Yes, ma'am.

The woman removed her oversized sunglasses and held them by one earpiece. She looked to be about thirty or so. Maybe thirty-five. Without sunglasses her face lost its resemblance to an oversized wasp. Her eyes squinted, dark with mascara. Pardon me? she asked.

Falk nodded. I'm going to mow.

Did you call me ma'am?

He shrugged. Well.

My Lord. I don't look that old, do I?

I'm sorry, he said. Just being polite is all.

She swung her glasses by the earpiece. So that's what you call it. Being polite?

I mean, well.

I call it ruining my day.

I'm sorry.

She gave him a look and made a gesture with her eyebrows that he didn't know how to interpret.

Can you do me a favor, Mr. Lawn-Mower Man?

Yes?

Could you mow behind our rooms? I mean, soon? First chance you get?

Okay.

That guy who used to do it always got around to us last thing. Now it's like a jungle back there. I complained to Gusef. But I bet he didn't say a thing, did he?

He didn't mention it.

That's like him.

I'll get to it first thing, said Falk. He started to move away, pulling the lawn mower backward behind him.

Don't you need to know where I'm at?

That he'd already seen her before, through her bathroom window, in the middle of the night, that he knew she was the woman in Room 17, suddenly seemed a secret revealed to all the world. He blushed.

Yes, I guess so, he said. Where would that be?

She told him. He nodded and again began pulling the mower

away. I'm supposed to mow the front near the office first, he said. Soon as I'm done with that I'll get right to it.

She laughed, the sound throaty and rich, like she knew he was hiding something from her, like she knew things about him without being told. You don't have to be in that big a hurry.

No hurry, he said. I mean, it's no problem at all. I don't mind. Really.

An hour later Falk trundled the sooty grass-stained lawnmower over the rough asphalt parking lot and parked the machine in the square of grass beside the back unit. Before he could pull the rope to start it the woman walked out of Room 17 carrying a rolled-up beach towel and a pack of cigarettes. She saw him and veered his way, hips swaying, wavy hair blown by the wind into her face, her hand slowly brushing some of it away from her mouth. She told him she'd been wondering about something and wanted to ask him a personal question. If he didn't mind.

Shoot, he said.

What do you do to your hair?

He made a face. I don't know. What do you mean?

Why is it so pale? You put lemon juice on it, don't you?

I don't put anything on it.

Then why's it so pale?

He squinted into the sun, trying to look at her directly. He said, I saw a ghost once. The ghost of my father.

She looked him over for a moment then smiled faintly. No. You're lying.

I'm not.

Where was it?

A few years back when we were living out by Humosa Bay. With my mother and stepfather. We don't live there anymore.

You mean your father was haunting his old house?

He never lived there. I couldn't even guess how he'd know we were there. But he showed up in the backyard once. I was walking out to the pier to go fishing and he was just standing there near the concrete bulkhead. Like nothing out of the ordinary.

What did you do?

I stopped and looked at him.

You're making this up.

I am not. He was real as you or me.

He was not, said the woman. She stepped a bit closer to him and turned into the crab-trap wind so that it blew her hair out of her face, made it easier to see into Falk's eyes. You're just in the sun a lot is all, I bet. That's what bleaches your hair like that.

Falk shrugged. Believe what you want to believe.

She grinned. You're full of it, this father baloney.

All I know is the ghost of my father, he was standing there talking to me plain as day, right? And he told me this wasn't going to work. The sea would rise and flood everything and then we'd have to move and I wouldn't like it. And he said there was nothing I could do about it because the pod people controlled everything and that the best thing to do is watch out for them and stay out of their way.

The pod people?

That's what he said.

Who are they?

I don't know. Falk made a motion toward the direction of Key

Escondida. Rich people. Fat cats. They have a lot of things. They drive nice cars and have shiny white teeth. But they got no souls.

And the ghost of your father told you all this.

That he did.

I don't believe it. You're lying.

I am not.

I bet your father is a fisherman. Is he out of work? Is that it?

My father is dead.

She laughed. You're such a liar!

I'm telling the truth, he said. His look backed this up. If he fishes for anything, he added, it's at the bottom of the sea. He drowned.

I'm sorry. I'm so sorry. And where's your mother?

She drowned too.

Together?

No. Many years later.

Now I know you're lying.

Falk shook his head. Remember last year when the causeway collapsed, the tugboat rammed it? My mother's truck fell into the bay.

I don't know about that. I wasn't living here.

Well, it happened. My stepfather was with her. He drowned too.

You're not lying?

I'm not. Around here, everyone drowns. Sooner or later. Seems like.

That's horrible!

He shrugged. It is.

She said nothing. Her face and body seemed to soften and melt in the afternoon sun.

Falk said, Maybe that's why my hair's so pale. You see a ghost, it'll happen to you.

The woman shook her head, put her wasp-lady sunglasses back in place on the bridge of her nose. You know what I think? I think you're a world-class bullshitter.

You do me wrong, said Falk.

Uh-huh. Well. The corners of her lips held tiny wrinkles, and Falk could see the pink of where lipstick used to be. She flipped the parrot towel over her shoulder. Well. I better be going.

I need to get back to work, said Falk.

She walked off with a little wave. Falk refilled the mower and didn't know what to think about the woman. He wondered why she would even talk to him. But mainly he wondered how he was going to get enough money to buy Una a car. As he'd mowed all day he'd calculated how long it would take him to raise, say, twenty grand. Billy told him you needed at least that for a decent set of wheels. At this rate, six dollars an hour, forty hours a week, he'd have to work, what? Like, forever?

By the time he was finished mowing the broad areas around the last two units in the U-shaped complex of the Sea Horse Motel the sky had darkened to the purple hue inside a grouper's throat, with low scudding clouds on the horizon of Red Moon Bay to the east. Nighthawks buzzed and flapped, hunting insects in the air. After one of the guests drove away, a small flock of herring gulls squabbled over a paper carton of French fries dropped out a car door into the parking lot. The pool was empty. The blue water sent wet fracture reflections in the shapes of white wings along the blue-painted cinder-block wall of the storage shed.

Falk cut behind Units 3 and 4 to the jungled back patio area dark now among the broad leaves of the banana trees and the waxy jumble of oleander bushes. He crept behind Room 17's bathroom window but it was dark. He waited there, mosquito-bitten and nervous, for nearly an hour before the woman walked into the shadowed room.

Through the glass he watched her turn on the shower and pull her hair back in a ponytail. The vanity-mirror light cast an aquamarine glow in the small bathroom, as if she were a bruised mermaid in an aquarium. She pulled her dress over her head. Falk held his breath. He did not slap the mosquitoes biting his arms and neck.

The skin of her breasts and bikini-strap lines glowed against the rest of her tanned flesh, set off the darker aureoles of her large nipples. She scratched her neck and looked at herself in the mirror, the water hissing in the shower, a faint steamy mist drifting above the pole holding the shower curtain. She blew her nose, tossed the Kleenex into a wastebasket.

She brushed her teeth and pinned up her hair. She adjusted the shower by reaching behind the aquarium-patterned shower curtain. Her hips were wide and tan-lined, her cheeks round and dimpled in the greenish glow, cleft and curved like a pair of half-moons in twinned eclipse.

Falk was late for his night shift at the Black Tooth Café. Gusef asked if he'd seen or heard the owl. Well, said Falk, tying on an apron, I'm not sure. I saw something.

THE NEXT DAY Una walked home from work in a hot, misty rain. She had forgotten her umbrella and didn't care. Cars passed her and passengers stared, tires hissed on the wet black asphalt. The faces of the people in the cars appeared gray and ghostly through the rain-streaked windows. In one yard a German shepherd barked as she approached on the sidewalk.

Oh be quiet, doggy, she said. It wagged its tail and rushed the fence close to her, until Una stopped and touched its black nose. The dog's fur was wet and it flattened its ears and cowered, licking Una's hand through the fence, its tail beating wildly with happiness in the warm rain.

You're a girl dog, aren't you? What a sweet, sad little girl you are. What's your name, doggy?

It stood up and put its paws against the chain-link fence, its warm tongue slimy on Una's fingers.

I'm going to have to give you a name then, if you can't tell me yours. What about Mariposa? You quiver like a butterfly, you know that?

Una stood there petting the German shepherd for several minutes, until she realized she was crying again. The dog wagged its wet tail and whimpered for more. When Una walked away it ran to the end of the fence and whined, turning circles frantically in the rain.

On her walk up the driveway of the trailer park Una felt a tightening of space, as if she were entering a sensory-deprivation chamber. When she walked through the door her blue dress was soaking wet, her lustrous hair pasted to her heart-shaped face. Her mother had just finished making a batch of tamales and was drinking a cup of coffee. She immediately shuffled to the bathroom and came back with a towel to dry her daughter.

Why didn't you call or get a ride with someone, *mi 'jita? Estás mojada y triste.*

I was ready to leave and I just walked out.

You could have called me. I would have picked you up.

I don't need anyone to give me a ride. I have two legs. I can walk.

Where is Gabriel? Have you had a fight or something?

I don't want to talk about it, okay?

You had a fight. I can tell. The other night he was *borracho, sí?*

I'm never going to ride in his car again.

Una's mother fell silent. She toweled Una's hair dry and told her to change clothes, that she would braid her hair while it was still wet, while it was easy to handle.

You like when I braid your hair, don't you?

Una nodded. I like it.

Maybe it make you feel better.

Una smiled faintly. Maybe.

As her mother braided her hair she described to Una her philosophy of woe and sorrow. A body must find a way through this treacherous path. She believed in the virtues of cooking and cleaning. These simple tasks had been a life raft and for many years had kept her from sinking into an ocean of anguish and bad times. She wove three plaits of Una's beautiful grackle-wing-black hair into and among themselves and explained her concept of *la virtud de simplicidad.*

She said, If your house is clean, no matter how humble and small and remote it is, it feels like a home. If the floor is swept and the dishes are washed you can look about the room and know you are not in the house of low persons. And if there is delicious food on the stove, the air in the house smells good. Your man will be happy with good food on the kitchen table. He will wrap his arms around you and keep you warm. *El mundo es frio, mi 'jita.* But it is not only for men you do these things. You do it for yourself. If your belly is full and happy, *un panza alegre,* what more can you want?

More, said Una. A full belly is not important to me.

What more do you want?

More? I don't want more. I want everything.

Pues, qué lástima. For then you will never be happy.

Maybe not. If I stay in this crummy town my whole life I won't for sure.

Una's mother had nothing to say to that, but Una could tell by the way she tugged at her hair as she did the braids that she thought her an ungrateful brat who would grow old and bitter and childless, most likely in some Northern city where people would use her only for their ugly lust. *Otra gente con ni corazón ni alma.* Strangers with neither hearts nor souls.

The doctors they tell me any day I might drop dead. Then you will be happy. Then you can leave this godforsaken town and never come to visit my grave. Weeds will cover it and no one will ever know I existed. Then you will be happy.

Don't be so melodramatic, Mama. You're not dropping dead anytime soon.

It could happen. The doctors they tell me I have diabetes and this disease it kills people.

Maybe you should eat better.

It makes your legs rot off. I do not want to live if I have my legs cut off. Put me to sleep like an old mother dog if that happens.

No one's putting you to sleep, Mother.

It makes you go blind too. I will sit here in this small house made of flimsy tin and listen for you to come home and you will never arrive and I will starve to death abandoned and lonely, heartbroken for the love of my foolish daughter.

No one's starving to death. If you go blind I promise to spoon-feed you *pozole* and *pollo con mole.*

An ugly thing it is to starve to death. What if I should end up like my Tía Paloma?

I don't know who that is.

Listen to you. You don't know your own family. And such a sad story it is.

You're always telling some story, said Una. I can't keep them straight.

If you can't remember them it is not surprising. Skinny ghosts do not remember anything but their own lives and their own pain. *Bueno. Olvide todos.* It doesn't matter to you anyway.

Would you stop that?

Una's mother had reached the end of her braid and into it had threaded a light chain of shiny red beads. She gave Una a mirror to look at the braid and the beads. Una thanked her and said she was lucky to have a mother who would braid her hair like that.

Now tell me about Tía Paloma, she said. She was your mother's sister in Mexico?

She died when I was just a girl. I don't remember her well but my mother mentioned her many times. In many ways she was like you. She was very beautiful.

Paloma is a pretty name. The dove.

Yes, she was like a dove. Her given name was Anna Maria, but they called her Paloma. Because she was so pretty. But her beauty was a sad thing for my family. Nothing was ever good enough for her. Especially no man. They tried to marry her to many men but none of them were good enough. They lived in a small village in the mountains northwest of Vera Cruz and the people there were country people. The men were farmers or woodchoppers and unsophisticated. She thought them all too stupid and brutish.

Sounds like the men here.

Claro. Lo mismo. And year after year went by without Tía Paloma finding a man who was good enough for her, and eventually she was too old.

I get it. That's what you think is going to happen to me?

Escucha me. I'm not finished. Tía Paloma had no man, so she put her heart into cooking. She made *lo más mejor comida.* Everyone in the village loved her food and eventually she had her own house where she lived all alone after your great-grandparents died. And this one year there was a great drought. There was no rain and the creeks that flowed down from the mountains dried up. Small birds fell from the sky like leaves. And on a day when the drought could get no worse a bear came down from the mountains. It was starving and needed some food. It must have smelled Tía Paloma's cooking, and the smell would have been wonderful, impossible to resist. The bear broke into Tía Paloma's kitchen and she attacked it with a broom.

Mother? Are you making this up?

I do not imagine such things. Such sadness. Tía Paloma's life was a waste. She should not have been alone. She should have been married and had a man in the house who could have fought the bear and driven him away. Perhaps the man would have had a gun and shot the bear. But there was no gun and no man to aim it.

So what happened?

Oye. You must remember this story. The world is a sad and

strange place. This hungry bear, he was not a bad animal. He was simply starving. And your Tía Paloma's food smelled so good! So he broke into her kitchen and he ate her. *Tu* Tía Paloma *fue comida por un oso.* Remember that the next time you decide to refuse another man.

What a horrible story! I don't remember ever hearing that before. Did you ever tell me that story?

No. You forget much of what I say but this is one thing I never told you. *Era un secreto.*

Why secret? Why didn't you tell me?

Because you were not ready to hear this story. Because you would not listen.

F A L K   S P E N T the whole day working. Gusef said he felt guilty, that a boy shouldn't waste his life, he should be having fun. During the evening shift he came to Falk and announced, I have gift for you. He held out a key attached to a sea-horse figure carved from wood. Think of it as bonus. This get you into spare room I keep handy in case I get lucky. Bed is clean and mirror across from it. Gusef winked. I call it nasty room. But you are young. Think of it as love room. He put the key in Falk's shirt pocket. If you are lucky, perhaps it is nasty love room.

Falk said, I don't have any use for it, really. But thanks anyway.

You are pathetic, said Gusef. If you do not lure female to room, then I am for certain you are gay.

It was after one by the time Falk made it home to his bunk bed above Leesha. He showered the fried-shrimp-and-oyster smell off his skin and out of his hair before he put on a pair of pajamas and walked down the dark hallway and into their room with the light off. He stubbed his toe and winced, letting loose a groan. Leesha flicked on a Daffy Duck reading lamp that sat on a wooden wine box beside the bed. It cast a yellow glow in the room and in this glow Leesha squinted at him, pushing her hair out of her face. What are you getting in so late for? she asked. You work too much.

I'm pulling double shifts to make some extra money.

She was quiet for a moment. She adjusted her pillows and watched him. It's not right, you working all the time like that. You should be in school.

That's not my doing.

Maybe if you apologized or something.

I did. They said they'd have a hearing next semester. If I keep my nose clean, they'll let me back in. I'll graduate in the spring.

He started to climb the little ladder to his top bunk bed. I really don't give a damn. I need the money anyway, and it would be harder to make money if I was in class. I kind of like being a JD.

As his legs disappeared up the ladder Leesha reached out and grabbed the cotton fabric of his pajama bottoms. What are you wearing?

Pj's, he said. Your mother said it isn't right, me walking around half naked in front of you.

Leesha laughed. She's one to talk.

She's all right, said Falk. I like to give her a hard time. You're lucky.

Yeah, right. She's a total pest if you ask me. She doesn't even want me to drive. She thinks I'm going to be a menace to the highways of Goodnight.

She's looking out for you. That's what she's supposed to do.

I guess.

Leesha turned out the light. They lay on parallel levels in the dark room, both with their eyes open, adjusting to the light. Falk remembered the woman in Room 17 of the Sea Horse, the image of her naked body through the bathroom window. He didn't know what to tell Leesha. He was about to say something when she said, You know I started driver's ed this week?

That's a tough one. They give you pop quizzes on the turn-signal indicator?

You wouldn't believe my instructor. He's like one step away from jail and a major hardass. Jason, this boy in my group? He's totally scared of him.

I had Mr. Buckthorn, the chemistry teacher? He'd fall asleep while we were weaving all over the road. It was easy.

This guy is anything but easy. He's cool though. I like him. I don't mind him being so strict. He told us his father was killed by a drunk driver and that he's on a mission from God or something to make us drive right. But I think he's really a softie. It's all an act, is what I'm thinking.

It's a game, said Falk. You play the game of the good student. Pretend to pay attention. Take the stupid test and ace it. They made us parallel park in the annex parking lot, on a course made from those silly orange cones. I mean, how hard can it be? Any retard over sixteen has a driver's license.

I can't wait, said Leesha. Once I get my license I'm going to sneak out every night and go wherever I want.

Falk laughed. You do and your mom will kill you.

In the darkness Leesha grinned. She'll have to catch me first.

. . .

GABRIEL WATCHED THE WORLD from behind the
wheel of the school bus, from his throne within arm's reach of the
shiny phallic handle that worked the doors open and shut and
the long black gearshift. He windexed the wide windows clean
before every drive because he knew they'd have his ass if he ran over
any of the little brats, whether he could see them or not.

He wasn't as good about sweeping the floors. He figured that
was janitor's work and by God he wasn't any fucking janitor. If the
floor was dusty and scuffed, littered with sheets of spiral-notebook
paper, too bad. The bus smelled of vinyl seats and Fritos and Anglo
brats going bad in a hurry. He watched himself reflected in car windows as he passed out of the parking lot, his bus a dark yellow shad-
ing to orange, No. 37. He wondered what the significance of that
number was. The age of his death? Then twelve years to go and,
what the hell, he might as well enjoy the ride.

He seemed to have fallen into a well of anticipation. He was at
the bottom amid the worms and the smell of moist clammy earth
and the roots, staring up at a small circle of sky, waiting for a face to
appear to save or doom him. He drove the bus down Pelican Av-
enue and Shoreline Drive and the children walked forward swaying
with the motion. When he pulled to a stop, the brakes screeching,
the teenaged kids swayed and held on to the pole behind him. He
watched the girls skip off and their skirts catch in the wind, and he
ignored the boys, no competition from those slouchy, pimpled
monkeyspankers.

He smelled the diesel exhaust and the asphalt dust and oyster-
shell smell from their driveways as they ran toward houses opulent

with lush grass, palm trees, and luxurious uselessness he could never afford. He felt himself morphing, brows growing heavier, hands outsized and nails ragged, the Bus-Driver Troll, opening his gate to let the privileged pass to and fro.

His route was a twenty-two-mile loop. Leesha lived off Humosa Bay Road, the end of the line. She was the last person on the bus.

After Una refused to have anything else to do with him, he did some investigating. He figured rightly that her new attitude had something to do with the kid who'd been kicked out of school, who worked with her at the Black Tooth. His parents were both dead now and she was sorry for him no doubt. Sorry enough to lie down in bed and show him a good time. Put a smile on his face.

He took to driving by Falk's house. His aunt's house. That was how he discovered Leesha Day was Falk Powell's cousin. That it wasn't so much his house as the place where he lived. Or was supposed to live. The cousin who didn't fit.

AND SO THINGS went on that way, with Gabriel lying in that well of anticipation, looking up at the sky, watching the girls' legs swish beneath their skirts as they got on and off the bus, feeling the stars and the sun swing by.

He told himself, There is always a point when you can turn back. The thoughts he had were unpleasant and some might say vicious and ugly, but they were just thoughts after all. He believed there was a feeling he'd get when suddenly he'd realize the direction of all his movements, a vision of the outcome. He expected a gut warning before any irrevocable and frightening act. It was too early to panic.

Yet perched high in the saddle of the Bluebird No. 37, he would brood. At the end of the line he would always be alone with Leesha, the teenaged *prima* of that smartass white boy who had stolen Una from him. He would brood while this yellow-haired girl leaned forward and prattled on about some utter nonsense, her sixteen-year-old breasts, soft and dewy, nestled against the back of his head. He would brood and stiffen as they rumbled down the back roads of Goodnight, snaking between the oak and saltgrass dunes near Humosa Bay, looking for a place to pull over.

She wasn't asking for trouble, she was begging for it. She was walking barefoot and short-skirted into a desert field of spiny cactus and not looking down at her feet, smiling, eyes asquint at the sun. Trouble, you get used to it and want it and expect it, and maybe at some level can't live without it.

A week after he started the bus route Leesha stood there, leaning against the stainless-steel rail, not exactly legit in that standing on the bus was prohibited. But he ran a loose ship, never having to do more than glare at the boys swatting each other in the head in the back of the bus. So no one said anything. He's the boss. If it's okay with him, it's okay with us. Leesha stood there, leaning against the horizontal stainless-steel bar right behind him, one hand on the vertical bar to steady herself, and started talking.

She said her birthday was November 17th and that made her a Scorpio. That was a fire sign. Did he know that? When was he born? Let me guess. I bet you're a Cancer. They're quiet and strong. You're like that you know. Or a Leo. A lot of movie stars are Leos. It's true! So did he believe in astrology? Some people said it was a bunch of nonsense. She didn't know for sure, but that sounded narrow-minded if you asked her. She hated narrow-minded people. The world was full of them.

She didn't know about those daily astrology charts in the newspaper. They were always saying something good was going to happen. She thought that was just wishful thinking. Nobody would buy the paper if they said, Don't get out of bed! Your wife's going to run off with the cable man and your house is going to burn down! You know what I'm saying? She laughed. She loved to talk, yes, she did. Her head was full of opinions, and she felt like if she was quiet too long it got all bottled up and that wasn't right. Teachers were always telling her to button her lip. What did they know? Lots of people make a good living by talking, like TV newscasters and reporters. That was what she wanted to be.

Had he noticed she was the last stop on the route? The end of the line they call it. Well I guess it's just luck. But it means I know the route, you wouldn't believe how well I know the route. The year before, this had been Mrs. Rugburn's route. Oh God that was sheer torture. She was a real sourpuss and he was so much better, you wouldn't believe. Kids used to cause such a ruckus and all she did was yell and scream and with him it was like peaceful and calm. She hated to hear people shout. He had a quiet strength was what he had. And that was a virtue.

Leesha Day would not shut up. It would take an operation to make that female quiet. A thick needle and some stout thread to sew up that yap of hers.

She stood so close her breasts nestled against the back of his head. He could feel her nipples hard as pumpkin stems through her flimsy blouse. He could smell her perfume. Her little woman scent. And with her wavy sunflower-yellow hair and wide mouth? She'd do in a pinch.

She was just peachy in driver's ed, wasn't she? She showed up for the second lesson wearing a skirt so short she had to keep pulling it down in the front seat to keep her cat from showing its fur. And when she was driving her hands were busy. Nothing to stop the hem from riding high. Nothing to stop her legs from being altogether a most wicked distraction.

A flower he might just have to pluck.

A WOMAN FROM the Associated Press office in Houston called and arranged a meeting with Falk at the Black Tooth. He waited for her at the bar at four o'clock, sitting opposite Leon. Mr. Buzzy drank alone across from them. The sunlight through the windows cast a bluish haze on the nautical world of ropes and mounted trophy fish. The countertop smelled slightly of cigarette smoke, beer, and ammonia. Leon's face was a bit puffy and gray as he considered a clipboard. He set it down and winced. I hate counting bottles of vodka, he said. It's so discouraging.

Falk bounced one leg and watched the parking lot through the front windows.

You think she's going to want the negatives?

Leon raised his eyebrows and looked out toward the empty row of parking spaces in front. She's going to want something real is what she's going to want.

Mr. Buzzy laughed. That woman take everything you have and you wish you'd of kept it.

How much should I ask?

I don't know. Leon checked something off on the clipboard. As much as you can get.

Ain't nothin' free in this world, said Mr. Buzzy. He finished his beer and carefully pushed it away from him on the table to take its place beside a stainless-steel container of white paper napkins and a bottle of Tabasco sauce. You know how much I got paid for this leg?

Well, I'd guess, I don't know, said Falk. Not enough I bet.

You right about that. Mr. Buzzy loosed a gargling laugh.

A white Volvo pulled into the parking lot. A woman got out and stood for a moment looking at the front of the café and the street. She wrote something in a small notebook propped against the Volvo's roof.

She's wondering what the hell kind of dump this is, I bet, said Leon.

She walked in and paused just inside the front door, near the hostess station, by the captain's wheel and the PLEASE WAIT TO BE SEATED sign. She was middle-aged, in a wrinkled tan pantsuit, with short gray hair and glasses. Falk shook her hand and introduced himself.

You're the photographer? she asked.

Well, yeah, um . . . He nodded.

She smiled and looked around. I thought you'd be older.

Well, you know. He shrugged. I will be. In a while, I guess.

She laughed. Let's take a look at your prints and see if we can make a deal.

He spread the photos out on a table in one of the booths. Leon and Mr. Buzzy were watching from the bar but were too far away to overhear the conversation. She looked at them, nodding, frown-ing, moving them around with her fingertips. Her accent was British. They aren't the best quality but they'll do, she said. The novelty of it, you know. It's not every day that something like this washes ashore.

Her favorite was the one with Una kneeling on the beach beside it.

This one, she said. She picked it up and held it toward the sunlight of the window, motes streaming in its smoky haze. The girl helps us get a sense of the size of the thing. We wouldn't want to be in the water with one of those things, now, would we?

Not me, said Falk. Unless I was in a boat.

How old are you?

Seventeen, he said. Almost eighteen.

Shouldn't you be in high school?

Well, yes, um, I should, he said. I mean I should be but I'm not. I was, I guess you might say, I mean, expelled.

The woman gave him a long look, then told him what they would pay. Falk said that sounded good to him. She asked if he could take her to the shoreline where the photo had been taken. To authenticate it. And I have some forms, she said. Legal things. Is that agreeable with you?

Of course. Sure. Where do I sign?

After filling out the forms they took a drive down Shoreline to the spot near the Sea Horse's fishing pier. The wind was gusty and the waves cast spindrift upon them. The Associated Press woman wanted to know if it always smelled like this and Falk said, Yes, well, most of the time. She compared the photos and the pier and seemed satisfied.

When they climbed back into her Volvo she took out a checkbook and a pen. Her hair was blustered and spiky from the wind so that she now resembled one of the crested cormorants that sat on piers and dove into the waves to eat mullet. After placing the photos in her satchel and handing him the check, she shook hands with Falk and congratulated him on a good bit of photojournalism.

If I'd been in school I wouldn't have been here to take the picture, he said.

Her smile was a bit lopsided. I suppose that's one way to view it.

She dropped him off at the Black Tooth and drove away. With a check in his pocket, Falk wasn't sure exactly what to do next. He went back to the wait station and got a cup of ice and filled it with Pepsi from the fountain machine there. His hands were shaking.

It wasn't that much, but it was something. He promised himself the money would go toward a car for Una.

LEESHA WATCHED GABRIEL driving the bus, pushing in the high clutch pedal, hooking the long gearshift lever with his thumb and pulling it toward him, his shoulder and biceps flexing, downshifting into second on the curves, banking his body into the sway and turning the black steering wheel big as a wagon wheel. She liked to watch him control the ungainly machine.

She wondered how he could shift with that cast on his hand. He'd told her the thumb and index finger were fine and that was all he needed. She thought the cast was cool. She wanted to sign her name but was afraid to ask. She knew that once she put her name there it would be something between them. A touch. A scrawl. It would make a faint but inescapable sound, like the softest hiss when a pair of lips part.

He glanced at her in the rearview mirror every so often but kept his focus on the road. Even when she leaned in to talk to him, standing behind him, behind his seat, separated by only the shiny stainless-steel bar that pushed against her belly. Raising her voice so he could hear her over the bus sounds but not loud enough for the rest of the kids, who usually sat a few rows back, to hear. They gave her some looks, the other kids, the ones who were scared of him. None of them said a thing. Directly to her, at least.

His presence was like an invisible bubble or aura into which she stepped and in which she was protected, lifted up, made more important and more alert. The temperature in his bubble seemed higher. But she was not uncomfortable. She liked it.

The only thing was her hands would sweat, turn moist and clammy, whenever he was around. Even if she only thought of him, which she did often, her hands would perspire.

She told him this. She said, Whenever I'm around you, my hands get wet. I wish they wouldn't do that.

He kept his eyes on the road, only a flicker of a look her way in the rearview. A hint of a grin.

I don't know why they do that. She smoothed her palms down the sides of her denim skirt. It bugs me, she said. Just nervousness, I guess.

They passed a white pickup truck hauling a trailer with horses, in the other lane. Gabriel raised a hand in a wave.

You know that man?

Maybe. And maybe I'm just being friendly.

Maybe you're just strange.

You're a nosy one, aren't you?

The word is "curious." Nothing wrong with that.

Didn't say there was.

She fidgeted against the railing, her body feeling so keyed up she couldn't help but move, twitch her leg, bounce her body softly against the railing.

I love horses, she added. If I had a horse I'd ride him every day.

You'd probably wear out two ponies a week.

She laughed and pushed the back of his head. Would not.

Cuidado, he said. Don't interfere with the operation of the vehicle.

You can handle it.

He shrugged. *Digame, chica.* How are those hands of yours? Wet and slimy?

I didn't say slimy. I said damp.

So are they damp?

She wiped them again on her denim skirt. A little.

Nervous?

A little.

No need to be nervous, he said. I don't bite.

I know that.

Well, not usually. 'Less I'm in a mood.

I bet. She watched his face in the rearview. Seeing if he would look her way. The almost smile on his lips.

He kept his focus on the road. Even when she leaned in close enough so he could hear her without shouting.

Even when she leaned in so close her breasts softly touched the back of his head.

She felt it and moved away, leaned back. She wiped her hands again on her skirt and watched out the windshield. The black asphalt, the amber highway stripes, the lush green fronds of the palm trees like fans in a harem, the branches of the live oaks, the white gulls gliding in the blue sky. In his bubble her pulse beat faster. Her very atoms and molecules seemed to move faster. Heat up. Her electrons speeding wildly in their valence shells that she had learned of in chemistry.

She told her friend Gloria that Gabriel Perez the bus driver and driver's ed teacher gave her the tinglies. Gloria said, You better watch it, girl. You play with fire, you end up scarred, you know what I'm saying? Or you put butter on it. One way or the other. Or both.

She leaned in again to speak. Again she touched the back of his head with her breasts. This time she stayed there. She knew it was trouble, but in his aura, in his bubble, she didn't care. She leaned her breasts against the back of his head, her palms wet, her skin goose-pimpled with the tinglies, and she said, I want to learn how to do this.

Do what?

Drive a bus. I want to learn how.

Gabriel made a face. Aren't you a little small for that?

I'm big enough.

Barely. Maybe after dinner. When your belly's full. He grinned in the mirror. But tell me this, *chica*. Why would you want to drive a bus?

No reason. Seems like a cool thing to do. Any lame-o loser can drive a car. You got to be special to drive a bus.

I don't know about that.

Well, it's true.

That would make me special, right?

I don't know. Maybe not. She was smiling. He saw it in the mirror. It's too early for you.

Sounds like you're making special rules to this game.

Maybe I am.

I don't know if that's fair.

Maybe yes and maybe no, she said. You want to be special, is that it?

He shrugged. It don't matter to me.

Liar. Sure it does.

Leesha leaned back. They had reached a bayside neighborhood where they let off most of the others. He slowed to a stop and pulled back on the handle to open the door. Three kids clomped up the aisle and down the steps. When they had moved off he pulled the door shut and shifted to first, revved the engine again, and let the clutch out. She watched it all. When they had reached third gear she leaned in again.

Tell you what, she said. You teach me how to drive this bus and then maybe I'll let you be special. If you're good, that is. How's that sound?

You trying to get me in trouble?

I didn't say anything about trouble. I said special.

I don't know, *chica.* Sounds like trouble to me.

I think you have a dirty mind.

You don't even know how to drive a stick, do you?

I can learn.

After two more stops he spoke. There were only the Miller kids at the back of the bus, and the McCullough girl in the middle. Maybe, he said. We'll see about that.

DRIVING THE PURPLE MONSTER tow truck with gigantic knobby black tires and airbrushed tongues of flame down the side, Martinez pulled into the parking lot of the Black Tooth about midnight. Gusef had left to give Una a ride home and had asked Falk to hang around and make sure the crazy taxidermist didn't set fire to the café or drown in Red Moon Bay. The colossal zebrafish perched on the flatbed like a traveling roadside attraction. The last drunken customer stumbling toward his car gave it a double take and said, Good Lord.

Falk walked outside to greet the mad blinker.

Martinez was already out of his truck and weaving in the oyster-shell parking lot, watching night terns float by the mercury-vapor lights. He stared at the great fish and beamed.

Falk told him Gusef had said he'd be back in a minute. Martinez looked at him and blinked three times. He wore a loud Hawaiian shirt buttoned haphazardly, showing a bulge of belly above his khakis. He smelled of beer and corn chips. He wheezed and blinked in Falk's direction as if peering through a thick bank of sea fog. He said, *Qué pasa*, surfer dude?

I'm all right.

Just all right? Not good?

Just working, is all.

Hell. Work. He belched. Seagulls in the sky above scattered. Nothing wrong with work. *Es* what an honest man does. He leaned against the truck's flame-red fender. What you think of *el pez*?

It's beautiful. Falk climbed up on the flatbed and felt the pebbly texture of its taxidermied scales. That's one fantastic fish.

What you think of it? Pretty mean mother, isn't it?

That's one great fish.

El pez gigantesco. Not bad, eh?

This must be the biggest fish you've ever mounted, right?

A great blue heron flapped by slowly in the penumbra of the mercury-vapor lights, at the edge of the shoreline across the road, its shadow sliding away into the darkness below. Falk watched it and when he turned back Martinez was staring at him.

You making fun of me, surfer dude?

Falk made a face of frustration. Not at all. This is a great job. It's, like, your crowning achievement.

Martinez blinked and nodded. Yeah yeah yeah. That's what you say. But what the fuck do you know?

They stood silent in the parking lot for a moment, the sound of the wind in their ears. Falk started to mention that Martinez must be drunk, but thought better of it. He had come to realize that when you point out their failings, other people often don't seem to take it with good cheer.

From the Dancin' Fool square-dance hall down the road came the hubbub of a Pimp & Ho Ball. A teenaged thing of curious organization, a community Say No to Drugs group trying to be hip. Kids in pickup trucks or four-wheel drives cruised Shoreline Drive. A limousine passed, filled with teenagers standing with their heads and shoulders through the moon roof and cheering. Girls in spangled low-cut slattern costumes, blond bouffant wigs and Cleopatra makeup. Boys in big hats with feathers akimbo, yellow leisure suits, hip-hop caps turned sideways.

They called it the Tards & Tramps Prom.

Standing in the hazy light of the Black Tooth's parking lot, Falk watched his ex-classmates' circus parade. People he knew waved or stared back. One gave him the finger and others followed with wicked laughter. A girl's voice called, Carter? Were you born an asshole? A beer can pitched out a Jeep backside skittered, spewing on the asphalt. Falk watched them pass without a word. The moon above was blue as the stone of a sea witch's ring.

Martinez put his arm roughly around Falk's neck and pulled him close, his beer-sour breath warm against Falk's cheek. You wish you were there instead of here, *verdad?* He tightened his grip, a soft headlock with his beefy arm. You want something but you don't know what it is. I know. Martinez kissed his forehead. I take you fishing soon, he whispered. We have a good time.

Falk twisted and stumbled, trying to get away. He rubbed his neck and backpedaled. Jesus, he said. You drink too much.

Martinez smiled. That's what I like about you. So nice and clean. He laughed then and scratched his stomach through the Hawaiian shirt. He stared at the platform Gusef had built upon the roof of the Black Tooth on which to mount the giant taxidermied fish.

Above the sound of wind and waves came the pulse of hip-hop music and the constant pinging of the pole grommets. What's that fucking sound? asked Martinez. It's driving me crazy.

Flag across the street, said Falk. It always does that.

Well make it shut the fuck up. Martinez laughed. Hey, surfer dude? He turned to Falk and blinked. You think the Soviet has a beer inside with my name on it?

Maybe.

Don't give me maybe. Give me yes sir.

I guess so.

Pues? Get me one. *Arriba arriba*, Señor Mozo. Martinez laughed. I wait here for your boss, I don't want to die of thirst, *claro?*

Falk returned in a minute with a bottle of Negra Modelo. He told Martinez that if Gusef asked, he didn't have anything to do with it.

Martinez nodded, put a gnarled index finger to his lips. *No problema.* Our little secret, right? But I bet that's not the only secret you have, little surfer dude. Let me guess. You look like the sticky-fingers type. Where'd you get that camera you carry around all the time?

Falk blushed. It was a gift from my mother.

Oh, right. *Un regalo de tu madre.* Likely story.

It's true, said Falk.

Nothing you say is true. But tell me this, surfer dude. What you stealing from the Soviet? I know you're stealing something.

I'm not stealing anything.

Sí, sí. Come on, *muchachito.* Our little secret, remember?

I don't know what you're talking about.

Maybe a woman, I'm thinking. You probably good at that. You steal women like candy. Let me look at your hands. *Tus dedos. Da me.*

He grabbed Falk by the wrists with his fierce hands, like the talons of a caracara, and turned them up to see the pink palms and fingers. *Mira!* They're sticky. Either you're stealing women or playing with your little Ramón. One or the other.

Falk jerked his wrists free and backed away. You shouldn't drink and drive, you know. They'll bust your ass.

Glazed with the yellow light of the parking lot, Martinez resembled just another drunken customer stumbling out into the night. The air was soft and he rubbed his face to clear off the cobwebs of his drink. You going to tell somebody, *muchachito?*

I won't need to. They'll see your ass weaving down the road a mile away.

The one working headlight of Gusef's mongrel Cadillac cut across the parking lot and the bald tires crunched loudly as he braked. He got out and beamed at them both. Let me see majesty, he said. Soon everyone will know Black Tooth Café and I be stinking rich.

Martinez said, I don't know about rich, but you already stinking. Martinez shook hands with Gusef Chicano style. They laughed and hugged. How you doing, you fucking Soviet?

Gusef shrugged. I have two legs, I do okay.

Martinez stared at his Cadillac drunkenly. *Diga me, mi amigo.* Why you drive this *cucaracha,* eh? He shook his head. What a piece of shit. A man drives that, he has no self-respect.

Is Cadillac, said Gusef. Best car in world. He noticed Falk lurking at the shadow edges and said, Are you harassing my cook again?

He's going to call the sheriff on me for enjoying a little brew, what he said.

Falk shrugged. We're just talking is all.

Martinez held on to Gusef, unsteady on his feet, breathing

loudly. *Qué puedo decir? Me gusta cerveza.* He held up the bottle of Negra Modelo in his other hand. Little surfer dude gave me this one. He said it was on the house.

You asked for it.

I already drank two, waiting here. I didn't even want this third one. He said, Go on, why not? Have another beer. The Soviet is a rich man. He won't notice.

I did not.

Gusef told Falk to go home. Our taxidermist friend here gives you hard time. Don't worry. Go home. He only fucks with you because he likes you.

What did I do? asked Martinez. I didn't do nothing. Hollywood, he's touchy, isn't he? Martinez blinked and nodded at Falk. *El joven es quisquilloso.* Me, I'm thinking he's a little iffy too.

Take car, said Gusef. He insisted he didn't need it. He had to wait for the crew with the cherry-picker rig who were going to lift the zebrafish off the flatbed and position it on the roof. He said, I must stay to direct this thing so they do not fuck it up. Martinez here keep me company. You take my car and this is good. That way I will get no ticket when I stagger home drunken ranting at God who does not listen.

Falk took the keys and started to leave. When he passed them, Martinez patted his back, telling Gusef, We'll go fishing soon, I'll teach this *crío* how to catch a big one.

Falk ignored him, still feeling the creeps in his neck where Martinez had touched him. He knew what it was and what Martinez wanted was never going to happen. He got behind the steering wheel of Gusef's Cadillac and cranked the engine. The car was something of a Goodnight legend, considered one of the rustiest in a town whose parking lots held more than their fair share of rusting junkmobiles. The tailpipe spewed a blue cloud of exhaust as Falk tooled through the glow of streetlights along Shoreline Drive toward his Aunt Vicky's house.

MONDAY MORNING a sight both outlandish and fantastic greeted the people of Goodnight. The first to see it were those who drove the hotel-and-restaurant drag of Shoreline Drive, but before long others heard and cruised by to gawk. Walter and India Hamilton parked their RV across the street and had a picture taken, posing in front of the Black Tooth, the colossal zebrafish seeming to float right above their heads. Walter told everyone who would listen that he'd actually discovered the thing. No one cared. He said it was because they weren't locals, they didn't get any respect.

No one thinks snowbirds can do a damn thing, he said loudly.

Hush, said India.

Before Gusef had mounted the fish on its roof, the Black Tooth had been a weatherbeaten white clapboard diner. The left side of the single-story building had four square windows that let in a glow of sunlight, while the right side, an original cinder-block structure that belied its origins as a drive-thru snack shop, had small windows covered with a blue cellophanelike plastic to dim the lighting. The bar was called the Captain's Galley, much agog with nautical gizmos. The entrance, a large brown wooden door, divided the two sides. In it was a round window, oversized, like one of the *Titanic*'s portholes.

The colossal zebrafish arrived stuffed on the roof like a supreme statement of defiance to Goodnight's slow demise. From a distance it resembled the giant bugs placed atop pest-control shops as gaudy advertisement. Up close it seemed the most ridiculous trophy ever mounted, a tropical fish on steroids, its zebra-striped sides bloated and beautiful, its palm-shaped dorsal fin like that of a coelacanth gone wrong. Tourists gawked. Traffic on Shoreline Drive slowed and snarled.

A marine biologist from the Texas Parks and Wildlife Department had examined the carcass while Martinez prepped it for taxidermy. He identified it as a species thought to be extinct for years, although a specimen had been hauled up in a net off Florida in 1983, another beached in Bermuda two years later.

Those who had seen the thing in the water or on the shore, or in Falk's photographs, insisted the fish itself seemed to have swollen. This was true. Martinez had stretched the skin so that it resembled an enormous zebra-striped pufferfish on the roof of the café, a pufferfish with a magnificent tail. There was a Moby Dick quality to it, a swaggering brazenness in its aspect.

From a certain angle the great fish actually seemed silly. Martinez had made the lips pink, as if it were wearing lipstick. A white papier-mâché horse head and hooves protruded from the mouth. From the parking-lot angle, the horse legs seemed like an insect in the process of hatching.

For several days Gusef could be seen outside in the parking lot, gloating. And he was right: It put the Black Tooth Café in Goodnight by the Sea, Texas, on the map. Within a few days the TV people in Corpus Christi did a follow-up story on it and more tourists came.

The weather that week mentioned a tropical depression in the Caribbean, churning the sea near Cuba.

. . .

HE WAITED in a grove of live oaks off FM 881. The sea wind rustled the fat fronds of palmettos. Bonewhite lizards the size of small birds skittered on the stalks shaped like sawfish bills. She was thirty minutes late and he'd begun to feel foolish and exposed, something new to him. He was having second thoughts. He leaned against his tequilagold El Camino and smoked a cigarette to kill the time.

The idea of plucking the rose petals from this *prima* of Falk Powell's had a delicious tang, yes. The unstated anger of a revenge fuck made it extra hot and bitter. But Leesha was also addictive. Already he knew he was playing lovesick. Gabriel always told himself, You don't wait for a woman, they wait for you. You don't give them the power over you. Especially not a girl, especially not a *gringa.* Walk away. When you see them next time, make them ask for it. Make them whimper. Want in their eyes. Hands fumbling at your belt buckle.

But when Leesha appeared, pedaling her mountain bike furiously down the dirt road, wearing a silly white helmet, forty-five minutes late, he wanted to smother his face in her breasts and touch every inch of her skin. He knew this was trouble and he didn't give a shit. That made it all the sweeter. Her brakes squealed as she stopped beside the El Camino where he stood, hands in his pockets.

She was breathing hard and took a moment to catch her breath. She unhooked her helmet and dropped it to the ground. Her lips were lipsticked red, her blond hair mussed from the helmet, her bangs hanging now in her face.

Do I look like a dork? My mother makes me wear this.

Little bit, he said.

She laughed. Thanks! She shook out her hair and squinted at him in the late-afternoon haze. It was cloudy and looked like rain, a blue light filtering down from the dark clouds and through the oaks. She said she was sorry she was late. You're here, she said.

I said I would, right? You're late. I was about to split.

I'm glad you didn't.

As she stashed her bike behind the oaks, she told him her mother had made her wash the dishes and vacuum the walls. Can you imagine? Vacuuming walls?

That ain't right, said Gabriel.

She is such an anal freak, said Leesha. Everything has to be so clean.

Mothers think it's important to be clean, don't they? Me, I like a little dirty now and then.

Personally, I think she's trying to cover up something. Like those crazy Christian fanatics who turn out to be sexually depraved. You know what I mean?

I've seen that.

She laughed. Seen that! You have!

Once or twice.

Right. I bet you've seen everything.

Not everything. Seen some things I like, though.

I bet you have.

They were quiet for a moment.

So, said Gabriel. Last thing I remember you wanted to learn how to drive a stick.

She nodded. I do. I mean, it's not that hard, is it?

Easy as pie. He took out his car keys, a skeleton-figure Day of the Dead keychain. What's in it for me?

I don't know. She leaned over and looked inside the El Camino. I'll owe you one. How's that?

Good enough. He handed her the keys and told her to get behind the wheel and make herself comfortable. He got in the passenger side.

Lesson number one, he said. See that third pedal to the left?

She was still adjusting her seat, scooching it forward, tilting the angle of the rearview, strapping the seatbelt across her chest, fumbling with the latch. When she was set she brushed her hair out of her face and looked at herself in the rearview.

I swear, she said. I look like death warmed over.

Cabrón, he said. You look pretty good to me.

She turned the mirror back. What again? she asked. You said something about lesson number one.

He gave her a look.

I wasn't ready!

Okay, okay. The pedal on the left. See that?

Is that the brake?

No. That's the one in the middle.

Okay. Yeah, I see it.

Push down on it. Then hold it down.

She did.

That's the clutch, he said. First thing you do before anything, before starting the car or touching the stickshift, you push in the clutch.

Okay. Then what? Now I put it in gear?

No. You push in and out on the clutch. What you need to do is get a feel for it. A touch. That's how you put it in and take it out of gear. And that's the most important thing.

She pushed in the clutch and let it out a few times. Her face with a look of concentration, as if learning a new game. You ever do this before?

Do what?

Teach someone to drive a stick?

Never.

You seem to know what you're doing.

He shrugged. I'm a driver's ed teacher, right?

She laughed. Yeah, right.

I never taught someone to drive a stick but so what? First time for everything.

Gabriel showed her the gears. The shape of an H. First up left, second down left, third up right, fourth down right. He told her to push in the clutch and put her hand on the gearshift. Her small hand there, nervous and wet, looking as if it were incapable of controlling such torque and horsepower. He put his hand over hers and directed her to keep in the clutch, then with his large dark brown callused hand engulfing her small white fingers he moved them through the gears, until he took his hand away and told her to do the same on her own. She did, frowning and addled.

My leg's getting tired. It's starting to shake.

He laughed. What, are you a scaredy-cat?

Don't laugh at me.

It's just funny, is all.

I've never done this before.

You'll get used to it. Trust me.

She let the clutch out and sighed. I don't know what I'm doing here. I really don't.

Outside it had darkened. The lush palmettos and saltgrass on either side of the road created a thicket that seemed to enclose them, cut them off from the rest of the world, the world full of people who would disapprove. For a moment Leesha thought about what they were doing, how beyond that wall of swampy greenery were people who could not see this. But if they could, she knew what they would think.

The sky above them, full of dirty wool clouds, began to rain. Huge clear drops spattered the windshield. They sat for a moment watching the raindrops.

Maybe we should do this another day, said Leesha. I don't know if I can drive in the rain. She wiped her hands on her jeans. I'm all flustered.

Nonsense, said Gabriel. You just need to do it. Push in the clutch and put it in first. Then turn the key.

They sat there. Leesha frowned. She turned to Gabriel and gave him a pleading smile. Do we have to?

It's just a little rain. You going to let that get in your way, you might as well give up now. Don't even bother.

She started the car. The engine caught immediately with a throaty deep idle. She said, How do I turn on the wipers?

Gabriel showed her and she switched them on, the blades slapping back and forth.

Is that better? he asked.

Uh-huh. Now what?

Now let out the clutch slowly. And I mean slowly. The same time, give it some gas.

She let the clutch out too quickly and the engine died.

Shit, she said. My leg's shaking too much.

That's okay. You just need to let it out slower. And give it more gas.

She tried again and this time the El Camino lurched forward. Leesha squealed in delight and surprise. The car bucked because she let the clutch out too fast, but it didn't die.

He told her to shift into second, then third. When they came upon FM 881 the engine died again.

Son of a bitch! she said.

Gabriel laughed. You ain't very convincing at that.

What?

Cussing.

She stuck out her tongue at him. It seemed a pink muscle between her glossy red lips, the bumps at its tip like the knobby hide of a starfish. She started the engine and let the clutch out again too quickly, again the engine died. That's the one I have trouble with, she said.

You're learning.

She got it going on the third try. They drove a couple miles down the road and he told her to take a right. It was a sandy palmetto-lined road through a swampy thicket of live oaks and palms and swampgrass, redwing blackbirds fluttering in the cattails. The rain slackened. She drove through puddles. A snake slithered in the muddy lane and she yelped.

Did I hit it?

I think so.

Oh. I didn't mean to. It's bad luck to kill a snake.

Gabriel shrugged. Maybe you didn't kill it. He raised his eyebrows. Maybe it's just a little bit dead.

They drove a quarter mile and came to a fork. He told her to take a left. She put on the brakes and forgot to push in the clutch. The engine died again.

I'm never going to learn this.

Sure you will. You're doing fine.

She got it started again and lurched forward, the back of her head thumping against the headrest. Where we going?

Nowhere. Just driving.

Why back here?

No reason. Nobody much comes out here. We won't be bothered.

They call this Thousand Roads Swamp, don't they?

They do. You been here before?

Once or twice. She didn't look his way.

You have?

Boys like to drive out here Friday nights after the football games.

Is that a fact.

You know that. People come out here to drink and party. She glanced at him. Couples come out here to *screw*.

Gabriel laughed. Is that what you were doing out here before? Once or twice?

No, she said. I got drunk once out here though. I got home late and puked my guts out in the bathroom. My mother liked to of killed me.

FALK MOPPED the linoleum floor of the Black Tooth Café, back by the coin-operated pool table, cleaning up a mess from the night before. It was humiliating work, holding a mop and pushing it around a honky-tonk floor, but then again, there wasn't much of anyone to see him. The only customers were a few regulars by the front counter, Mr. Buzzy and the tackle-shop owner. The rest of the place was quiet.

It was another bright and fishless day. Sunlight made the blue-shaded windows in the dining room seem to glow. In the back of the place, Falk labored in the neon god's light of beer signs and the country-western crooning of the jukebox. The ammonia smell of the mop water was sharp enough to make him blink and breathe through his mouth.

A motorcade pulled into the parking lot.

Mr. Buzzy waved his cane toward the windows and said, Look what just dropped into our net.

Una quit rolling her silverware. She slipped out of the wait station and glided to the bank of enormous aquariums opposite the front door, where you could look out the portholelike window. Outside a line of four cars had pulled in, the black limousine in the center looking monumental. It was flanked by an alligator-green Ford Explorer and a pair of anonymous government sedans. After a moment doors popped open and out stepped a crowd of people, all wearing suits.

Una touched at her hair and smoothed her dress, positioned herself behind the captain's wheel in front of which stood the sign that read PLEASE WAIT TO BE SEATED. The group outside gawked at the colossal zebrafish mounted on the roof, one of them taking snapshots, getting everyone to line up for a group photo.

When they entered Una smiled and asked if they preferred Smoking or Nonsmoking. She collected a stack of lunch menus. Eight men and two women stood gabbing as Gusef and Falk scooted three tables together. In the middle of them all was a large man about whom the others seemed to be orbiting. Within a couple moments Una realized it was the governor. After ordering a round of gumbo and iced tea, he got up and began to walk around the restaurant, shaking hands. He was a large man in blue jeans, boots, and a plaid Western shirt. He shook Mr. Buzzy's hand and asked him how he was doing.

That depends, said Mr. Buzzy. He leaned back and squinted at the governor. Depends on what you sellin'.

The governor laughed. He had a pink fleshy bloodhound face and coyotegray hair. I'm not selling anything today. I've heard about trouble in the fishing industry down here and I came to see for myself how folks are getting along.

We do, said Mr. Buzzy. We do. Like always. He waved his cane at the governor. You a Republican ain't ya?

That I am. The governor laughed again. You won't hold it against me, will you?

That depends, he said. Republicans never did a thing for me. I ain't rich so what you want to hear from me? Nothin'. And not much of it.

Falk returned to the back of the café and finished mopping. He hauled the mop bucket out the back door so he wouldn't have to walk by the gaggle of slicks in the dining room, not wanting too appear too Quasimodo. He took to loading cases of beer into the cooler and keeping an eye on Una. He heard her laughing at something one of the men in dark suits said. He was jealous. He saw the bloodhound governor shaking hands and didn't like it. He overheard the governor say, I understand you have a photographer here.

You mean Falk, said Una. You want me to get him?

At first Falk refused to go out. Una had to plead with him. What are you? she asked. Chicken? She tucked her thumbs in her underarms and flapped her arms, a black-haired teasing bird. Cluck cluck cluck?

I'm not chicken, said Falk. I just don't like politicians. They give me the creeps.

Me too, said Una. But he's here, so deal with it. Come on. How often does this happen? The governor wants to meet you? You're famous.

No, I'm not.

Minutes later Falk found himself shaking hands with the hulking, puffy-faced man. Una stood behind him, smiling.

So you're the one who found the sea monster? said the governor. That's really something.

Falk nodded vaguely, then shrugged. Well I wasn't the one who found him first. A snowbird did that. I was just the one who took the pictures. We heard about it and walked down there.

I was with him, said Una. It was so huge, you wouldn't believe.

You think that's what's eating all the shrimp?

Falk shrugged. I doubt it. I think they just caught too many. We're the ones eating them all.

You think people got a little greedy, caught too many, said the governor. That makes sense. Sometimes you have to look at the big picture, but we don't always like what we see.

Falk shrugged. Well, maybe. But it's just my, you know. My opinion. What do I know?

The governor shook hands with him again and moved on. He and his entourage left the Black Tooth after eating only half the meal and glad-handed their way around the boat basin, shrimpers eyeing them suspiciously as they approached, a pair of Mexican illegals hightailing it across Shoreline Drive, fearing the border patrol and a bus ticket to Matamoros.

WHEN FALK LEFT WORK that day Gabriel Perez followed him like a shadow. Falk drove Gusef's cruddy Cadillac to his Aunt Vicky's. Behind him trolled the low-slung body of Gabriel's El Camino. He followed Falk along Shoreline Drive to the turn at Curlew Way, where Falk took the shortcut across Highway 35, then down the back road toward Humosa Bay.

When Falk pulled into the driveway Leesha sat on the hood of her mother's car, talking on a cell phone. Leesha saw Gabriel's El Camino drive by slowly on the dark road, and recognizing it, gave him a wave, though she couldn't see his face.

Falk waved back.

Leesha wore blue-jean cutoffs and a tank top that read SOON TO BE A MOVIE STAR in sequined letters, a retro '70s look. She thought to tell Falk about her driver's ed instructor passing by, but didn't. She liked having secrets. If anyone knew about her meeting Gabriel on Thousand Roads for extracurricular stickshift training, she'd get her bottom spanked but good.

Falk got out of the car and asked, You eat already?

She kept talking to her girlfriend, shook her head to answer him.

He made a feint to grab the phone and she pulled away, swatting at him like a cat.

Leesha sashayed her hips as she walked toward the house. Hurry up. Everybody's talking about the storm. Hurricane Tanya, my lord. She turned around and walked backward. We're all going to blow away, you know that, don't you?

I wish.

That evening Falk helped Uncle Ed clean up the yard and nail plywood over the windows in case the storm actually hit. Aunt Vicky thought they were overreacting, but Ed frowned and said, Better safe than sorry.

They didn't finish until ten at night. He and Falk heated up leftover pizza, and Falk said it was good they got this done ahead of time. He had told Gusef he'd help board up the Sea Horse tomorrow.

When they were done eating Falk rinsed the dishes. Ed told him to get some sleep. It was late and he had a busy day ahead. Leesha was already in bed in their darkened bedroom, watching a TV propped at her feet. She was giggling and told Falk to come here. Quick, you have to see this.

The TV was plugged into an extension cord stretched across the room to a wall outlet, and Falk tripped on it, almost jerking the TV from the bed. He grabbed it just in time, and she laughed even louder, saying, Careful, you goof.

She was watching *The Simpsons,* one of her favorite episodes, and told Falk if he wanted to, he could fit himself in the bunk bed. No tongue kissing, though, she said.

He frowned. Well, I don't know. I mean, I have to get cleaned up first. At least.

Leesha laughed and threw a handful of popcorn at him. I was kidding!

Falk nodded, put his wristwatch on the dresser top. I knew that.

But hurry up anyway. You're going to miss the whole episode.

After his shower he squeezed into the tight space next to her on the bunk bed, and she told him to be quiet. They didn't want her mom poking her nose beneath the covers. She pinched his arm. Mom would put a stop to this right quick.

Falk shrugged. She's cool.

I heard you got a visit from the governor today.

Falk nodded. That we did.

What's he like?

He shrugged. Oh, you know. All just bullshit. He just pretended to be interested. We made the news. He was jealous, I bet. Probably didn't like a bunch of nobodies getting all the attention.

Was it fun? Meeting someone famous and all?

Falk shifted his body. His left arm was touching her shoulder, and the silky feel of it made him anxious. It was hard to take Leesha's eyes. She looked at him so directly he had to turn away. I guess, he said. Not really.

Why do you look so serious?

He shrugged. No reason. I guess I'm still in the work mode.

Oh, come on. Work work work. It's just fried food, right? That's not really a job.

What do you think it is?

An elaborate favor. A smelly, elaborate favor.

Well that's what I'm doing then. A cooking favor.

I said smelly.

Same difference.

Leesha stretched and yawned. I got an idea why you're so serious all the time.

You do.

Yes, I do. What I heard is you got girl trouble.

Falk made a face. He rubbed his pale hair until it stood up straight off his face in a comical fashion. Girl trouble? Not me.

You're not very good at lying, you know that? You got it written all over your face. You want that Una chick and she's playing hard to get. Either that or just playing.

So who told you that?

Leesha shrugged. Personally, I don't think she's right for you. She must be, what? Six years older? Seven?

Five. He worked his feet out from under the blanket and said he should be heading topside.

You ever get the feeling we're, like, sailors, trapped together on a long voyage?

Falk smiled. Ahoy, matey. He stood up and climbed onto the upper bunk. Maybe we are trapped. But I don't have time to think about it right now. I need some sleep.

I'll be listening, said Leesha, her voice a half step above a whisper. I'll be watching you in your dreams.

THE END of the bus route was what they waited for, with an impatience and excitement as if a cast were about to be removed, a tingling limb to be released, itchy skin eager to be free. They waited for when they were alone. The last two bodies on that behemoth of a machine. And in that time of waiting they grew careful. Leesha sat now in the second row and did not ask his opinion on anything, like did he think the storm would hit Goodnight? Hurricane Tanya it was. What kind of name is that? Sounds like a hillbilly sweetheart.

She wanted to talk about it. She wanted to ask his opinion. He seemed to know things. She wanted to tell him what the news said. Ask if he'd heard it. That Tanya could make landfall in two days anywhere from Pascagoula, Mississippi, to Matagorda Bay, Texas. Her not asking what was on her mind. Her trying not to even look at his dangerous face. His brown eyes and dark eyebrows. The hair on the back of his neck. The bulge of muscle in his arms. On his wrists, blue mesquite-thorn tattoo bracelets.

For a time she gave in on that ride and stared at them, the muscles. The center of her body grew warm and wobbly in imagining. If she could just wait. If she could just hold this burning in her lap. After the McCullough girl got off she would rest the back of his head between her breasts, pretending it wasn't happening.

The bus route wound its way like a great gray snake through salt marshes and oak thickets full of palmettos and the long white necks and ostrich heads of yucca. At the last stop the McCullough girl, awkward and lumpy about her middle, large glasses and small eyes inside not looking at anyone directly, clomped down the steps, faded toward her palm-tree yard. Leesha waited until Gabriel pulled the bus away and they turned a bend in the road. She waited until Mary McCullough was out of sight before she moved to her perch behind him, the faintest of smiles on his lips in the rearview.

So I thought you wanted to drive this thing? he said.

It's raining again.

So?

Why does it rain every time I want a driving lesson?

I'm beginning to think you don't need any lesson.

Is that so?

That's so. I'm beginning to think you already know how.

Maybe I do and maybe I don't. You certainly don't know everything.

Gabriel pulled onto a side road. The pavement was potholed and weedy, bordering a swampy field full of roseate spoonbills. Tall cranelike birds, awkward and beautiful, like illustrations from a Japanese calendar. Their dark spatulate beaks dipped into the marshy water between their elongated sticklike legs and primordial pitchfork feet. He slowed the bus to a stop. The headlights reflected into a mizzle of rain.

Leesha's heartbeat was loud as the slap of wipers. Louder than Gabriel's voice when he yanked the parking brake, left the gear in neutral, stood up. Yawned.

Take the wheel, *chica.* Let's see what you can do.

The seat warm from his body heat. Her denim skirt hiked high so she could reach the pedals. She fussed for a moment, turning back the sleeves of her Western shirt. The flock of spoonbills beat heavily as they flew off in the silver rain.

Gabriel said, You remember how, right? Clutch and gas, clutch and gas. Give it a little gas and let off the clutch.

They lurched forward and she stayed in first, wrapping out the gears. The engine whined loudly. What do I do now? she said.

Gabriel laughed. Second. Shift to second.

Which she did, jerkily, swerving as she took her hand from the wheel.

He called out, Don't run off the road! He stepped forward to steady the wheel.

They went perhaps two miles this way, never over twenty-five miles an hour, just reaching third gear, before she pulled over and stopped. A vicious squealing of brakes.

She smiled at him in the rearview and blew a sigh. It lifted her sunflower bangs. She said, I think that's all for now.

That wasn't so hard, was it?

Oh, I love it, she said. It's kind of scary but I love it anyway. She stood and wiped her hands on her skirt.

He didn't move. Outside the rain grew harder, shimmering in great rippling sheets. She asked if he thought the storm would hit.

I don't see why not, he said. He pulled her close enough to smell her hair, hear the sound of her breathing, the blue pulse of her veins beneath the silky skin of her neck. It'll probably come and wash us all away, is what it'll probably do.

Her voice faint and breathless. Aren't you scared?

Not at all. He pulled her onto his lap in the front-row seat, kissing her neck as he worked the pearl-snap buttons of her cowgirl shirt. Each of them made a tiny metal click. Her eyes half closed, her faint voice saying her knees were so weak, her feet numb. When half her shirt was open, he pushed back the fancy-stitched collar, slipping one white bra strap off a thin shoulder.

Truth is, I'm not scared at all, he said. About time something happened to this town. Wind like a terror. Lightning. Thunder. All the fucking tourists running like scared rabbits.

He parted her legs and put his hand between them. Hellacious waves, he said.

She stared groggily at the rain spotting the windshield. Her lips parted, her breathing fast. I don't think we should, she whispered.

He worked the cowgirl shirt off her shoulders, bunched at her elbows, deliberately but without hurry, as in slow motion. In the tunnel of the empty school bus, he exposed her china-white skin. The blue veins in her breasts like rivers flowing beneath fields of snow.

She tried to whisper for him to stop. She seemed to have lost her voice. She made no sound. When he kissed her nipples, she closed her eyes and whimpered.

After a moment he looked up. The expression on her face was pleading. She started to speak and he shook his head.

Shhhh, he said. Quiet now.

By then he had his fingers where she knew they shouldn't be. She loosed a faint moan, as if in a fever, squirming within a bad dream.

We might not even survive, he said, putting her hand on the tightness between his legs. We might all be drowned.

Don't say that, she whispered.

He grinned and said, Me? I'm looking forward to the storm. Wind and rain and flood. The whole shebang.

The rain hissed in great squalls on the metal roof of the bus. They were enclosed in a vapor sheen. It misted the windows and cut them off from the world. Leesha's face blushed pink, her blond bangs damp with sweat.

When they were done she lay on the front seat of the school bus, tears matting her eyelashes. Gabriel stood and buttoned his jeans.

We better get going, he said. People be looking for you.

Let's not go yet, okay? I don't want to leave. Not yet. Okay?

He took off his shirt and rubbed their heat clear from the foggy windshield. Well, sorry, *chica*. I don't make the rules.

He let her off at her bus stop an hour late. Afterward he told his supervisor the engine had died. A problem with the carburetor, he said, but explained that he had fixed it.

At home Leesha drifted giddily. Her cheeks pink as the evening primrose blooms that grew in her backyard. Nothing she could do about it. She hid in her room until it went away, the guilty blush. Hiding there and changing her clothes three times and feeling him seep out of her. She began to worry. What if? In a matter of moments she was defiant and eager. Well, what if? It wouldn't be the end of the world. Why not, even? Her mother called through the door. Alicia Ann? Girl? What in the world's the matter with you?

Nothing, she called. Just watching TV is all.

In his tumbledown home, Gabriel sipped a Dos Equis and stared out the window at a flock of gray herring gulls. He remembered how Leesha's skin had felt and wanted her all over again. Twice as bad. Like an infection it was.

Telling himself he'd done nothing wrong. Or if he had, it was worth it. You can't live a life worth living if you don't do the wrong thing now and then.

Keeps you on your toes.

THE NEXT DAY Falk mowed the picnic area behind the pool, and behind the courts, parts he hadn't reached before. When he was done he bought a can of root beer from the vending machine near the pool. He put the mower up and returned to the back fence behind Room 17, where he'd left the weedeater.

He was tired and walked slowly, drinking the root beer. Behind the guest-room patios, behind the motel, behind the gray wooden fence that encompassed the wild bamboo clusters and banana-tree thicket, stood an abandoned convenience store gently rusting and rotting in the tropical heat and sun. He poked around in the rubble. The asphalt of the parking lot was cracked and full of weeds, littered with broken beer bottles. The windows were spray-painted ugly with graffiti, elaborate leering wolf faces, and the scrawled announcement: *Sheila B. is good pussy.*

A ladder led to the roof. Falk climbed it. From there the air was sea-soaked and balmy. It glowed with a tangerine light as the sun filtered through the rustling palms. The sky turned violet, the world filled with a smell of beached catfish, cut grass, and tar. Dusk morphed all in the overgrown border to wind-whipped silhouettes. In the abandoned land below, the blinking fireflies seemed as big as hummingbirds.

From there he could just see into the glowing windows of Room 17 and behind the glass the woman being slapped. The act unfolded in dumb show, the sound of hand on cheek muted by the distance. Falk's heart quickened. He saw her husband walk into another room, heard a faint sound of shouting.

He heard the clap of doors slammed and a rough voice shouting, YOU GODDAMNED WELL BETTER FIND IT! The skirl of the woman's softer feminine voice pleading. A pause of quickened breathing and dread. The hope it was all over. Then more stumblings, the crunch of a door being kicked. The sound of crying. The man's voice shouting, WHY DO YOU BRING THAT UP? HUH? WHY DO YOU BRING THAT UP? YOU WON'T EVER FORGET WILL YOU? YOU GO TO HELL. I MEAN IT. YOU GO TO HELL. Another door slammed. YOU THINK I WANT YOU FOR A WIFE? IS THAT WHAT YOU THINK? WHAT A JOKE. WHAT A FUCKING JOKE.

He wondered if he should call the police. He could call Sheriff

Littledog, but he wasn't eager to do that. He went to the motel office and Gusef wasn't there. Billy Wright sat at the counter watching the lobby TV. Falk asked, Did you hear something?

Hear what?

That couple in 17. They're having a fight I guess.

Billy shrugged. So what else is new? That dude's a creep.

Should we call somebody?

Like who?

I don't know. The police?

Billy made a face. You're on your own there, pal. That falls under the category of None o' My Business. And my advice to you is stay out of it. Most likely all that will happen is you'll make an enemy of that dude. And I know for a fact that he totes a gun.

Falk started to go. He stopped at the door. When is Gusef getting back?

Later. He went to Corpus for supplies. You heard about this storm in the Gulf? Weatherman says it might come this way. Gusef went to the lumberyard there.

Why Corpus?

The ones in town are either sold out or charging too much.

Falk stood with the door open. Still, it seems wrong not to do anything.

About what?

About that woman. He hit her. I heard it.

Billy nodded. Yeah, well. She should of left his ass a long time ago. Some women like that sort of thing.

I don't think so. Not her.

Go home.

Falk picked up the phone, Billy frowning and shaking his head. He called Gusef's cell phone and told him what was going on. Gusef said he'd call the police, to just come on to work and pretend like he had seen nothing.

When Falk pulled into the parking lot of the Black Tooth, he saw the sheriff's car pass down Shoreline Drive.

❧ 6 ❦

Una Drove Her Mother to the doctor's office. The voice of her *mama loca* rattled and bounced in the old car as they drove through town. She had something wrong with her, she said. She just knew it. She was seeing spots and feeling faint. She'd almost passed out in the Wal-Mart the day before while shopping for mouse traps.

No puedo vivir en una casa con los ratónes, she said. I won't do it. I'd rather live under this miserable trailer than live with disgusting creatures. I'll live under there, where you keep your money. If I stay in this miserable trailer, *esta chozuela,* I'll become *una ratóna* myself. You'd like that, wouldn't you? You could bring your boyfriends over and laugh at me. You could toss me cheese. That would be nice. Maybe you would. And maybe you wouldn't. I never know about you. *Mi hija ingrata. Mi alma flaca. Mi mocosa.*

Una held her tongue. She couldn't stand driving her mother's stinky Chevrolet. The only thing holding it together was rust. Black rosary beads swung from the rearview mirror and a plastic Jesus stood looking rather discount-store beatific on the cracked vinyl of the dashboard. With holes in its muffler the engine chuffed with a guttural cough. The motor mounts were broken, making the entire car shake when idling. At the stoplight on Highway 35 Una cringed as the car vibrated, growling like a ragged old dog sitting beneath a Beware sign.

Qué pasa con tu novio, Gabriel?

He's not my boyfriend.

You should get back together with him. *Es un hombre, me gustale.* He's just a little rough around the edges. You don't appreciate that now. You will later. Maybe.

It's over with us.

Una's mother sighed, picked at a thread on her plain black dress. *No lo creo. El tiene tomado contigo.* She laughed. He's under your skin, like a chigger.

Una refused to look in her direction. She knew the smile on her mother's face, what she meant, how she envisioned her life. It was a false vision, but one her mother nursed like an ugly baby that would grow to be an uglier teenager.

Mama? Enough. I don't want to talk about it.

Ay, you never want to talk. You would like me to shut up *siempre,* wouldn't you? You'd be glad if I lived down there with the mouse droppings, wouldn't you? said her mother. *Con la caca de los ratónes.* She laughed bitterly. You'd be happy. I could guard your precious money like a pit bull.

Mama? Do you have to do this every time we go somewhere? Keep it up, I'm getting out of the car. You want to drive, is that it?

Una's mother stared out the window at the palm trees and the blue sky. It was hot and both of them were sweating in the car without air conditioning. Oh, *sí*. I'll be quiet. Like a little *ratón*.

Oh, Jesus, said Una.

They drove in silence the rest of the way. The doctor's office was in a sunbeaten, faded wooden building in a ragtag strip mall on the southern edge of town. It seemed to be constructed from the wood of bleached fishing piers salvaged after one of the many storms that swept the coast. They went inside and took a seat on the plastic chairs of the waiting room.

Dr. Arispe specialized in treating the poor. His was not a glamorous *consultorio*. Two plump white women sat across from them, discussing the coming storm. They'd heard it was headed for the panhandle of Florida and at most Goodnight might get some more rain. They hoped it would come closer. It might cool things off. The weather had been so hot and here it was almost October.

You know the joke, said one of them, her neck wrinkles damp with sweat. If I owned hell and Texas, I'd rent out Texas and live in hell.

Una and her mother listened to the conversation of the women but pretended not to. Dr. Arispe's office was too warm, the air stagnant. Una could smell the women across from them, could smell her mother, could smell herself.

No tengo miedo por la tormenta, whispered Una's mother. *Tengo miedo por los hijos de ese mujeres, como se sabe.*

Mama? Would you speak English?

Why? *Me gusta la lengua Mexicano.*

Well. We're in public, okay? It's rude.

179

Una's mother stared out the window. Outside all they could see was a patchy sunbaked yard and a pile of broken gray cinder blocks. In the center of the rubble three huge lizards, the same color as the cinder blocks, sunned themselves, their backs zigzagged with black stripes. Two of the bigger lizards jostled for position and tried to mate with the smaller one. One of the males made an obscene humping motion on its surprisingly long legs. Una and her mother watched this nature show and Una swore to herself that if her mother made any comment about the lizards, she would walk out of the doctor's office and leave her to take care of herself.

Her mother shook her head and grimaced. *Los lagartos están hiciendolo en las piedras, qué repugnante.* She reached up to her shoulders and straightened her black braids. Reminds me of you and your boyfriends, eh?

Mama? Okay. That's it. I'm leaving.

Her mother put one hand on Una's arm. I'm kidding. Quit being so sensitive. You're becoming just like all the little *gringas* you work with.

I'm not becoming like anyone. I'm me, understand? And I'm just sick of it. That's all.

Okay. Fine. I'll shut up. *El huracán* will probably come and blow me away, and then you'll be happy.

They waited for a half hour before getting in to see Dr. Arispe. Her mother made Una come and sit in the doctor's office with her because she didn't want to be alone if she had to unbutton her dress. Una walked back to the patient's room, feeling foolish, following her short, chubby mother down the hallway. The nurse made Una's mother stand on a scale.

It registered two hundred and sixteen pounds. Una tried not to act shocked. She was slightly taller than her mother but the woman weighed twice as much as she did.

In the patient's room, Una's mother sat on a vinyl bench covered with a strip of paper. She had to step up to the bench slowly and when she sat there her puffy legs dangled. She looked foolish and forlorn. Una sat off to the side and picked up a stethoscope from the white countertop nearby, next to a box of rubber gloves.

Put that down, said her mother. It might have germs.

Dr. Arispe arrived and nodded at them, asked, *Qué tal?* He was a heavy gray-haired man with oversized eyeglasses. He asked Una's mother how she was feeling. She said she was really not so good. Her back was killing her and her feet were swollen. She could barely wear shoes anymore. She saw splotches of purple before her eyes when she woke up in the morning. What were these splotches? She had chest pains. Like someone was jabbing her in the heart with a tiny knife.

Como un cuchillo pequeño, she said, looking right at Una as she spoke. Sometimes she couldn't get her breath and had to just sit there and be still for a while.

Dr. Arispe made a concerned face, took off his glasses, rubbed the bridge of his nose. Una could hear him breathing. She wondered who examined the doctor. If he was in good health. She doubted it. If he could be trusted.

He put the stethoscope prongs into his ears and placed the tip against Una's mother's chest, listened to her heart. He asked her to inhale deeply and exhale. Over and over again. He listened from her back as well. He looked in her eyes with a small light, into her ears. He asked her to lie on her stomach and palpated her back.

As far as Una could tell, he seemed to be examining a small and overfed dog. She half expected him to rub her mother's belly and give her a treat when it was done.

HURRICANE TANYA was a cycloptic swirl of wind and rain two hundred miles across, stalled in the middle of the Gulf. The forecasters didn't know for certain where it was headed. Hurricane warnings were posted from Pensacola to Browns-ville. The Weather Channel talking heads predicted that it would most likely make landfall west of Lake Charles.

There was still a chance it would hit Goodnight, but most people seemed to think it was at least two days away and nothing to worry about. When FEMA ordered a precautionary evacuation it didn't sit well with the locals. Gusef had an Evacuation Is for Wimps party aboard his boat, the *Crazy Jane.* He invited everyone and anyone who was planning to stay and ride it out. He enjoyed himself by insulting his guests.

Falk sat alone on the bow of the *Crazy Jane,* his legs dangling over the side, watching the dock lights shimmer on the water's surface, watching for Una. When she came walking up through the harem-fan shadows of the palms, he waved to her and got to his feet.

She had a rushed and wide-eyed look about her. Her black hair was windblown by the walk to the marina, and her eyes were dark with mascara and eyeshadow. Falk took her hand to steady her balance as she stepped aboard. I don't know what it is, she said, holding his hand as she made the wide step over the gunwales. I just feel so weak. Maybe it's the barometer falling or something meteorological like that.

Falk thought she was beautiful, with her thick black hair like a fluid cloak against her spice-rich skin. She seemed as if she'd been born to spend her life near the ocean, on coral islands in the South Pacific, with white sand beaches, sky-blue water. She wore faded blue jeans and a red cardigan sweater, a white scoop-neck blouse beneath.

Falk told her he had a surprise for her later that night. Something that was going to make a difference in her life.

Gusef overheard him and shook his head. Whatever it is he planned, you do not deserve.

And what's that supposed to mean? asked Una.

He burped, then added, I am foolish. You deserve more than what you receive, yes? He handed her a paper cup, then filled it with champagne. Soon the boat was packed with people, all talking too loud. Most of them were older, friends of Gusef's, but a few teenagers straggled in, and some hangers-on from Una's time in high school. She and Falk hid in the cabin belowdecks, lying in hammocks and drinking champagne from paper cups. They could feel the boat rocking when people stepped on and off. The motion seemed more noticeable the more champagne they drank.

There was an ice chest full of bottles within reach if Falk leaned over and stretched as far as he could with one arm. Una rocked back and forth in her hammock, her foot pushing against Falk's body.

I feel kind of sloshy and warm, she said. Like a jellyfish or something. Like that fish you found. Like I got a horse in my throat, you know what I'm saying? Is that what you feel?

I don't know what I feel. Maybe like a jellyfish. Or a squid.

Don't just agree with me to be agreeing. I bet you're the kind of guy who agrees with a girl all the time when they first know each other, just to be pals, and then after they know each other a while the real you comes out.

Someone opened the door from the deck and looked down on them. It was a girl Falk knew from high school, one of the cheerleaders. Is that Falk Powell the bad boy with a bottle of champagne in his hand?

Well if it isn't the pep squad calling, he said. Hello there, Stacy.

She waved and smiled brightly, then looked at Una. Looks like you have a little private party going on.

Invitations only, said Una.

Stacy said, I get it.

Behind her someone asked what was going on below, and as she closed the door, she said, Lovebirds.

Una said she had an idea. They should lie side by side in one hammock. It would be easier to sip the champagne. After a moment they slumped together, her warm body pressed against his.

You know what I think you should do?

Una laughed. I have no idea. She took another sip. What is it that you think I should do?

I think you should leave.

Here? Now? She put her head on his shoulder. I thought you liked me.

No no no. Not here. Not now. But soon. And I mean Goodnight.

Goodnight?

He burped. Excuse me, he said, smiling. I mean Goodnight, the town. You know.

You want me to leave? Really? Una nuzzled in closer against his chest. Why is that?

This town, Falk whispered. It's too small. Life's too mean.

Una closed her eyes. I like small. I'm a small person.

Falk nodded. That you are. Then he frowned and shook his head. No. No. That's not true. You're big. You're a big person. In spirit, you know? You're huge.

And you're crazy, said Una, patting his face, her hand on his cheek, warm there, an act of utter affection.

Falk started to speak but before he could get the words out Una leaned over and kissed his ear, touching the tip of her tongue inside it. His eyes closed and he felt the cabin spin. After a moment she leaned back and smiled.

What were you saying? she asked.

I don't remember.

You still have that key to the motel's nasty room?

He nodded.

Then, she whispered, staring at his mouth, why don't you take me there?

They made their way topside on champagne-woozy legs. Most of the other guests had left. Gusef was sitting on the sundeck at the bow with the woman from Room 17, talking in hushed voices about her husband in jail and court orders. When Falk and Una approached they stopped talking and sipped their champagne. Finished with heart-to-heart? asked Gusef.

We're just starting, said Una.

Gusef laughed. What is this? Schoolboy makeout time? Camera boy? You going to ask her to pose for nasty photos, this I bet?

Falk laughed. I didn't think of that.

No, said Gusef. You are type to ask her to be wife.

Una shook her head at both of them. She said it was time they should be going, that much was obvious. Falk stepped toward the gangplank and stumbled, almost falling into the boat basin, then steadied himself. He looked at Gusef and said, I can't do that. I don't have a ring.

I tell you what. I let you borrow ring for one night. Then Una be happy. Then she will let you touch her lovelies.

The woman from 17 clucked her tongue. Gusef? You have no class. She looked at Una and told her to ignore him. You know Gusef. He makes being a pig a virtue. But we see right through that, don't we? He's just trying to bully everyone with his Boris Badenov routine.

Una frowned. Yeah, thanks, Boris. You really killed the mood.

Come on, said Gusef. Falk is healthy boy. He deserves woman's touch. Right? Am I right?

Una made ready to step off the *Crazy Jane,* getting her footing on the gangplank, holding on to the guyline. You, said Una. You should quit while you're ahead. Or behind.

Speaking of behinds, said Gusef. Show camera boy yours and I predict even he in time will lust for greatness. He winked at Falk.

Come on, Falk. She pulled him by the hand, and added, We're leaving. And Gusef? You're full of it.

As they left, Gusef called out, Greatness I tell you! Greatness!

They crossed through the marina and the docks. This was Falk's favorite time of night to be near the waterfront. The marina was ablaze with light, shining like a cathedral surrounded by the sea. The boats tied in their slips were stately and beautiful. Una and Falk walked down the marina pier and admired the cabin cruisers, yachts, and sailboats, fitting their tongues to the names like *Phoebe's Plaything, Lil' Red Nasty, Suzy Q.* The snaky trails of lights curled and shimmered across the water's surface, and the lines of the moorings were reflected on the water's surface.

The sounds of water lapping against boat hulls and the creak of mooring ropes lulled Falk and Una into a mood. An atmosphere of exotic privilege hung over the marina, of wealth and abandonment, of desires given in to and to hell with the cost. Falk imagined owning one of the boats and sleeping on it, rocked to sleep, lullabied by the calls of seabirds. In the dimness of the empty docks, surrounded by light reflections on the smooth surface of the basin waters, the winking of the scattered lights on the quiet shrimpboats, they kissed, leaning against the dented Caddy. When they parted Falk kissed Una's neck, but she pushed him away softly.

Wait, she said. Just wait a second.

She held her small hands against his chest. Falk struggled to catch his breath, stared hypnotized with her beauty. At that moment she could have asked him to jump with her into Red Moon Bay and he would have leapt.

Beyond them a vision of the moon on the water. Una leaned her small body against him, her fingers tugging the fabric of his shirt. I don't feel so good. I need to go home. Is that okay?

Falk groaned. Are you sure?

Don't pout, said Una. She stood on tiptoe to reach him, her mouth warm and luscious, the smell of her kisses drowning him beneath a wave of this moment and nothing else.

She stopped and put a hand to his chest. We shouldn't be doing this, she said. You're too young.

No, I'm not, he whispered.

Yes, you are. I can tell. You kiss young. She was smiling, though, her face in the moonlight.

. . .

IN THE UNHOLY guts of the night clear and warm, Martinez drove his purple monster truck slowly down Shoreline Drive. It passed beneath the lighted signs of the motels, past the amber mane and emerald curlicue body of the Sea Horse Motel, past the plain black-and-white-lettered sign of the Driftwood Motel, which proclaimed, FREE HBO, COLOR TV! The streetlights could not pierce his dark-tinted windows. The painted tongues of flame along his fenders licked orange and red.

He had drunk many beers, yes he had, and yes he should not be driving. A man does not always do what he should do. A man has the right to view his masterpiece. The duty. Before it was destroyed forever. He had a bad feeling about this storm. As everyone drank and laughed a foreboding in his soul began to squirm. Like a worm trying to break the surface of his skin. He had seen the weather reports and he did not believe them. This Tanya was *extraño. Como una bruja.*

He parked on the cracked asphalt of the docks across Shoreline Drive from the Black Tooth Café, took a seat on his car hood, and opened another bottle of Negra Modelo. To him the colossal zebrafish looked *fantástico.* Amber spotlights directed on it from the roof made the zebra stripes glow eerily. The pony's legs protruding from the giant mouth cast weird shadows across the roof, like a tangling of antlers. It was magnificent. He felt a sentimental rising in his throat. He wished he could have kept it. But the Soviet had bought the thing and wanted to make money off it. This world was too much about money. A sea monster should not become an advertisement.

There is a world that should be. There is the world that is.

Perhaps Gusef was right. He should rename the café. He'd said the Swallowed Angel Café. But it was a horse, not an angel. Maybe El Caballo Tragado. No, that was too Mexican. The *gringos* liked words they could understand. The *gringos* didn't like to think too much, to learn something new. They liked to take the world and rename it for themselves. Make a horse an angel. Make a man a queer. What did they know? Cell phones and shopping malls, high-tech crap. Their souls were full of numbers, their hearts pumped Coca-Cola.

La tierra es por Mexicanos. La gente de mar, con huesos blancos, pelo negro, y piel moreno.

He lay back against the windshield of his monster truck and stared up at the stars in the sky. It was too warm for a night in late September. A sign of trouble. The air should be cooler by now, not warm like a dog's breath. The seawater was warm as the blood of a dying man. Warm water like this fed the storms in the Gulf, fed Tanya. *La bruja. La tormenta.*

Martinez unbuttoned his Hawaiian shirt to let his belly breathe. He wanted to save the zebrafish but could not muster the effort. He wanted to save the world of Goodnight but it would end anyway, so what was the use? He felt the sharp pressure of his full bladder but was too dizzy and too tired to climb down from the car and give the parking lot a good piss. A car passed by on Shoreline Drive and honked. Its headlights washed him in annoying blue light. He closed his eyes and relaxed his body against the hard warmth of the truck's windshield. He held up one hand to block the light in his eyes.

A hand tugging his shoulder. Yo, Martinez. Wake up.

What?

Wake up, Oscar. This ain't good.

It was Sheriff Littledog. The man himself. Martinez blinked slowly. I know you, he said.

Yeah yeah yeah. You're going to know me a little better by the time you post bail, *entiende me?*

What?

Public intoxication. The name for it. It's against the law.

Turn off the fucking light, would you?

Look at yourself. Sheriff Littledog shook his head, kept his huge flashlight trained on Martinez.

What?

You want this pretty truck impounded? Is that what you want?

Martinez rubbed his face with his hands. He ripped off a long and satisfying burp. He smiled. That's better.

God, you stink. Look at you. You pissed your pants.

Martinez grinned. Not the first time, he said. He leaned forward, slid off the truck, and stood uneasily on his legs. He turned and looked Sheriff Littledog in the face. The black eyepatch gave the sheriff the look of an Indian desperado. You are one big son of a bitch, you know that?

Sheriff Littledog sighed. He turned off the flashlight and slipped it into a loop on his black leather belt. Yeah, I know that. We all know that.

Martinez shook his head. No, I mean you are big. You know? *Como el hombre más grande* I ever seen?

That may be.

Martinez smiled at him, blinked three times with both eyes, still weaving a bit. I'm sorry, he said.

That's okay. Let's just get back to the office and sleep it off.

You taking me in?

Oscar? I'm tired. It's late. *Vaya te, mi amigo.*

You don't have to take me in. I don't like jail. I don't like the cage.

Not many do. Sheriff Littledog yawned. Come on. I'm getting sleepy.

Martinez put his hands on his knees and leaned forward. He rested his weight against the monster truck's front fender. He burped again. I don't feel so good, he said.

Sheriff Littledog shook his head, walked to his patrol car. From the front seat he called the dispatcher, told her what he was up to. He leaned out the door and called to Martinez, Are you going to be sick?

Maybe.

If you're going to be sick, why don't you go around the back of your truck? That's not something I want to see.

Martinez nodded and walked back there. He clumsily tried to fold down the tailgate but it was too complicated. He ended up sitting on the weedy asphalt, staring at broken glass. He vomited a great gush of liquid, holding on to the shiny massive bumper. He wheezed and spat. He vomited again. He could hear the crackle of the sheriff's radio in the background, the big man talking to the dispatcher.

After a while he was breathing better. He leaned against the bumper and groaned. He saw Sheriff Littledog's cowboy boots approach.

Yo, Señor Borracho? You feeling any better?

Maybe.

Okay, well, let's get rolling. I don't have all night.

You could just let me go.

I could. But I won't.

Gracias.

Sheriff Littledog pulled Martinez to his feet. You need a cleaning, he said.

Martinez patted his pockets. *Necesito los llaves.*

I don't know where your keys are. God, you're a mess.

Sheriff Littledog walked around to the driver's-side door and opened it, trained his big flashlight in the cab, searched around.

They're not in the ignition, he said. You probably dropped them somewhere.

Martinez walked slowly toward the front fender. I can't leave my truck without those keys. Somebody rip this thing off for sure.

Goddamnit, said Sheriff Littledog. He rummaged around in the cab of Martinez's truck, pulled out a small duffel bag, dropped it at Martinez's feet. The zipper was open and revealed two cellophane bundles. It looked like weed. The fuck is this?

Martinez leaned against his truck, rubbed his face. *Es nada.*

Nada my ass. That must be a couple pounds, right?

No sé. I never seen it before, really. Some dude borrowed the truck the other day. Maybe it was something he left.

Oscar? You need to straighten your ass up, right quick.

What? What'd I do?

Come on. Let's get in the car.

Martinez held out his hands in supplication. I'm a victim of circumstance, he said. It wasn't me.

Sheriff Littledog led him to the patrol car, opened the back door, put his hand on Martinez's head to push it down as he coaxed him into the car. He shut the door and Martinez sat there, blinking at the window. Sheriff Littledog got behind the wheel and started the engine.

What about my keys?

I'll send a deputy to tow the truck. It'll be impounded.

Well fuck me.

You said it.

They drove down Shoreline in the emptiness of the night. Sheriff Littledog asked the dispatcher about the storm. She said latest info had it headed for New Orleans. They figured to get some rain probably tomorrow.

In the backseat, Martinez glowered. You don't fool me, he said. You're just like all the others.

Button it, Oscar. I'm not the bad guy here.

Martinez laughed. *Sabes nada. Solamente números de teléfonos y cosas a comprar, cosas para las turistas.*

Keep it up, Oscar. I put you in the cell with the broken toilet? You'd like that, wouldn't you?

This is bullshit, said Martinez. I'm a U.S. citizen. I pay taxes. Where were you when my house was broken in to? Huh? They broke my fuckin' windows?

It's news to me, said Sheriff Littledog.

Oh, yeah. Well, me too. I never seen that weed before. Somebody must of planted that. Really. I bein' framed.

We'll dust it, is what we'll do. You never touched the thing, maybe you be okay.

Martinez blinked and said, Yeah, okay. Whatever.

❧ 7 ❧

In The Morning the sky bloomed a marvelous shade of green. It resembled the color of a watery margarita. All across town people pumped their cars full of gas at the convenience stores, stared up at the beautiful pale green sky, and decided it was time to get the hell out of Dodge. The margarita sky did not last. Before long a liquidy iridescence replaced it. It rippled above the people of Goodnight, undulating and pulsing in the time it took to put your credit card in the gas pump, press Regular, pump, and get your receipt. A fishbelly sky, the shimmering clouds like schooner sails luffing in the wind, coated with mother-of-pearl fish scales.

The winds began to gust and swirl. Across Red Moon Bay, to the east, in the direction of the open waters of the Gulf, a squall line of clouds loomed blue and purple as enormous bruises, shot with snake-tongue sparks of lightning. The hard rain hissed and passed, hissed again. Lingerers dashed to their cars and trucks in the parking lots of lumberyards and supermarkets and hardware stores, splashing through deepening puddles. Each lightning flash illuminated rain drops plunging earthward like schools of white minnows.

Walter and India Hamilton should have been gone already. They had an evacuation plan. They were not foolish people. Walter stayed up late plotting the best route north. They would have to leave in the RV, which was like riding an elephant to war.

They had been slower getting ready than Walter had anticipated. India puttered about, packing the kitchen of the RV neatly. She believed in order. If a body leaves things a mess and takes off helter-skelter down the road, chaos will ensue. She washed the breakfast dishes and put them away. She told Walter to take Cosmo for a walk so the dog wouldn't have to go on the road for at least an hour or two.

Walter should have been watching Cosmo more closely. The spaniel skittered down the steps and took off before he even got the leash attached. He didn't worry. Cosmo did this most every day and he usually caught up with her in the grassy back lot of the RV park, where she went to do her business. This morning he was distracted. He walked along staring in openmouthed wonder at the sky. He thought it the color of key lime pie.

He didn't realize the time.

Inside the RV India sat at the foldout kitchen table and did last week's Sunday *New York Times* crossword. She did it with diligence and commitment, as mental exercise, like some people work out on the Stairmaster or run miles on a treadmill. She was not going to let her brain go to mush. She didn't fear the storm. Her life and Walter's were in the hands of Jesus. She had only recently come to realize that, and since she had, a peacefulness had settled upon her like fog upon a marsh.

Walter followed Cosmo into a palmetto thicket behind the dog-walking area of the Sea Horse Motel's RV park. He stumbled against a Spanish dagger and gave his calf a nasty scratch. He had to remove his glasses and wipe them on his shirtsleeve, and was breathing heavily before he found the dog. She was barking herself sick over an armadillo. She stood with her front paws on the animal's plated hide, scratching as if she would dig a hole in its armor.

The odd creature barely paid the dog any mind. It kept snorting in the mulch around one of the palm trees at the back of the area, near the fence. The wind began to gust. It blew Walter's hat from his head and snatched it farther away as he hurried to catch it. Fat drops of rain then spattered against Walter's bald scalp. He shouted Cosmo's name and told her to get back. Enough of this foolishness. They had places to go and they couldn't spend the morning chasing armadillos.

By the time Walter returned with Cosmo the wind was a pummeling shriek, ripping the American flag in the Sea Horse's parking lot, shooting geysers of white spume as the waves crashed and sprayed over the shoulder of Shoreline Drive. Red Moon Bay was swollen and whitecapped, with skeins of foam streaking from one wave to the next, like tentacles reaching up from the deep. Traffic backed up along Shoreline Drive.

WHEN FALK ARRIVED in the morning the Sea Horse was a scramble of guests packing their cars or pausing in the parking lot to stare at the sky. Gusef had spent the day before in Corpus, driving from one place to the next to get storm and party supplies, expecting a false alarm. Now the weather people predicted the storm would cross Goodnight by afternoon.

The front office was empty, so Falk walked back, calling for Gusef. The woman from Room 17 was in the back office, two rooms behind the front desk. It appeared she had been crying but was over it now. She sat across from Gusef's work desk, the area where he paid bills and did the accounting, in a white wicker chair. Whenever she moved, it squeaked. A small suitcase sat at her feet, beside it a yellow beach bag. She was smoking a cigarette and considering a bird skull that Gusef kept on his desk. It was a fantastic thing with huge eye sockets and a long bleached beak. The air-conditioned air smelled of her cigarette and her perfume. What in the world is this? she asked.

A heron skull, said Falk. Gusef collects stuff like that.

He's been waiting for you, she said.

I helped my uncle get a few last-minute things ready for the storm. Everybody's crazy out at the house.

He heard the bells tinkle at the front door and went to meet Gusef. In the front of the office the Russian was breathing hard and pouring water into the coffee maker. With his wild gray hair and hooked nose, he looked like a sea eagle. He turned to Falk and smiled. This will be big day. I will need coffee in many cups. You have keys to Caddy?

Gusef took them and walked down the hallway toward the back office. As the coffee dripped Falk could hear them talking, Gusef giving her directions. The woman protested she would never be able to thank him enough. Gusef told her to forget that, and assured her everything would be fine.

Falk eavesdropped. The man who had slapped her was gone and not coming back. But she had nowhere to go and no money. She swore she'd return the Cadillac so clean Gusef wouldn't recognize it. Plus she would make him dinner. Gusef mumbled something, and they both laughed. Falk couldn't catch it all. He put out three cups and poured coffee. He was sipping his cup when Gusef and the woman emerged from the hallway.

Now I need to wake up, yes, said Gusef.

I poured some for y'all, said Falk.

Thanks, but none for me, said the woman. I better get.

Go, said Gusef. Hurry now and do not look back.

She gave him a quick hug and kissed his cheek, thanked him again. He told her to forget this. As she drove away in his Cadillac, Gusef stood at the office door and waved. As soon as she was gone he turned to Falk.

If madman boyfriend ever escapes from jail and come here with gun in hand, you did not see this, right?

Falk grinned. See what?

Gusef nodded. He smoothed his wild gray hair and sighed. Maybe this I will regret someday. It could be much trouble. But it is right thing to do and so I say, Fuck it. Fuck it! He laughed. Now drink your coffee and let us hurry.

They tied nail aprons around their waists and carried sheets of plywood to board up the windows. The blows of their hammers shot loud and sharp in the humid air. They hurried, each trying to keep up with the other. Falk held the sheets of plywood in place over the bayview windows of the Sea Horse while Gusef held up one edge with his knee and nailed. Before they had been working an hour the rain plastered Falk's hair in his face and trickled down his neck where he'd tossed back the hood of his rain jacket in order to hear Gusef's instructions. Gusef was soaked as well, his face bleached ashen gray, frazzled hair darkened to another shade of gray, droplets dripping down his nose.

He yelled that if things got bad they might regret not leaving. But is worth it just to see show, yes? Falk allowed that theoretically it was. But at the moment he wasn't so sure. He worried about the rising tide and storm surge, the town being swallowed by the sea. He imagined Una in her mother's trailer home, floating intact and alone as on a prefab ark. Gusef said she should be fine, that far from the bay.

They worked all morning, making progress, covering the windows, the sky morphing from pale green to fishbelly, the wind moaning and whipping the palm-tree fronds, the rain shooting into their eyes like a blizzard of pins. They had reached the second-floor balcony of the Sea Horse and were nearly finished, both of them soaked and bedraggled, struggling to nail the plywood over the last few windows of the outermost rooms.

They positioned a four-by-eight plywood sheet over a window. A fierce gust caught the corner and flipped it. Gusef stumbled and grabbed his head, pinned the plywood against the window with one meaty shoulder. The constant wind now filled their ears with a deep buffeting sound, the gusts shrieking with a higher pitch. Gusef managed to hold on to his end of the plywood sheet.

Falk shouted, Are you okay?

Gusef's forehead was bleeding. He didn't answer but got the sheet in place and nailed his side.

The wind blew a beach umbrella from the patio of the Drift-wood Motel next door onto its side so that it popped open, then tumbled into the deserted driveway. A wooden picnic table slid across the same patio, until a gust lifted it, spinning it end over end.

Falk urged Gusef to get inside and let him fix up that scrape. Gusef waved his hand as if it were of no importance and struggled along the balcony toward the next set of windows, gripping the railing. He shouted something that Falk couldn't hear.

What's that? Falk shouted back, trying to catch up with him.

Gusef turned and gave him a frenzied smile. I said this is really something, yes?

His face was drenched in blood, the wind-driven spray creating a halo of pink froth around his head and shoulders.

You're bleeding! shouted Falk. We need to get you to a hospital!

Gusef wouldn't hear of it. He said all he needed was to get cleaned up. They nailed the last sheet of plywood in place, then struggled against the wind, down the balcony hallway, down the stairs, and tumbled through the wind-pressured door of the office. Falk found a towel to wipe off Gusef's face. A flap of skin was torn loose from his scalp. Blood oozed from it and runneled down his cheek. He looked wildly at Falk with eyes that seemed incapable of focusing or moving in synchronized motion.

This is no good, he said. I need to pull out *Crazy Jane*. She not going to like this one bit.

It's too late for that now, said Falk. Besides, you lashed it down last night, remember?

Gusef lay back on the floor. My head hurts, he said. This is okay. I be all right. Yes. This is better. But he winced and blood trickled into his ear. More bright blood had seeped into his gray hair and stained it pink, matted to his ragged flap of scalp. A dribble of blood crossed under Gusef's nose. When he breathed the air from his left nostril formed a pink bubble.

Falk pressed the towel against the wound and tried to think. He had Gusef hold the towel in place and crossed behind the front counter to the telephone.

UNA'S MOTHER COOKED a breakfast of *huevos con migas* and watched the sky from the window above her kitchen sink. Una said they shouldn't bother to eat, they had to leave. She watched the small TV in their living room as the news channel from Corpus Christi broadcast hurricane warnings and an evacuation notice for the coastal sections of San Patricio, Nueces, and Mustang Counties.

I'm not going anywhere, said her mother. *Éste es no mi primero huracán.* They come and go. You stay you save what you have. You know what happens if you leave? *Los saqueadors van a venir.* Her eyes were wide and dramatic. She waved her wooden spoon in her hand, indicating the rooms about them. They take everything you have. Two years ago remember that storm in México? My poor cousin. An old woman living in Veracruz, the sweetest woman in the world. She left when a storm came to her *aldea,* and when she returned? *Todos perdido.* Una's mother shook her head. She stirred the eggs-and-tortilla mix. They took her underwear, *quién sabía?* They took her false teeth! The poor woman.

Una frowned, dividing her attention between her mother's story and the news reports. Why didn't she have her dentures in her mouth?

Her mother shrugged. *No sé.* She didn't. And they took them, *bastardos.* Her underwear even? *Qué pervertado.* If looters come to my house, I will throw boiling water in their face.

Mama? No one's going to want to loot our trailer park. If they loot anything they'll go after some business. Some rich man's house. Not a trailer.

You never know. *Mi prima,* she didn't think anyone would touch her house either.

That was Mexico. It's different there.

Not so much. You think so. You don't know.

Oh, please. Una sat on the worn fabric of their chocolate-brown sofa, sipping a cup of coffee. Her black hair was pulled back in a ponytail and her tiny body was lost in a plain white T-shirt and a pair of cotton capri pants. She watched her mother and thought how crazy she was. Their trailer was worthless. It was nothing to anyone but them. Nothing but a box of resignation.

Still she feared the storm could blow it away. She had lived here for years, she had grown up here, and as crummy as she knew it was, it was still home. The sunflower curtains tied back over the louvered kitchen windows were pretty. She liked the clock in the shape of an Aztec calendar, the scratched dinette, the silly turtle cookie jar in the kitchen.

Sometimes she hated Goodnight and felt as if she couldn't breathe. Sometimes she felt that if she lived there one day longer she would die a miserable and bitter woman. But it was her life, her home. The *huevos con migas* smelled good. Her mother washed her hands at the sink and shook her head at the threatening sky. She wiped her hands on her apron and told Una, *Basta.* Quit watching TV like a zombie and set the table.

They ate breakfast and listened to the television, the evacuation notices, the constant annoying throb of the National Weather Service warnings beeping as they rolled across the bottom of the TV screen. They filled mason jars and an Igloo ice chest full of tap water and found a flashlight with weak batteries. Una walked outside to look at the sky. It rippled above her in eerie iridescent greenness, as if she were looking through the water surface of a flooded yard.

A light rain fell and made her blink, coated her forehead warm and wet. The palm fronds began to bow in the wind. The rain grew harder. Una saw the curdled blue clouds of the squall line over Isla Pelicano in the distance, at the edge of Red Moon Bay. As she blinked into the wind and rain, the people in the trailer next door climbed into their old pickup truck and drove away.

She walked down the driveway for a better look. The trailer park was fast becoming abandoned. Another pickup passed her, splashing mud. The parking spaces beside the trailers were empty. Some had windows covered with plywood, many did not. As she covered her face against the rain and wind, Una realized she and her mother were left alone there. She ran back to the trailer, struggled to close the door against the wind.

She told her mother they needed to leave. Now.

I'm not giving my house to *los saqueadors*. You go without me.

Don't be crazy. No one would want to loot this miserable place.

What do you mean, miserable? Why do you call it miserable? Why are you so ungrateful?

They argued for a while. The wind shuddered the thin walls. When Una's mother felt the trailer rocking, she said, Okay, I'll go. But we must take my sewing machine. *No voy a dejar la máquina de coser.* Una helped her carry the sewing machine out to her hulking rusted car. She got behind the wheel, but it wouldn't start.

I can't believe this, said Una.

Her mother nodded. It's been acting up lately. Sometimes it starts, sometimes it doesn't.

You could have mentioned that, Mama.

Well, I forgot. Don't blame it on me.

I'm not blaming you. It's just that we need to get out of here, you know?

You didn't ask.

They sat in the car and felt it wobble in the wind, the rain now gushing in silvery sheets across the cracked windshield.

Let's call Alonzo. He'll come get us.

I hope so.

They went back inside. Una called her Uncle Alonzo on her cell phone, but he didn't pick up. She left a message on his machine and asked him to come as soon as he could to get them. She called 911 and was told they would try to send someone to help evacuate them, but couldn't promise anything. Una's mother was quiet now and looked worried. *Santo Dios,* she whispered. My sewing machine is all wet. Now it's going to rust in the car. It will be flooded and ruined there. She shook her head sadly.

We're the ones who are going to be flooded, Mama. We need some help.

Una went to her bedroom closet and started rummaging around. She wanted a jacket. Something rarely needed in Goodnight, with weather usually so fair. She found a raincoat decorated with Snoopy cartoons. It still fit. She had grown no bigger since the seventh grade, when she'd begged her mother to buy her this raincoat. She put it on and walked into the living room, where her mother had the phone to her ear.

The lines might go down, said Una, so I gave Uncle Alonzo this number to call. She handed her mother the cell phone.

Una's mother had never used one before. She looked at it with disgust. I cannot use this thing, she said. What are you doing? You should stay here with me.

Una explained that if it rang, press Talk. I'm going to the motel, she said. We need some help and I bet Gusef is there at least. He said he'd stay as long as he could, to try to save it, even if the storm got bad. He's just crazy enough to be there.

Gusef will know what to do, she said.

THE SCHOOL DISTRICT woman called at dawn to tell Gabriel classes were canceled. He answered the phone with a scratchy voice. He listened to what she said and blinked into the gray stillness of his room. His head split with a hangover, his eyeballs burned as he blinked. Looks like we're in for a blow, she said. That damn storm turned and is headed right for us.

He had to clear his voice twice to reply.

That's fine with me, he said. I could use a day off.

He hung up the phone and lay in a daze, wondering if he'd get paid for today or what. He needed the money and if they tried to stiff him, he wasn't going to let it slide. His eyes came to focus on the ceiling, staring at a water stain the shape of a horse's head. He fell back to sleep.

At ten o'clock Gabriel was awake again, standing on his back porch naked, scratching his nuts, watching the wind whip the salt grass in his backyard. Raindrops fat and silver drummed against his tin roof. Before long it became a constant sizzle. He wondered where Leesha would be in all this, if she'd be safe. She had told him her father swore he'd stay to protect his house. No way he'd leave. Come hell or high water.

He thought of Leesha with her skirt lifted, the bus windows fogged, her eyes closed, a soft sweet heat enclosing the two of them.

The rain fell in gray curtains. Gabriel stood flat-footed on his back porch with a hangover, watching the first kisses of Tanya on the edges of Goodnight. The phone rang again. He answered it, amused to be talking on the phone naked and hard.

The school district dispatcher woman again. She was talking too fast now and he wanted to tell her to just calm the fuck down but he held his tongue and listened. She wanted to know if he'd be willing to drive the bus in the storm. She wanted to know if he would help evacuate fools and goofballs from bad spots along the coastline.

I guess so, he said. I get a little overtime for this maybe?

You help us out here, they give you Bus Driver of the Year Award is what I bet.

All right then. I like the sound of that.

By late morning Gabriel was making shuttle trips from the swamped areas of Mustang County to the high school gym and auditorium, which had been converted into a storm shelter. He followed the debris-covered roads through Little Bay Shores and Key Escondida, stopping at any house that looked as if someone were still home. People waved at him from their front porches, held their hands up as if telling him to wait.

A bald man with a distended belly bulging out his T-shirt helped a white-haired grandmother wade through the knee-high water along Tortuga Street. They clambered aboard and told Gabriel they were glad to see him. The man was excited and talking too fast. We saw you drive up and I said, Thank God help is here. That water rising so fast I never saw the likes of it. This town's going underwater I shit you not.

The woman toiled with each step. Her chubby son held a black umbrella over her head and Gabriel stepped down to offer her a hand. The rain pounded on the roof of the Bluebird school bus and in the wind gusts it rocked and shuddered. On Palacios Street they stopped at a small house where a Latina woman waved from the front porch. She and four children scuttled through the rain and wind, holding newspapers over their heads, and scurried aboard the bus.

With its tall tires the school bus managed the high water in the low-lying neighborhoods, but as the day wore on the wind shrieked across the bay and the crowds inside the high school gym huddled against the walls, children crying, mothers fussing over them, fathers at the doors looking out, predicting nothing less than an apocalypse now.

A man Gabriel knew who lived out Farm-to-Market 881 told him the road was flooded high and houses along the Humosa Bay Road might be underwater by nightfall. Gabriel asked about the subdivision where Leesha lived with her parents. He was told that was one of the worst of all.

He asked the men lingering by the door to stand aside.

You can't go out there, said one of them. It's too late for anything like that now.

I know a family that might be stuck, said Gabriel. They might need some help.

A man by the door said, Be my guest. But I don't think that bus is going to make it.

That wind's so high she'll pitch over, said another. Then what will you do? You'll be up shit creek without a paddle.

I'll see, said Gabriel. If it's impossible, I'll just give up. He gave the cluster of men a sorry look. Like the rest of you chickenshits.

Out the auditorium doors the wind howled and pushed him toward the schoolbus parked on the lee side of the building. The storm seemed to be egging him on, daring him. He got in and shut the doors, but once he left the protection zone of the building the bus heeled over to one side with the worst gusts, close to flipping. He took a roundabout route through the torn-up neighborhood streets to skirt the strongest wind. That way he reached FM 881, then gunned the bus and shoved it right up the belly of the storm. Fallen mesquite and live-oak trees littered the roadside, their branches stripped by the wind.

It was hard to see at first, so much rain fell against the windshield. Then it eased. The winds slackened and he could see the road before him. The flood was deepest near Leesha's house. The rain had slowed to a steady hum, but streaks of sunlight shone through and illuminated a double rainbow huge and arcing over Humosa Bay. Floodwater reached the second step inside the bus. The current pulled against it, but the vehicle kept moving.

When he walked up to Leesha's parents' front porch he couldn't help but smile. Her mother opened the door, smiling, saying, Am I glad to see you!

Leesha hovered behind her, wearing hiphugger jeans and a tight T-shirt cut short to show her belly button. She gave him a wink and said, You would not believe how close we came to drowning.

He felt like the Seventh fucking Cavalry there to save the stage-coach.

WALTER AND INDIA Hamilton decided not to flee and save their own lives in a selfish and self-centered way, but to take on the humble role of saviors. They had a quiet talk about it and decided that the civic thing to do would be to save the lives of the unfortunate, and they reasoned the best place to troll for unfortunate souls in dire need of saving from a horrific storm was in a trailer park. It always seemed the news programs focused on trailer parks to show the lost and destitute victims of storms in the aftermath footage. It's hardly surprising, said Walter. Look at how they're made! What shoddy construction. You don't build like that and expect it to last. Those things could be destroyed with a good sneeze.

It's all that some people can afford, said India. And it's our Christian duty to help them out.

I suppose, said Walter. But they haven't been particularly welcoming or caring to us since we've been here, so I don't see how we owe them anything.

We don't owe them anything, said India. Is that the motivator of our behavior? What we owe or don't owe people?

I didn't mean it that way, said Walter. Don't twist my words around.

It's a matter of compassion, she said. A matter of helping out people who are less fortunate.

I think it's a matter of lunacy, said Walter. One big gust of wind and this bus is going down, just like those trailers.

We better hurry then, before it gets worse.

After owning it for a total of seven months, Walter and India had begun to consider their recreational vehicle something of an absurd monstrosity. It was thirty-eight feet long and complete with TV set, bathroom, dinette, and sleeping accommodations for six. Its name, the Hitchhiker, made no sense whatsoever. They rarely voiced this opinion to each other. The thought occurred to them separately, but each sensed the other shared this feeling. They were hesitant to express their opinion for fear of admitting the depths of their foolishness. The price had been outrageous. What they'd paid for it could have bought a winter home in Goodnight.

Plus the thing was impossible to park. Walter was always hitting shopping carts, mailboxes, and trash cans, so that India experienced a perpetual state of anxiety whenever they were rolling upon the pavement.

The idea of using the Hitchhiker's roominess to save the unfortunate trailer-park dwellers of Goodnight gave some meaning and offered some redemption to this absurd vehicle, this dinosaur with wheels.

Still Walter was slow to flee. He didn't want to seem the coward. Ever since Gabriel Perez had threatened him in the Black Tooth, had branded him an irrelevant old fool, Walter had become one of the many defiant and disgruntled haunting the shorelines of Goodnight. He had never run away from a single thing in his life and he didn't want anyone thinking he was using the storm as an excuse to turn yellow. He took a good thirty minutes to get the Hitchhiker started and ready to shove off. India didn't notice. She was fretting over what to wear and what to take along, despairing over what to leave behind.

By the time they left the Sea Horse the rain was a pulsing squall and the wind made the Hitchhiker rock like a ship at sea.

They did not see Una heading toward the Sea Horse. She was taking the back way, along Church Hill Road, which paralleled Shoreline Drive, but was sheltered by a sandy hill and not as windy.

When they knocked on Una's mother's trailer door, she did not want to come out. She said she was waiting for her daughter, who'd gone for help. They urged her to come. She made them coffee and they sat and tried to decide what to do as the wind began to rock the trailer. Finally Walter lugged her heavy sewing machine from the old car into the Hitchhiker.

They decided they would return to the Sea Horse to try to find Una. By the time they were back on Shoreline Drive, water covered much of the road. They crept slowly toward the motel. From the east of them, the waters of Red Moon Bay surged forward and surrounded them. The road disappeared. Waves rose to the windshield and the vehicle wobbled.

It was as if they were driving toward the bottom of a murky sea.

FALK PRESSED the phone to his ear, but it made no sound. Jiggling the clear plastic post on the receiver, he watched as a figure approached through the billowing waves of rain. The office was situated at the end of the motel, the room closest to Shoreline Drive, right across from Red Moon Bay.

The figure stumbling and struggling against the wind moved closer and Falk wanted to open the door and shout, Are you crazy? Until he recognized her and rushed to hold the door against the gusts.

Borne by a burst of rain and wind, Una staggered inside. She shucked the hood off her black hair and wiped her face.

I thought I'd never make it, she said. I mean, the wind. It's . . . She wiped her face again. When she spoke her voice was hoarse and weak. We need help.

Okay, everything's okay, said Falk. He stood beside Gusef, who was still lying on the floor, like the victim of a beating or worse, his head wrapped in the blood-spotted towel. He seemed to be sleeping, but with his eyes closed he spoke to Una and Falk, standing above him. Do not worry. I'm okay, he said. It look worse than it is. It just little headache.

Una crouched beside him and touched his swollen forehead with her fingertips, telling him he should be careful and not move around too much. She got Gusef to tell her where the first-aid kit was, then cleaned up his wound and put a gauze bandage on it. Falk helped her, tossing away the bloody towel, tearing open the package of gauze bandages when she was ready. The wind shrieked a tremendous gust, causing the plywood and glass of the windows to tremble. An aluminum folding chair went by, clattering and tumbling end over end.

The lights died, all the white noise of the office quieted, which seemed to amplify the seething of the wind. Gusef got up on his feet, staring out through the gap of one of the windows that were too wide for the plywood to cover. He said these would be the first to break.

We go upstairs to second floor, said Gusef. We are safe there.

Before they left to head outside, Falk grabbed his camera. Una frowned. What? You want to get us all killed so you can take a picture of it?

No one's getting killed here, said Falk. It will only take a second. Besides, this is important. I bet there's no one else this close to the storm.

Once they stepped outside, the wind pushed them forward, whipping ripples over the puddles beneath the frantic awning, casting spray off the pickup's hood. On the walkway outside the first-floor rooms, spindrift billowed and hissed in the eddy of a constant gray squall. Gusts pummeled the windward side but here only swirled. The maroon outdoor carpeting of the walkway was soaked and the decorative sea-horse railing trembled and vibrated. The air itself was warm and wet.

Gusef climbed the stairs slowly. Near the landing he tripped and fell to his knees. Falk and Una took his arms and helped him to his feet. On the balcony outside the hotel rooms perched a flock of gulls. They fluttered and waddled sideways on the metal railing. When Gusef fell forward they called out and swooped away, a blur of black-and-white wings filling the space before Una and Falk as they supported Gusef and helped him to his feet.

Go, said Gusef. Get pictures now.

I don't know, said Falk. It might ruin the camera.

Good, said Una. Gusef is more important than any stupid picture.

They opened one of the rooms and made him lie down. Within moments he seemed to sleep, his eyes closed, his breathing even.

Falk returned to the balcony to find the water level of the bay had risen several feet and reached halfway across the road, just a foot or two below the level of the driveway. The force of the wind almost planed the surface of the waves flat, only the whitecaps at the shoreline breaking into tremendous spume. Una appeared in the doorway to watch.

Falk took photos from the rain shelter of the balcony, turning his back to the wind, trying to keep raindrops off the lens. After a moment he gave up and put the Nikon back in the room, saying he had better not press his luck.

Both then felt a curious shift. The gusting wind eased. The torrential rain diminished to a light dimpling of the flooded parking lot.

Is that the worst of it? asked Falk. He took the balcony stairs down to the parking lot, turning his face to the pewter sky. Maybe this is it, he called up to Una. Maybe we've seen the worst. You think?

The light seemed queer, the clouds dark blue and bunched above.

You be careful, said Una. She followed him down, stepping out into the open space cautiously. She wiped the dampness from her forehead and cheeks. Her long straight hair bowed out in curves where it bunched against the collar of her clear plastic Snoopy raincoat, and it shone with a blueblack luster in that storm-charged light.

In the east, over Red Moon Bay, mist still drifted down in shimmering veils. Behind it an arc of rainbow appeared above the bay.

We must be in the eye, said Una.

I don't think so, said Falk. That would be too fast, wouldn't it? Maybe this is just a lull.

Falk noted how the water was still rising. Shoreline Drive was completely swamped with waves, lapping up to the entrance to the Sea Horse itself.

It was then that Una grabbed his arm and pointed toward the bay, pulling him toward the office, saying simply, Look.

They watched a frothy swell of water. Una pulled on his arm, saying, Move. Go. Let's get out of here. Falk scuttled backward, Una yanking his shirt.

As it grew closer the ocean swell morphed from a frothy mound on the surface of Red Moon Bay into a Japanese illustration of a tidal wave Falk had seen years before in a children's book.

Una and Falk ran, pursued by a whirring, roaring hiss, until they were engulfed, tumbled and flipped, fighting the drench and bubbles, born aloft as if on a cloud of wet foam, hurled forward into the tangle of windswept oaks that covered the low rise of dunes above the Sea Horse and into which the enormous storm-surge wave swept them, dying finally to a spent debris-filled wash. It was a blinding world of brown seawater that swallowed then spat them out against the rough trunks of the oaks they grabbed. It did not then suck them back but rather stalled and seemed to merely dissipate and give them to the sandy land as they came to, close to each other, drenched and dizzy, astoundingly alive and whole.

Falk made it to his feet first and helped Una. With her face cloaked by her wet black hair and her body wrapped in the raincoat, she resembled nothing so much as a mermaid once wrapped in cellophane, now cast loose by an incantation from the sea.

THAT MORNING, inside the Mustang County Jail, Oscar Martinez sat on the sheetless yellowed mattress of his seedy bunk. He watched the green sky outside the bars of his windows facing the bay. A deputy sheriff brought him breakfast, a honey bun and black coffee. He said a hurricane was going to hit and they should be okay here, but if worst came to worst they'd head inland in a patrol car.

Sheets of rain hissed and splattered in the courtyard outside Oscar's barred window. By noon the light in the cell had become a deep-sea blue. Martinez lay awake on the miserable fleabag cot and breathed in the smell of ammonia and the beached-fish breeze of the storm.

The rain gushed so loudly the voices of the sheriff and the deputies were drowned out. Martinez was left alone in his cell with the feeling that no one gave a damn.

Through the bars and past the screen of his cell window he watched the waters of Red Moon Bay. Dark curdled clouds rolled in until the rain gushed so hard he could see nothing but a blue-gray curtain of water. The roar of it filled his ears.

Faintly the sound of a radio crackled and at times voices shouted in the sheriff's office down the hall. The odor of mildew and damp concrete suffused the hours of constant rain. At some point he could no longer tell what time it was. The wind throbbed and whistled through the screen and bars, spraying his cell with a fine mist full of the ocean.

Martinez watched with more pleasure than dread as the hurricane winds swept the dockside area visible from his window. Huge white plumes of sea spray shot into the air and were blown over the docks. A white car became submerged up to its windshield, its headlights glowing beneath the water. The next time Oscar looked it was gone. A telephone pole fell and power lines exploded in sparks across the parking lot.

The clamor of rain and wind changed to a roar and shriek by midmorning. In a fit of resentful pique Martinez wished that the hurricane would wash the entire town away and drown his enemies and accusers, whom he cursed with biblical vindictiveness. In another instant he second-guessed his wish. For all the innocents. The people who did not and would never deserve this fate, this punishment.

As if in answer to his kinder impulse, sometime after noon the wind weakened. Martinez wiped the salt spray from his face and stood in a puddle of water near his window, looking out on the disastrous world from which he was locked away. His body stank of the sweat of excitement. He wanted a shower and believed the worst was over, the rest of his misery about to begin. He called for the deputy sheriff, Steve, and got no answer. Finally a short, wide woman, the dispatcher, came to the door. She told him to hush.

All the sheriffs is out, she said. You just hush and sit tight. They evacuating folks. It ain't over yet.

He lay on his cot but could not sleep. A smell wafted through the windows. A gumbo smell of beached catfish and mullet. When he looked out the windows again the scene was disorienting. As if he'd walked through one door and returned to enter a different world altogether. The sea had risen over the docks and its brown water flooded the parking lot that stretched along the east side of the jail where his windows faced. A lone patrol car sat there.

Oscar watched as the water rose and soon the patrol car had water up to its windows. Seconds later only the roof lights marked its place in the widening sea.

The waters of Red Moon Bay were the color of aluminum streaked with rust. The waves hurtled head-high toward the jail and the window from which Oscar watched as if he were on a skiff, until a large swell capped with white foam tumbled across the parking lot, engulfing the street signs and a SeaFest festival billboard. It rushed forward and slapped against the building.

Before Martinez could react the water gushed through his barred window and waterfalled into the cell, dunking his face and shoving him off his feet, smashing his head against the toilet. His head throbbed and ears rang. He struggled to his feet, pain making his left cheek and eye feel as if they were glowing with heat. He spat out a mouthful of saltwater, the bay now discolored brown and cascading through the window.

The cell filled with water. He tried to climb onto the top bunk but slipped and fell into the water again as the second wave hit and the flood level in the building rose three feet in a matter of moments. The current sucked him against the bars and he screamed for help. Something grasped his arm with a clammy touch and he jerked away, flailing his arms wildly, as if he were being attacked by a shark. It was only the blanket, soaked and undulating in the current toward the bars like an eel.

The water kept rising. It reached the top of the bunk bed and gushed in an undertow toward the cell bars leading to the hallway. It flowed a swift current toward the sheriff's and dispatcher's offices. As his airspace shrank, Martinez kicked his feet and struggled to spit the water out of his mouth and breathe. He shouted for help but there was none. He shivered in the water and clung to the bars as the last wave hit and narrowed the space to the gray ceiling to only a couple feet. He reached up and touched the ceiling as if he could somehow push it away.

He knew he was being punished for something. He wished that before he drowned he at least could discover the what and why of it.

❧ 8 ❧

I T W A S A S I F the sea suddenly rose by over fifteen feet, higher than it had ever been in the history of the town. Falk and Una held on to each other in the sudsy froth at the waves' end, soaked and covered with seaweed. In the wind of the storm's eye a flock of laughing gulls floated over the flooded stretch of Shoreline Drive. One dove into the waters now covering the Sea Horse's parking lot and speared a small fish floating dead on the surface. The body of the motel's neon sign floated over Shoreline Drive like a giant sea horse from a '50s horror film.

Waves sloshed high upon the glass-walled office at the end of the building closest to the waterfront. The waves' force ripped the plywood sheets loose and they flapped in the current, the waterlogged sheets of wood slapping against the windows with each swell. For some time Falk and Una huddled at the edge of the newly swollen shoreline. Falk's T-shirt clung wet and heavy to his chest. He pulled it over his head and wrung it out, a gush of brown silt and seawater dribbling through his hands. Gray bleached planks from the destroyed fishing piers floated in the sloshing waves.

Una moved away, staring vacantly at the water-logged catastrophe around her, only turning back when she stepped to avoid the soaked and limp body of a drowned orange tabby cat.

I have to get home, she said. I have to get out of here.

Falk was too far away to hear her, only saw her lips moving as if she were mumbling to herself.

Across Red Moon Bay loomed a bulging biblical sky. The storm's eye closed quickly, sweeping inland and westward. For a time the air was still, wet, heavy and warm, like the fetid breath of an animal. Then the wind once more began to increase. The waves' crash filled their ears.

Falk waded into the brown water of the parking lot toward the office. When the waves lapped over his hips and splashed his chest, he slowed. He had no idea what to do. He felt confused and disoriented. A fresh surge of foamy brown waves lurched a drowned body into him, the limp hands touching his, the blanched face surfacing out of the slosh, eyes wide open and staring. A gash gaped at the drowned man's throat, exposing dark thready tissue, a piece of wire from a crab trap entangled in the torn clothing that drifted beside him, still connected.

Falk staggered back, away from the cold touch of the dead man's hands, slogging in what seemed like slow motion toward the high ground from which he had come. When he reached the waves' edge, he collapsed in the mud, shivering.

Una appeared beside him. The wind gusted and sent clots of brown spume into their hair and upon their wet clothes.

The limp body of a drowned Whiteface steer clattered against the motel office, floating sideways in the water, its split hooves tapping the windows. It reminded Falk of the zebrafish with the colt in its maw, a foretelling of the disaster.

They climbed the stairs and found Gusef on the second-floor landing, shouting at them to hurry. The winds gusted again, shaking the building and making a high-pitched rasping sound as asphalt roofing shingles peeled loose and went flying.

Falk turned to Una and saw she was also shivering, her arms dimpled with goose bumps. They had been wet for too long now. Una's eyelids were a shade of blue. Falk's teeth chattered as he sipped a glass of vodka thrust into his hand.

We must get you two warm, said Gusef. This is crazy water. Come.

Gusef led them to the room where the last guests, a square-dance couple, had been staying. Inside they found suitcases lying atop the bed. Gusef said the last time he'd seen the couple they'd gone to the Duck Inn for breakfast, insisting they would ride out the storm, that they'd been through tornadoes all their lives in Abilene, and a little wind and rain weren't going to hurt them.

Gusef said, I told them no. You must leave. And before I can say chicken yellow, they are gone.

The suitcases held dry clothes, but the only outfit for Una was a peach-colored square-dancing dress with puffy sleeves and a knee-length pleated skirt meant to be worn with frilly multilayered underskirts beneath, designed for the whirl and twirl of the Carolina Wheel or for kicking the Cotton-Eyed Joe. Falk found a plaid shirt and wide-body blue jeans that he had to cinch to his waist with a cowpoke belt.

Gusef used a pass key to open the connecting door to the next room. He said he was going to try to reach someone with his cell phone and see if they could get out.

But I think we must stay put until storm dies down. Come join me and we will finish bottle and listen to wind.

Falk and Una said they'd be there in a moment. They dried with towels before dressing, Falk in the bedroom, pulling on the cowpoke getup, Una in the bathroom, shivering as she hurried into the square-dance dress. Falk opened the door and watched the wind-blown debris skittering over the flooded parking lot, shingles flying off the roof of the Driftwood Motel next door.

He went to Gusef's room, wanting him to step outside and watch. The Russian was lying spread-eagled on the bed, snoring. He still clutched the bottle of vodka.

As the wind shrieked and shook the Sea Horse, Falk and Una curled against each other on the bed, barefoot. Una was still cold. They hugged each other and tried to warm themselves by lying close beneath the bedspread and sheets.

Una closed her eyes and curled against Falk. Warm me up, she said. Please please please. I'm so cold. Feel me. I can't quit shaking.

Shhhhh. It'll be all right. Don't worry. He smelled her hair and squeezed her so close their bones crumpled against each other.

The light in the room was the deep blue of shadows in closets in which something important, perhaps life shattering, is hidden in a shoe-box. The battened-down motel room smelled of must and mildew and the brine and musk of the storm itself, of saltwater whipped into a fine mist by the wind, blasted through the cracks in doors and windows.

The wind shook the building and squealed as it whistled through these cracks and gaps. Falk and Una shivered and trembled, hunkering under the thin tropical motel bedspread. Outside came the sounds of things breaking, cracking, splintering, dull concussions and watery thuds.

We should pretend this isn't happening, whispered Una. We should pretend that everything will be okay.

Falk closed his eyes and listened. He kissed the hollow of her slim and salty neck. Their body heat suffused the pocket of sheets and blankets after some time so that they felt enclosed in a delirious, blood-warm cocoon. Una unzipped the side of her dress and guided Falk's hand to her center, so hot it felt as if he were blindly touching the lips of a torch. Falk was swollen and feverish and Una brought his lips to her nipple, kissing his eyelids, telling him, Warmer. You are so warm.

They grew entangled in her loosened dress. Una broke away from a kiss and tried to calm Falk's squirming body. Maybe I should take this thing off.

Falk gulped for breath and nodded. He had lost the ability to speak.

Beside the bed, she squirmed out of the rumpled square-dance outfit, her figure standing there suffused with the room's bluevelvet light. She made a face he could faintly see, a comical frown. I hate that thing. Wriggling out of its puffy sleeves and frilly-necked bodice, she let it fall to the carpeted floor, kicked it away.

Streaks of watery light coated the curves of her hips, the softness of her belly, the half moons of her small breasts. She stood for a half instant, her long black hair over one shoulder and hanging forward, like a ceramic sea nymph in an aquarium's blue glow. Behind her crisscrossed the patterns of the taped windows, the curtains pulled open, the wood trembling in the blasts of wind, the rough tan hide of nailed plywood buckling and heaving.

Back beneath the covers, she told Falk to warm her again, that it was the only thing to make her feel good. The feel of his skin, the sense of being alive despite the storm and waves. The sense that for a moment this was all that mattered.

They curled against each other again, opened their lips to each other. Falk shimmied out of his clothes while still under the sheet and bedspread, and kicked them out the side. Una asked if he wanted her and he whispered, Yes, I do. Very much. Do you?

Very much, she whispered.

He drowned in her delicious heat, engulfed in the smell of her wet hair, while she whimpered, twitching and trembling, until he asked if he were hurting her. She told him to hush. Whatever you do, don't stop, just keep touching me.

THE WINDS DIED in the middle of the night. Falk woke in the warmth of Una's orbit and emerged into a world sea-tossed and tangled. The storm had moved inland and left behind the steady undulating hiss and guttle of rain. He lay awake, eyes wide open, feeling the smooth warmth of Una's skin, the smell of her hair. He stayed there motionless for some time, eyes wide in the still and stuffy room, listening to Una's breathing, feeling the soft tidal shifts of her lungs and heart. Finally he slipped out of bed to find even the second-story balcony had flooded. Ocean debris and seaweed clotted the wrought-iron railing and floodwaters soaked the wood. The carpeted floor of the hotel room was squishy, his steps leaving footprints.

He realized dawn would expose the tableau of devastation, a scene that must be photographed. He dressed quietly in the oversized jeans and plaid shirt, collecting his camera, the black vinyl bag of extra film and lenses. When he squeaked the door open, it released with a gasp.

The sound of rain splattering against the soaked balcony walkway grew louder as he stepped through the doorway. The water had receded but the slush of the waves in the flooded parking lot below moved with a lapping sound and a slap as they rocked against the motel's doors and windows. Falk's eyes began to sting from being opened so wide, from straining to see into the mystic darkness. His eyes stung from the yearning to count the bones of tragedy and smell the breath of destruction.

The latticework lumber of a house roof floated over Shoreline Drive. Beneath the mopwater sky, the sea level had receded many feet and was retreating still. In its wake it left behind sand and seaweed and a population of the drowned.

In the ditch beside the Driftwood Motel floated the body of a Vietnamese woman. At the water's edge bloated cattle rocked back and forth in the slow waves. Falk waded through the streets and photographed everything he saw, toppled signs and telephone poles, drowned women and fishermen, bloated whitefaced cattle, rafts of plastic bottles and trash cans. A palm tree stripped of its fronds jutted from the water like a forgotten idol.

Wading down Shoreline Drive beyond the Driftwood, Falk came upon a white RV. Dark green clumps of Sargasso seaweed tangled in the windshield wipers. It lay on its side in a flooded ditch littered with storm debris. He recognized the couple who had found the zebrafish. He looked inside briefly. He did not take any photographs.

. . .

When Falk returned to the Sea Horse, he crept quietly into the motel room. He thought to return to bed but could not do it, so much was behind him, behind the door. He loaded a fresh roll of film into his camera. Una lay in bed still asleep. She awakened to the click of his shutter as he took her picture. She covered her face.

Don't do that, she said. Please? Okay?

Falk looked away from his viewfinder and in the milky gray light of that boarded guest room on the second floor of the Sea Horse Motel he saw Una, the woman he loved, holding a hand before her face with her fingers spread wide and starfishlike to hide. He lowered the camera.

I'm sorry, he said. I didn't mean to bother you.

Una pulled the sheets to her neck and smiled.

I don't like that thing pointed at me. We shouldn't always have to worry about the way we look.

Her face was small and ghostly in the shadowed light of the boarded room, her eyes like twin black holes pierced with a point of light, her long hair splayed on the white pillow beneath her head.

I can't help it, said Falk. Taking pictures. It seems important.

It isn't, said Una. But if you have to. Well. Okay. Just not of me. Okay.

Or I'll never be able to relax around you. You know. I don't want to be that deer in the headlights. They usually get hit by cars.

I'll stop. Falk sat beside her on the bed and through the sheet he gently touched her belly. He heard her breathing slow and stop as he touched her.

You have to see what happened, he said. Nothing looks the same.

Una told him to go outside. She needed to dress and she wanted privacy. I have to find my mother, she said. When I left she was waiting for my uncle to give her a ride.

Moments later they stood together on the balcony. Before them lay a landscape drowned and flattened by the wall of water. Gusef had already left to see about the *Crazy Jane*. The cut on his forehead looked nasty, but he told Falk he was fine. He was sure there were others much worse off.

Una and Falk tried to make plans. It was as if the sea had swamped not only the coastline but their minds as well. Falk said he would go with her to find her mother. Both of them worried about Mr. Buzzy. The old man had only one leg and would have ridden out the storm in a bar like the Alibi Lounge or the Canoe Club at best, or in the boxlike trailer he called home at worst.

You should go find him, said Una. I can take care of my mother. Maybe Uncle Alonzo came to get her. I don't know. But Mr. Buzzy doesn't have anybody to care about him. It has to be you.

Una stood on the balcony, barefoot, looking for all the world like a twelve-year-old girl, with the puddled parking lot full of beached fish and drowned gulls below, a white sailboat resting on its side in the middle of Shoreline Drive not far from the motel's driveway.

You might need some help, said Falk. I don't know. Maybe I should go with you first. Then later go to Buzzy's place.

He did not want to leave Una. She knew this and shook her head. She told him to find Mr. Buzzy. She didn't need him. She'd been following her mother for years. She would find her. It would all work out.

Now go.

. . .

FALK HEADED NORTH on foot, in the general direction of Mr. Buzzy's trailer park, a cluster of rusting rental units hidden in the live oaks. It was known as the Tombs. The morbid nickname arose from the propensity and likelihood of its elderly inhabitants to expire in their flimsy homes and be discovered by concerned if often neglectful relatives or bill collectors.

Falk weaved his way through an obstacle course of fallen palm trees, great scaly trunks blocking the roadside path, frogs leaping into the mud puddles as he neared, a drowned ridley sea turtle upended and motionless on the shoulder of the road, the plates of its belly geometrical and bonewhite. He passed beached catfish and sea gar the size of dolphins, with rows of horror-show teeth, buzzed by flies. He tried breathing through his mouth, but that only seemed to coat his tongue with a fishy paste.

He resigned himself to inhaling the rank odor of rot and drownage. He stopped to relieve himself in the flooded ditch beside Shoreline Drive. Standing there with his fly open, a shrimpboat stranded on its side nearby, he felt as if he were witness to an end of the world.

North of the Sea Horse the strip of beach homes and motels was sagging and soggy. A terrier stood upon a roof, barking at gulls that floated untouchable and effortless above the wrecked yellow bungalow. A Jeep lay upside down in a front yard, draped with wreaths of seaweed like garlands of spinach.

At the corner of Pirate's Lane Falk headed uphill toward the Tombs, taking a wide detour to avoid a splotchy red longhorn standing smack-dab in the center of the road. Falk shot a photo of

the steer with a wind-ravaged two-story home in the background.
As he focused and clicked the shutter, he noticed a man at the front
door of the house behind the longhorn. The man walked backward
with a five-gallon red plastic gasoline can in his hands, splashing the
front steps and porch. Falk snapped another picture of the longhorn, the man on the porch only an unfocused blur behind it. He
shifted the focus to infinity just as the figure on the porch struck a
match and dropped it to the ground. A gush of flame erupted
silently in the image of Falk's viewfinder. The man hurried backward until he was safely beyond the reach of flames, then turned
around and saw Falk pointing a camera in his direction.

What the fuck you think you're doing? he shouted. He hurried
toward Falk, the house in flames behind him. Give me that fucking
camera, kid. I'll rip you a new asshole. By God I will.

Falk kept moving. The man's voice grew fainter. He stood in the
middle of the street and threw his gas can onto the asphalt. Behind
him the longhorn had turned in his direction and was watching, as
if considering whether to gore or not to gore.

Don't make me hurt you! he shouted. Don't make me do that!

Falk's breath sounded labored and rough to his own ears and he
seemed to be running in water. When he reached the first trailers of
the Tombs he turned to look back. The arsonist stood now in his
yard on the street below, his home in flames, a dense black cloud of
smoke curling up the sky above the murky green bay.

Falk walked the final stretch of driveway into the Tombs. The
storm surge had reached its summit at the park's edge. A low wall of
debris now marked the eastern side, and Falk clambered over and
through this jumble of splintered lumber spiny with nails.

A human arm, its skin almost bluish and doll-like, protruded from beneath a toppled SPEED LIMIT 35 road sign. Falk's stomach felt nauseated, his mouth too full of saliva, as if he would be sick. Near the sign the wall of debris held a black-and-white soccer ball, an Igloo ice cooler, a tangled mass of coat hangers and clothes. Falk set his Nikon on the ground and took hold of the road sign. It was wedged tight. He struggled with it for several moments before he worked it free. His stomach felt as if it were floating up through his chest. His head was dizzy from the heat. He lifted the sign off the body and pushed it away, although the metal pole remained entangled and the best he could do was push the face of the sign to one side.

He recognized the teenaged girl, a sophomore, two years behind him, but he wasn't sure of her name. He noticed his hands were shaking. He had scraped his wrist somehow. It was bleeding. He did not take a photograph. He took off his shirt and covered her face.

Mr. Buzzy's small trailer was old and meant to be pulled behind a pickup. Falk rapped on the door. There was no answer. A dog next door began to howl. Falk rattled the door again and stood on the cinder blocks of the front step to peer in the window. This time he heard a muffled sound.

Inside the place was dark and cluttered, smelling of Mentholatum and mildew. Puddles of water soaked the warped linoleum of the floor. He found Mr. Buzzy on his back in bed, eyes closed.

He thought the old man might be sleeping. Yo, Mr. Buzz. How's it hangin'?

The old man did not move nor open his eyes. It was quiet in the powerless trailer park but for buzzing flies. A pair of them landed on the old man's grayish-white fuzzhead. He didn't move to shoo them.

Mr. Buzz? You still among the living?

At that Mr. Buzzy slowly put a bony hand to his forehead. God-damn flies got no respect. Among the livin'? I hope so. I do hope so. Yessir. 'Cause if I dead and be gone to heaven, I don't plan to see your skinny ass, that's for damn sure.

Now what kind of thing is that to say to a rescuer?

Mr. Buzzy nodded, closed his eyes again. What I want to know is what you be doin' here? He nodded again, as if someone were de-bating him. Yessir. Here. In my trailer after that crazyass storm be blowin' the world around.

Well, the thing is, I mean, I hate to tell you this, but you are dead, Mr. Buzz.

The old man opened his eyes.

Falk kept a stony face. Jesus was busy. He sent me instead.

The old man smiled. That be a fine kettle o' fish. He leaned on one elbow. I be goddamned on a Sunday. That was some blow, wasn't it?

UNA MOVED AWAY in the streaked light, a small dark figure with long hair, weaving her way through a battlefield of the fallen. She headed south, down the muddied sidewalk beside Shoreline Drive, toward her mother's trailer, her straight posture conveying a sense of beautiful remorse and steadfast refusal to be diminished.

The yards along Shoreline south to the Bay Breeze Trailer Park were now swamps. Ponds and puddles filled the low-lying areas, jumbled with what the sea had stranded. The *Maria de las Lagrimas* lay on its side in the road, covered with croaking frogs.

What remained was wreck and garbage. The plywood and timbers of Krazy Karl's Krabhut were scattered over the inland side of the road. A black cottonmouth slithered out of the broken boards and disappeared into a weedy puddle, only its head visible. Una had to fan the air before her face to keep mosquitoes out of her eyes.

Nothing looked the same. She grew disoriented, afraid of encountering more snakes, pestered by the mosquitoes, irritated by the constant sound of the croaking frogs resting atop everything.

Finally she reached home. The trailer door was open and the floor soaked with water, filled with even more of the gruesome frogs. She called her mother's name. Picking her way through the rooms, her eyes clouded with tears. From her bedroom, a sound as of rats scurrying. A scuttle and scratch. She moved slowly down the narrow hall, around the corner. And smiled. Fa-lo and Toong, her red canaries, bedraggled and hungry, waggled from side to side on their wooden perch dowel. She found the bag of birdseed in her bathroom and filled their tray. They chirped and fluttered, the sounds of their wings like the beating of feathered hearts.

On her hands and knees beneath the trailer, breathing hard, her heart beating wildly and her vision cloudy, the world seeming darker than it should be, she scrambled to find the metal box, her crude and impractical bank. Coils of chicken wire from the neighbor's garden were blown up against the tires, and as she tried to pull the wire away it cut her hands.

Squirming into the crawl space, she scooched forward on her elbows and knees. Everything was dim and she whimpered when she saw a snake flee at her approach. She reached where she thought the metal box full of her money should be.

There was nothing. She pulled out an aluminum cooking pan. A dog's plastic water dish. Handfuls of mud.

9

THE NEXT DAY, Gusef and Falk picked through the rubble outside the Black Tooth Café. Nighthawks buzzed above the debris-strewn roadway like origami birds. Their bodies appeared in silhouette, only the white bands of their wings clear against the hazy blue sky. Clouds of gnats and mosquitoes zizzed the air. Gulls swooped and kited. The storm surge had reached halfway to the café's roof. The high point of the waterline sharply divided the outer walls, making it resemble vertically arranged before-and-after photos.

Gusef told Falk how the zebrafish had been found on the Key Escondida tennis courts, like the giant goldfish in the children's book about the boy who feeds his pet too much. The Russian walked beside Falk and shrugged. This is not so bad, he said. I will collect insurance money and take vacation. Plus now I will not have to listen to stinking shrimpers and fishermen complain about how they cannot catch fish. Fish that no longer swim in water because they were too greedy and caught them all to last minnow and shrimp to feed their ugly children.

A sludgy coating of sand and silt covered Shoreline Drive, and their passage left footprints in the brown sand, which appeared pale, almost whitish, in the veiled daylight, as if they were scoring a lunar surface or some other world, newly formed and fresh, ready for its own rules and customs. Falk snapped photographs of the devastation and said very little. He listened to Gusef and kept close to him, felt a bit safer in his orbit.

Thank Jesus for nothing, said Gusef. This is stinking fucking mess.

They pushed open the door to the café, now draped with dark seaweed. Inside the tables were jumbled against one wall, the trophy marlin fallen from its wall perch, huge forked tail pointing into the air, as if caught in the act of plunging into the deep, as if diving to feed or to escape some dread quality of this terrestrial brightness.

They made their way through the stricken building, past the tumbled tables, soaked tablecloths, strewn dinnerware. Falk ghosted his way beside the older man. Gusef grabbed at things and flung them aside, wiped his hands on his pants, sniffed and grimaced. He touched the new bandage on his forehead with his oversized warted hands.

Inside the café he dropped his Russian fatalist bravado and stared around him as the owner of a property marked by catastrophe. This is fucking horrible stinking mess, he said again. He turned to Falk. What you think, photo boy? What you say for this?

Falk grinned. It's a stinking, fucking horrible mess. I think you nailed it.

Gusef nodded. I nailed it. Some big accomplishment. Big fucking horrible mess. Good for me.

Falk wondered when the café might reopen. Gusef tugged a flood-soaked checkered tablecloth from a toppled table and pulled it slowly into the air. Two months to never, said Gusef. In the gloom of the wrecked dining room, he gazed at the warped wooden table-top with an expression of disgust and resignation. Why should I open again? There is no use. It is hopeless. Do you not see nose on your face? Hopeless!

Oh, come on. You can't just close down. Where's your fighting spirit?

Gusef hissed in disgust, shook his head.

When the going gets tough, the tough get going?

Gusef dropped the tablecloth. To hell with spirit.

Falk wouldn't let it go. He said, This town won't be the same without the Black Tooth. It's an institution.

Institution, yes. You should be in such thing. For madness people. For people who hear voices and talk to dead and see Virgin Mary in pickle jar. Talk to dead, yes. That's what we have here. Res-urrection of dead.

What about Una? She's been working here for three years and you're what? Just going to let her go?

Una is not my problem. She is your problem. Yes. This much is obvious. For me she is no problem. She loses this job she find an-other.

But—

It is hopeless, I tell you! Do not argue and say such words any longer. There is no hope!

Falk straightened the chairs around the warped table, brushed the clumps of seaweed from their ladderbacks. You always exagger-ate. There's always hope.

Bullshit, said Gusef.

Falk brushed off his hands. We've got a little saying here in Texas. Where there's a will there's a way.

Texas is stinking ruined redneck shithole and to hell with stupid hick sayings.

Gusef rubbed his thick fingers over his high forehead and winced, touching his scalp wound. But he grinned. Crazy person. You are. Crazy person in love with this impossible girl Una and even this storm, this colossal fucking mess, means nothing to you. He tapped his palm against Falk's brow. Your head is filled with pussy.

Maybe, said Falk.

Maybe nothing. Gusef nodded. This is good thing. You are young. If you think of anything else, I know for certain you are fairy.

UNA'S TRAILER resembled an abandoned ruin hidden in a jungle or left over from a cataclysm in a tropical wasteland, the way ships from the tidal waves of Krakatoa were later found stranded miles inland. It sat twisted on its frame, wrenched off-kilter by the wind, the back end higher than the front, the door at a listing angle, a great jumble of torn palm fronds clustered against it on the wind-ward side. Falk parked in the sandy mud. By the sound of the truck tires in the silt, he suspected he was now stuck. Mired in Una's proximity literally if not metaphorically.

The air thick with swarms of mosquitoes. A rattling of broken glass and loose wood when he knocked.

Una answered as if in a dream. Barefoot, wearing a simple blue dress patterned with green ivy leaves. Her hair loose and black, trailing on her shoulder like a horse's mane.

I just woke up, she said. I can't sleep. Or I couldn't. And then I did. For too long. She yawned.

Falk told her he'd just come from the Black Tooth. What was left of it. Gusef bitter and gloomy in the rubble.

She told him to hurry inside. Quick. You're letting in bugs, she said, swatting the mosquito-bedeviled air.

Inside she cleared a place for them to sit at the dinette. Everything small and cramped in this world. My mother is lost, she said. She left a note, that tourist couple from the Sea Horse picked her up.

Falk nodded and told her how he'd found their RV on Shoreline Drive. Your mother wasn't there. Maybe she got out. Maybe she went someplace else.

Una shook her head. There's a tent full of bodies downtown. She looked out the window and blinked at the bright sunlight, rubbed her eyes. I'm going to find her.

Una was thin and haggard. She looked smaller than ever, as if she could fit in the cup of a seashell. An Asian sea spirit who steals the hearts of befuddled sailors and hides them in a coral box. The room smelled of spice and mildew. She had called the hospitals and the sheriff and had been told to check the FEMA tent by the harbor, where the bodies of the drowned lay sleeping forever now in rows. Like children just born in a hospital room, come full circle now, waiting to be named.

First we should eat something, she said. I have some cold macaroni. I think it's still good.

The trailer seemed quiet with no buzzing refrigerator or whoosh of hot-water heater, no radio burble, no flick of digital clock-radio numerals card-counting the minutes. A chirping at the other end.

That's the birds, said Una.

Falk had no idea what she was talking about.

She opened the refrigerator, yawning, and no light came to life. A smell of old food. From the darkness she pulled a Tupperware bowl and set it on the table. She opened it and sniffed inside. Put two forks on the table.

Is that good? Falk looked doubtful.

She shrugged. I don't think it will kill us. And if it does, we'll join our friends and family, right?

The macaroni was blood-warm and gluey with cheddar cheese. But it tasted good to Falk. He had not eaten since a donut at the bank's disaster relief tent earlier in the day. The taste of it made him lose himself in the eating. He wolfed down forkfuls like a dog fed once a day. Una ate a few bites and watched him, then stared out the louvered windows, an attitude of waiting for someone to reach the door with news perhaps good but most likely not.

Wind stirred the raspy palm fronds storm-blown against the trailer. They scratched the metal siding, a faint keening.

Halfway through his bowl of macaroni, Falk yelped and winced, put a hand over his mouth. He closed his eyes and groaned. Una asked what was the matter. Was there something in the food?

I bit my tongue, he said. I'll be okay.

You should slow down. Be more careful.

I didn't realize I was so hungry.

He kept eating as Una told him about the search for her mother, what they should do next. When he was finished eating he could taste the metallic tinge of blood in his mouth. He showed Una his tongue.

Oh, my God, she said. You really gouged yourself, didn't you?

He looked in the mirror. In the center of the tongue was a groove oozing blood. She told him to put ice on it. When he did it simply melted. She cut a piece of gauze and folded it into a square. He felt woozy and suffused with warmth, protected and fortunate to be within the realm of her nursing, the smell of her skin, the touch of her hands.

He placed the gauze atop his tongue, then held it there with pressure against his teeth. I think thith'll work, he said, the gauze sticking out his mouth and garbling his words.

Una almost smiled. You look like one of those dogs with a white cone on its neck to keep it from biting its wounds.

He barked weakly through the gauze.

They walked outside, Falk stooping to get through the small, crooked door. Into the humid and mosquito-filled air. The sunshine blinding. It baked the destruction and was not unlike putting your face near one of the heat lamps that used to grace the kitchen countertops of the Black Tooth Café, where Gusef now poked about and cursed a God he had believed in all his life, albeit secretly, since leaving the home of his mother and father many years ago.

The truck tires spun in hot mud. Falk shifted into first and gunned it, then put it in reverse and managed to rock the vehicle, shooting rooster tails of mud against the side of the trailer, until the tread caught and lurched into the traction of the oyster-shell road through the trailer park.

Two fat sunburned men labored over a large hydraulic jack to raise the near end of a fallen house trailer, swatting mosquitoes. They stopped what they were doing to stare as Falk drove by, nodding to the high school expellee with the local beauty who thought she was too good for them.

. . .

On the drive Una talked about her mother, herself. How she had been an ungrateful daughter for too many years and now was going to pay for it. How she had wished and prayed to be somehow rid of her mother. How she had never really appreciated all the things her mother had done for her. How she now feared it was too late, you never see the end coming. Falk, trying to talk through the gauze on his tongue, insisted, No, you were a good daughter. Everyone geth irritated by their family now and then. It'th no big deal. It happenth.

No, I wasn't, said Una. I was hateful and vain and it's too late now.

Maybe not, he said.

She just looked at him. They had arrived at the city park where they would search for her mother's body. A crowd of people milled about as in a county fair of the dead and grieving. He parked the truck in the grass as she stared.

You're too sweet, you know that? she said.

I'm juth opthimithtic.

In the city park of Goodnight a makeshift morgue was demarcated by the quivering purlieus of yellow tape: CRIME SCENE DO NOT CROSS. Falk turned off the engine. Una kept staring ahead and did not move. A slow and somber procession of survivors entered and exited the olive-green canvas tent. Women sobbed, supported by leather-skinned shrimpers who had seen their share of grief, had seen more than they could handle. Their feelings were now sunken within their chests, their eyes shadowed in deep sockets.

Falk took the gauze out of his mouth, a white oval shape of soggy blood in the center. We don't have to go in there, he said.

Yes, we do. We don't have a choice. That's just an illusion, you know. That choice business.

There's always a choice.

Who do you think I am? If you think I'm leaving my mother . . . Una's voice broke, eyes wet and pink. Think I'm leaving my mother alone on a tarp in the middle of a park somewhere because it's too . . .

I didn't mean that.

Una got out and walked away, leaving the truck door open. Falk replaced the gauze in his mouth. He could feel the blood start to ooze in the few moments he'd had it out to speak clearly. He took his 35-mm camera from the glove compartment. He tried to sling it over his shoulder inconspicuously as he walked away, nodding to the convenience store owner he knew, who walked unsteadily, leaving the tent, like someone stricken.

The crowd was quiet, though he could hear muffled sobbing among the sad and shuffling men and women who were mostly middle-aged or older. Tattooed shrimpers in T-shirts and jeans stood in a group, discussing whose boats were lost. The children and teenagers were quiet.

Inside the dim tent a relief from the radiation of tropical sunlight. Community hospital women in shapeless green smocks and mouth masks asked whom he was looking for. He answered, I'm with her. Her mother is lost. They nodded, one touching his shoulder softly, telling him to watch where he stepped. If he felt like he would be sick, please go outside.

Bodies lying supine and shoulder to shoulder, several dozen in three rows. Grim-faced survivors with their hands to their faces or covering their mouths shuffled down the rows. Crouching. Peering. Shaking their heads. Among the bodies Falk recognized two of his classmates, boys he had never liked, and an old kooky woman who ran the bait stand, Krazy Karl's, the one destroyed and washed into the fields above Shoreline Drive, near Una's trailer park.

The bodies already identified were covered with blue sheets. Workers hefted one blue-sheet-covered body onto a stretcher and carried it through a V-shaped makeshift door at the rear of the tent.

The row of bodies appeared as so much mortal flotsam. Ragged and seabitten, buzzed by flies and dusted with sand. A hand outstretched, clutching a scrap of cloth, a bare foot split with a dark gash. Una stood motionless in the shadows, poleaxed and heartbroken. Out of respect, she stepped carefully, her feet trying to avoid touching the flesh or clothes of the dead and silent of Goodnight.

This darkened tent had become a shrine, the pitched tarp *una iglesia de los ahogados,* a hut for ghosts wherein they whispered the error of our ways. The stiff and immutable shape of things to come. You will laugh when I am old and lonely, she had said. *Mi alma flaca. Mi mocosa. Mi hija ingrata.* You do not, have not, and will never appreciate the pain and toil the world sucked from me *por tu piel*—here she had pinched Una's skin—to make *tus huesos*—here she had grabbed Una's arms.

The tent canvas flopped in the wind, a freak show come to town, the smell of popcorn not here, not now, the scent of ammonia to mask the smell of the decay. She had been standing near a body and was about to pass it when she realized she would need go no farther. Here was her mother, who would not be saved in this world but perhaps in some life everlasting. Her mother who had joined the snowbirds and had not made it out alive, caught by the waves. Her mother's eyes puffed and swollen, her mouth agape, her braided hair like a ship's rope coiled beneath her head, a rough pillow. Her mother's ghost who could haunt her for the rest of her days and then into the afterlife *en el día de los muertos, en la tierra de los olvidados.*

She reached down to close her mother's eyelids. With her fingers she worked them down, but when she let go they parted, as if opening of their own accord, as if her mother wanted to watch the world and her daughter, with whom she had now lost touch.

A hospital worker called to Una, Miss? Miss? Please? Please don't touch them. It's not safe.

Falk crouched with his camera, froze an image of Una stroking her dead mother's face.

Una ignored the hospital worker's pleas. Her long black hair hung beside her like a curtain of charcoal. She stroked her mother's hair, and again closed her eyelids. This time they stayed in place. The hospital worker said nothing more. Falk snapped several photographs unnoticed. When he was finished he walked over to Una and touched her shoulder. He said he was sorry. He said he knew that was not enough.

Una looked at him for a moment, but it was as if she wasn't seeing him. Some reflection of him or someone else. She nodded. The worker came to them and took Una by the elbow, made her stand erect. She asked Una to fill out an identification card. She assured Una her mother would be taken to the morgue in Gregory-Portland, a town twenty miles away, before evening. There were so many dead. The living were doing their best.

Outside the tent the glaring sunlight had softened with late afternoon. The wind blew Una's hair in her face. She got in the truck and folded her arms on the dash, resting her head in them. Falk took photographs of the tent and the people walking out of it. They appeared haloed by the late-afternoon sunlight. He imagined that no one could see him and for the most part they seemed not to, except one woman who glared, her look accusing him of sacrilege.

When he replaced the camera in the glove compartment, he expected Una to scold him. She had raised her head and watched him chronicling the moment. But she said nothing. He started the truck and backed up.

We have something in common now, said Una.

Falk waited. He put the truck in gear and eased across the grassy park, driving slowly through the crowd. The faces anguished and stricken, heading toward the tent of the dead.

We're all alone, she said. We've got no one to watch over us.

He wanted to say, That's okay. We'll watch over each other. We'll rely on ourselves. We'll become independent. We'll become strong.

But he didn't. He didn't know what to say. He drove Una home, taking much care to use his turn signals, merge with the flow of traffic, negotiate the darkened traffic-signal intersections where the power was still out. As if he were the chauffeur of a princess. A mere underling with an unimportant role.

AFTER THE HEAT of summer and Tanya's humid after-breath, puddles lingered in the driveways for weeks, ditches were high with swampgrass, white water lilies bloomed yet in late October. The air finally turned cooler after Halloween, after *las calaveras* candles of the Day of the Dead had been lit and burned. With this cool air of autumn came the fogs.

Mornings and evenings a white wispy air would drift in from the east, from the same bays whose great waves had engulfed the seaside edge of the town. Now a tremendous reverential calm descended upon the waters. Banks of fog floated inland in the blue light of dusk. Through the evening haze the full moon of November appeared only as a ghost face.

It was as if the dead and the lost from Tanya were returning to Goodnight in spirit form. Their bodies were lost and washed out to sea or interred in one of the many cemeteries, boneyards filled with freshly dug graves, adorned with flowers, poems, mementos. Great blue herons perched on the tombstones.

And the living refugees made their way home. The woman from Room 17 of the Sea Horse returned with Gusef's Cadillac. Her name was Carol, and she moved into the Russian's house. Gusef said that if he could get the motel repaired, she'd be taking over as manager. In mean time, he added, she feeds me morning and night. So what if all I own is ruined? I get fat and happy.

The *Goodnight Gazette* ran many of Falk's photographs of the storm's aftermath. One of them showed Una in the tent of the dead, her hand to her mouth as she stared at the rows of bodies. It revealed their faces and figures grainy and indistinct in the gray light. Behind her, framed, backlit by the light of the exit slit in the tent, stood a faceless figure, opaque and undeniable as the angel of death itself.

The black-and-white prints had a silvery quality to them, the swollen waters of Red Moon Bay tinged an almost pearlgray. One series of images showed the waves slamming into the Driftwood Motel's second-story balcony. Another showed the neon sign of the

Sea Horse loose from its pole and about to be swept under, the gigantic curled sea-horse shape looking strangely proportional to the fantastic waves, rafts of sea foam about to swallow it.

When the fogs of November arrived, Leesha feared her life would soon change. After the storm her daily routine had quickly returned to normal: boredom in class, fever on the ride home. The high school itself was not greatly damaged, being five miles inland. She helped her mother clean their flooded house and kept a secret. She planned how she and Gabriel would be happy together. She took to eating Cheetos and drinking root beer. Her fingers would often be stained orange from the food dye coating the cheese that goes puff. The root beer only made her burp. The school system forbade students to bring food or drink aboard the buses, but considering she had sat in Gabriel's lap with her panties pulled to her ankles, that became another rule most honored in the breach.

She clambered aboard the bus one autumn afternoon and loosed a conspirator's sly smile as she passed him. He kept his place in the driver's seat and pretended to ignore her. He was doing his ex–juvenile delinquent best to look less a criminal and more an honest citizen, not the tattooed fisherman driving the bus who was tasting one of his charge's forbidden fruits each afternoon before dropping her off as the last on the route. Still she was perhaps the least of the many crimes he'd committed without blinking, without looking back.

This day she wore a white cotton blouse, a Wonderbra beneath it, a baby-blue wool sweater, one button hooked at the top, the only button, the way the cool girls did, even though she was anything but cool. Just the opposite. She wore a blue-jean skirt that was loose on her no matter how many Cheetos she ate and root beer she drank. She had lost eight pounds since September. By now she was developing an angular waiflike look, her sunflower-yellow hair hanging straight, parted on one side, pinned in place with dragonfly barrettes, the tips frizzy, often tucked into her mouth as she chewed on them.

She kept the root-beer bottle hidden beneath her sweater and lifted it to sip only after the bus lurched to life, gears grinding, the swaying motion making her giddy, giving her a fresh outbreak of the tinglies. Now the feeling had reached such a pitch she could barely stay in her seat until the last few kids remained on the bus and, to hell with what they thought, took her place behind Gabriel to rub her body against the back of his head.

She sometimes thought back to how foolish she had been, weeks before, but even now, with a child in her womb known only to her, she was not remorseful. She imagined an entire conversation, telling her mother, insisting that there was nothing wrong with it. There's nothing wrong with love, is there? But she was scared. Once she had almost worked up the nerve to confess everything, but felt like she was about to vomit.

She tried not to think about it. Today she chose a bench on the right side, second row, as the bus swayed and whined. She faced the window and watched a floppy T-shirted goon racing beside it, out of sheer exuberance, making faces at someone in the back rows.

Outside the window images revolved like microfiche of her life: the brick buildings of the high school, the faded stripes of the American flag, the gray asphalt of the parking lot, the weedy ditches, the stop sign. Pigeons fluttered about the water tower, seagulls glided overhead, disappeared into the billowy clouds of November whiteness.

The fog muffled sound and mood. Today the students seemed quieter, subdued, sleepy. They trundled off at each designated stop until at last Leesha and Gabriel were left alone.

She leaned her body against his head and made him smile. She caught his eye in the rearview and mock-threatened to pour her now warm root beer over his head.

You better not, he said.

What you gonna do if I do?

That would deserve a spanking.

She grinned. Tipped the bottled till it dribbled on his head.

Goddamnit, he said. I told you not to.

Yes, master.

I mean it.

Okay, grouch.

They stopped the school bus on one of the deserted lanes of the abandoned development known by the locals as Thousand Roads. This was where Gabriel had taught Leesha how to drive a stick, how to drive the bus, how to love a man. She thought of it as their secret place.

She enjoyed this now more than ever. She had given herself up to it, reveled in it, this new world of heat and flesh, believing it to be something extraordinary and hypnotic. An exotic love that made her special if not exalted.

She wanted to tell him. She tried to find the words for it.

She caught Gabriel staring at her in the rearview, made a face at him.

What are you looking at? she asked. What is it?

That's what I was thinking of asking you.

She shrugged. Oh, nothing. Six weeks exams are coming up. I hate to study.

THOUSAND ROADS was no secret to Sheriff John Littledog. He knew its reputation as a Lovers' Lane of the swamps. That didn't concern him greatly. If he gave it any mind, it did stir unpleasant memories. But the problem of Thousand Roads was contraband. As far as law enforcement was concerned, it was equivalent to a rum-runners' alley. There were rumors it had become a spot for drug shipment transfers, bundles of weed coming up from Mexico, being offloaded onto boats and taken into Humosa Bay, out-of-town couriers waiting in the Thousand Roads area for the pickup. Littledog had never caught anyone. He didn't know if the rumors were true.

But it was his duty to keep an eye out.

That afternoon he drove down Humosa Bay Road, listening to the radio crackle, making his usual afternoon loop across the wide sweep of Mustang County. Near the Thousand Roads area he noted the number of ducks and geese that side of the bay. Duck season had recently begun, and that could be trouble. He worried about drug couriers transferring the merchandise right in front of hunters in the marshes. With both sides holding firearms, it could get ugly fast. As he passed in the patrol car he caught a brief glimpse of something unusual in the swamp. It was visible only for an instant, blocked by trees before he could even put on the brakes.

It was not much more than a faint blur of orange through the haze of fog and green live-oak trees. A glimpse of something bright through the branches. Most likely a vehicle. He reversed until he pulled up beside the turn-in to a rutted road. It appeared to have fresh tracks through its mud and puddles.

He turned down the unmarked lane and rolled forward slowly. Before he reached the oaks he stopped the patrol car and got out. If it were a vehicle and up to no good, it would be stuck behind his cruiser for now. He crouched down and considered the zigzag pattern of tire treads in the muddy ruts.

He continued on foot, stepping in the grassy marsh a few feet wide of the road. The swamp was fog-shrouded and quiet. The only sound was the beating wings of ducks rising from the brackish ponds as they sensed him coming, the honks of Canada geese on the wing. Not fifty yards past the first squall line of oak and mesquite he got a look at the school bus. He left the road and moved into the woods, where he could approach without being seen. He noted the legend on its side, MUSTANG COUNTY INDEPENDENT SCHOOL DISTRICT, the number, the condition of it.

He passed out of the woods and back onto the road as he neared the bus, close enough to peek in the back window large and square. A mottled image of leaves and branches was reflected in the glass. From his low angle, he could see no one inside. Walking beside the bus, he considered its amber paint, its black stripes and painted number 37, its Bluebird insignia. It wasn't an old one that had been sold to hippies for living quarters, as far as he could tell.

The doors were closed. He realized he was at a disadvantage. If there was someone here up to no good and ready to do him harm, they would probably see him before he would know much about them one way or the other. He drew his gun and readied to knock on the door.

He considered climbing onto the insect-spattered bumper, getting his tall frame high enough to have a look through the windshield. He pictured that and imagined the white sky's reflection would block any view inside. Law enforcement has to know what can be seen, what can be guessed. Carefully he moved closer. He didn't like the mud. If he had to backstep quickly, he'd probably fall on his ass.

He leaned in close enough to see through the door windows: an Almond Joy wrapper on the rubber-mat steps, a baby-blue sweater upon the empty driver's seat. He then saw the front bench. And two people, looked to be a teenaged girl beside a boy. Fully dressed and sitting pretty as you please, like they were on a school picnic. Maybe they had returned to the bus early and were now waiting for the others to arrive.

He gave the door a loud rap. He watched them react, watched the girl scoot away. She smoothed her hair and grabbed her sweater, like she had something to hide. The boy stood up and looked his way, hitched his jeans, then reached for the door handle and opened it.

Afternoon, Sheriff. What can I do ya for?

Littledog recognized Gabriel Perez. He'd ticketed him more than once, heard something about trouble between him and Pedro Alamogordo, the meth-lab casualty.

Sheriff Littledog hauled his lanky frame up the school-bus steps and nodded. He removed his cowboy hat and looked at both of them for a moment. Anything wrong with the bus? he asked.

Gabriel raised his eyebrows. He looked at the dash, at the array of instrument panels, as if it were a breakdown to be diagnosed. Well. No. Not really. Bus is fine.

Sheriff Littledog asked to see both their IDs. Gabriel took his out of his wallet and handed it over. When Leesha fished hers from her purse, she mentioned it was only a learner's permit. Mr. Perez is my driver's ed instructor, she said. I'm about to get my regular license, soon as I pass the test.

Littledog looked at both the IDs. As he did so Gabriel said, I been tutoring her a little extra. She wanted to know how to drive a bus. I told her I wasn't allowed to do that, you know. To let her drive it herself. But she kept bugging me, so I let her come along on an extra training run.

What would you be doing here? The two of you, an afternoon like this?

What I told you, said Gabriel. Tutoring.

Tutoring? You mean bus-driving training, one on one?

Yessir.

The middle of a swamp?

Well, yes. You gotta learn to drive all kinds of roads, don't you?

When I walked up here I didn't see no drivin'. Littledog handed the IDs back. Looked to me like you were just sitting here. Like maybe you two were having a heart-to-heart.

Leesha rubbed her right eye. Her hair was in her face and she held a dragonfly barrette in her hand. I just wanted to learn, she said, her voice choked and wobbly. No harm in that.

Gabriel shrugged. That against some law?

Sheriff Littledog stood there tall and implacable, holding his cowboy hat in his hands, looking at the two of them. He didn't say a word. Gabriel spoke up after a moment and said they had better be going, they hadn't meant to be this long.

You two alone here? asked Littledog.

You bet, said Gabriel. We didn't think anyone else would be interested.

Interested in what?

Driving a bus, said Gabriel.

I don't want to get in any trouble, said Leesha. I was just curious, is all.

Littledog said nothing to that. He walked the length of the bus, checking every seat. When he returned to the front of the bus he told Leesha to pick up her things and come with him. I expect you need to return this to the county lot, don't you? he asked Gabriel.

Yessir.

I expect you should do that. Immediately if not sooner.

Yessir, said Gabriel. I promise. Soon's I leave here.

Leesha followed Littledog toward the patrol car, her legs weak, heart beating wildly. She had trouble finding a way in the high grass beside the muddy lane. After a few moments Littledog noticed her lagging behind. He waited.

When she caught up to him, she almost fell in the mud, and grabbed his arm.

Careful there, he said. Wouldn't want to dirty those pretty clothes now would you? He could feel her trembling as she gained her footing.

Am I under arrest? she whispered.

Should you be?

I don't know, she said. I don't think so.

Well, then. Not as far as I know.

Thank you, Sheriff.

When they got back to the patrol car he opened the passenger-side door for her, had her sit in the front seat. He called the dispatcher to report his location and record the license plate of the school bus, mentioning that he was escorting a high school student home. His legs were wet to the crotch from walking in the swampgrass. If there was a thing he didn't like, it was a wet crotch in the patrol car. If he'd heard about that with one of his deputies involved, he'd think it was either cowardice or inappropriate behavior in a county vehicle. Either way, trouble. With him it was unpleasant.

Something about the moment, calling the dispatcher, reminded him of Oscar Martinez, that arrest, and how he'd never felt right about it. He wondered if maybe he should have looked the other way. A man shouldn't drown in jail. That ain't right. Littledog felt he was at fault, though he tried not to blame himself. He had a job to do. That storm was one bad motherfucker. It was to blame, not him. Still.

He drove Leesha home, cruising slowly down Humosa Bay Road. He said he wasn't there to judge. A person's private life is their business. He didn't see himself as the town snoop. Then again, he said, there are laws, and consequences for people who break those laws.

So I have to ask, he said. You got anything you need to tell me?

About what?

About this tutoring?

She shook her head. No, sir.

He kept driving. Okay then.

After a moment she said, I never been in a police car before.

He smiled at that. Maybe you oughta keep it that way.

Yes, sir.

When the patrol car pulled into her driveway, she was glad to see her mother's car and her dad's pickup were both gone.

· · ·

THE PHONE RINGING in his mosquitoed ranch house. An odd noise. He had expected a call from Sheriff Littledog but it had not come. The longer it took to come, the greater his hopes grew that it never would.

Things could be the same. Things did not have to turn to shit.

It was the woman from the school calling. She was Chicana and he liked her. Her name was Rosa. Since she had called to tell him classes would be canceled because of the storm, and later to ask if he would help evacuate people, he had become friendly with her. She was part of his being a hero. Hi, he said. *Qué pasa?*

I'm sorry, she said. They told me to call you. I don't like doing this.

They who?

They, the school superintendent. Mr. Mitchell. Plus Mr. Hinajosa. My boss.

Gabriel's hands were sweating. He wiped them on his jeans and switched the phone from one hand to the other. He said, Where we going with this?

They want me to tell you that we won't be needing you anymore. I'm sorry.

What do you mean?

Well. You know. It's not my decision.

I mean, why not? The kids are going to walk home now? Is that it?

No. Someone will drive your route.

I get it. Someone will. Not me.

I'm sorry. Really.

You know, I didn't do nothing. People think I did something, but I didn't. I didn't do nothing.

Gabriel. Listen.

Yeah.

It's not up to me.

I know.

He held the phone hot against his ear, stared out the window. Fog drifted over Humosa Bay. He couldn't see the dark line of houses in the distance. Not with fog like this. A hazy white cloud drifted across the green water. He couldn't see the line of houses that marked Yucca Beach. He couldn't see the abandoned world in the distance.

Maybe if I explained something. Maybe if I talked to them. You think that would help?

There was a pause on the other end of the line. This was a good woman. He knew she wanted to help. She finally said, No. They won't listen.

Okay then. Fuck it.

I'm sorry.

Yeah yeah yeah. I don't need this crummy job anyway. I get something better than this tomorrow.

I think so. Really.

I never liked driving that bus. The pay sucks.

Listen, she said. The tone of her voice changed: a sense of business being conducted, a job to do. I'll just mail it to you.

What?

Your last check.

I could just come pick it up. Isn't that what I always do?

She was silent. Then she said, They don't want you to.

To what?

Come in here. To get your check.

What's their problem? Like I'm going to fucking pollute the hallway or something? I don't get it.

I'm sorry, she said. I have to go now.

Yeah. Thanks, he added. I mean, shit. I know it wasn't you.

Forget about it, she said. You can do better.

She hung up with him still holding the phone. He listened to the dial tone for a moment, the realization of being out of work again settling upon him like a spell.

There was hurricane cleanup work. There was that. Shitwork, was what it was.

But he had to find something else. Again.

⤬ 10 ⤬

ON GABRIEL'S BIRTHDAY, they ate German choco-
late cake and French vanilla ice cream, neither of which Gabriel
gave a rat's ass about. He didn't have a sweet tooth. In his book,
people who made a point of indulging in sweets were weak and
flabby. Sweets were fat food. The last thing in the world he wanted
to be or would be for that matter was another fat *pendejo* standing
in the checkout line at Wal-Mart just waiting until he made it out
the door to rip open a box of Fiddle-Faddle or chocolate malted-
milk balls. The streets of Goodnight were full of fatties. Gabriel
knew that one way to draw a line between himself and that herd of
losers was by staying lean and mean.

Of course he kept all this to himself when Leesha sat him down
at the dining room table for a birthday celebration. It was late afternoon and a school day, Leesha dressed in a tight white turtleneck
sweater and low-rider jeans that showed a stretch of skin beneath
her belly button and above her charms. Any lower riding and she'd

be fit to be tied, was what Gabriel thought, though the knots would be loose and gentle-like.

Gabriel smiled awkwardly at the fat wedge of cake Leesha placed in front of him and felt the warm, damp touch of her hand on his leg as she asked if he liked it or not.

The light in the dining room had the gray, washed-out quality of the fogs of November that hovered and drifted outside the windows, obscuring the elm oaks that bordered the yard. It was a light that seemed to leak through the sky. The oak branches glimpsed through the ripped wet sheets of fog looked like the writhing arms and legs of souls in torment. Or at least that was how Gabriel saw it. He was aware, now and then, that he seemed to have developed a rather morbid mental vision of late. It must be all the ruined appliances he'd been hauling to the dump as part of the hurricane clean-up brigade. For a day laborer, Tanya was a gold mine. He and every *mojado* in South Texas had all the work they could handle.

Goodnight by the Sea had become famous all across the country as a place of hardship and abandon, decay and collapse. The Forgotten America, it was called, often enough to remind whoever it was that the sad-sack fishing-village-without-fish still existed. New York media people came to stay in the hotels far enough from the shoreline to have remained undamaged. Even the Sea Horse Motel made it on the NBC Nightly News, although if you blinked you missed it.

Now the town was full of disaster tourists creaming their jeans to tour the "war zone." For Gabriel, one of the surprises of the aftermath was the sheer number of strange horny women in town. Between doing news reports on the devastation and the failure of FEMA and most branches of government, they killed time in the

Holiday Inn lounge. If an enterprising local like Gabriel got cleaned up and pulled into the Pirate's Cove halfway into Happy Hour, he'd have no trouble finding a woman both liquored and lonesome.

The day before this silly birthday hoo-ha celebration Gabriel had tasted the sweets of a mousy blond personal assistant to a Dallas TV reporter. He felt somewhat guilty about this, what with her crying while they were doing it. She told him she always cried when she did it, especially when it was good. It gives me a tremendous release, she said. When I come I cry. I can't help it.

Gabriel just nodded like that was the most natural thing in the world. For all he knew, maybe it was. Maybe that was a natural thing for all those Bible-thumpers in Dallas. Humping like escaped convicts on Saturday and speaking in tongues on Sunday. She made so much noise he could hear people giggling in the hallway outside the motel room.

With the sheets kicked to the floor and the pillows propped under his head, Gabriel was channel surfing with the remote through the cable TV lineup when the Dallas girl put on a T-shirt and went over to the sliding glass door to the motel-room balcony, like she was about to walk out there half naked and moon the reporters from Houston and parts beyond. The tight T-shirt barely reached the small of her back, leaving her naked bottom pointing toward Gabriel, who felt himself go half-mast in the looking. She didn't notice. She stood at the sliding glass door and stretched, raising her arms high and yawning.

You don't talk much, do you? she asked.

Maybe. Maybe not.

No one's going to accuse you of being a chatty patty, are they? She turned to look at him after she said this, and the expression on her face seemed to record her slowly dawning realization of just exactly who and what she was dealing with.

Maybe I think you should come back here and take off that blouse.

It's not a blouse. It's a T-shirt.

He shrugged. Like I give a shit. Take it off.

She took a sideways step, hiding behind the sliding glass door curtains, tugging her T-shirt hem down a bit in front. And why should I do that?

Because.

Just because?

Because you look better with it off.

That made her smile. Gabriel knew it would. He knew a just-been-loved, half-naked woman in the motel room of a disaster zone can't resist a compliment. Plus the promise of more where that came from.

Her name was Cheryl and she had attended SMU, where she said she'd felt out of place, it being so conservative and all. Gabriel said he'd heard it was a boarding school for Baptist brats.

Well, she said, partly it is. She asked if he'd been to college.

Gabriel shook his head. I'm too old for that.

That can't be true. How old are you?

He told her. He also let it slip that his birthday was around the bend, banking on sympathy, and she gave it good. He even promised this mousy Dallas Cheryl with short bangs and a big bottom that he would spend his birthday night with her.

At the moment he sat at the dining table, the festivities he imagined in the Holiday Inn seemed a whole lot sweeter and hotter than German chocolate cake and French vanilla ice cream. Besides, how was German chocolate cake any different than Mexican? What was so special about vanilla from France? What was next? Balloons?

Leesha sang "Happy Birthday" solo. There was something sad in that, yes, there was, like Gabriel didn't have enough respectable friends to populate a real party. That realization hung in the air like a bad joke. He was the Invisible Man. And if not, if anyone found out what he was up to with Miss Honeypie? He'd be doing time for stat rape, was what he'd be doing.

Leesha sang sweetly and softly and a bit off-key, two fat candles in the shape of the number 2 in the middle of the cake. Gabriel endured it as best he could, like a defendant being read the verdict of his crimes by the foreman of the jury, loosing a tight and tortuous smile as a matter of guilty protocol.

When she was done and reached the "and many more" part he leaned over as required and blew out the candles with the idea that in so doing the worst was over.

Would it hurt you to smile? asked Leesha. She stared at him and frowned. She said the look he had on his face, you'd think he was being forced to eat turnips. In the back of her mind she imagined what her mother would think if she could see this scene, how she'd be shaking her head, saying, I knew it. Once a rat always a rat. If she could see. And lucky it was she couldn't.

Right after she cut the cake, Leesha's cell phone rang, and she rolled her eyes. My mother, she said. I better take it. She put a finger to her lips, giving Gabriel a look, before she answered. He stood up from the table and walked down the hallway. She listened to her mother telling how she and her father had visited Leesha's grandmother dying in the old folks' home. But Leesha's mother was worried about a message she'd gotten from her real estate office, something about a meeting tomorrow, and wondered if any other messages had been left on the answering machine. I don't know what we're going to do if I get laid off, she said. That's the only money to speak of coming in this household and now with the storm and the insurance rates going up nobody's buying. I know it will turn around, but when? You're lucky, young lady. You don't have to worry about such things.

You do enough worrying for the both of us, said Leesha. Gabriel came up behind her and reached under her shirt as she was talking, she had to slap him away and struggle. Her mother asked what she was up to.

Just making a grilled cheese is all, said Leesha, feeling Gabriel's warm hand under her shirt again, touching her belly, his lips on her neck.

You better not eat too much, said her mother. Nobody loves a fat girl. I hate to say it but it's true.

A blue northern was blowing in that afternoon. When Leesha folded shut her cell phone the north wind blew the front door open and popped it against the wall with a loud smack. A gust whistled in and blew a stack of mail off the small table in the hallway. Leesha started for the door but Gabriel held her back, his arms wrapped around her, and she struggled to get free. Jesus, she said. The wind is making a mess of things. Could you let go?

Gabriel watched her kneel down and pick up the scattered envelopes. He wondered when her cousin would be home. He was looking forward to that. The icing on the cake. It would be sweet to wear the girl cousin's pussy on his chest like a Purple Heart. He had entertained ideas of delivering a serious ass-kicking over this Una business. Now he realized that was beneath him. More than one way to skin a cat. The boy comes home to find Gabriel sitting in the living room, a shit-eating grin on his face? That would make him squirm.

As soon as the front door closed, the wind whistle slowed to a sibilant hiss. The house turned quiet as a funeral home before the service. Gabriel stood with his hands in the back pockets of his Levis and looked Leesha up and down in a direct way he figured she'd know he meant business.

You going to give me a little sugar or what? he asked.

She knew what was coming, but she wanted to make him wait. Just thinking of it made Leesha blush and bite her bottom lip. Gabe?

Gabe what? He put his finger to her belly button and poked it gently, working his thumb inside the top button of her low-rider jeans, feeling the heat there as if he were putting his hand over a tea kettle. Come on, he said. You know that's the only thing to make me happy.

But I think we should wait, she whined. I mean, I don't know.

He pulled her to him, his fingers hooked into her jeans. You love me, don't you?

You know I do, she whispered.

You want me to be happy, don't you?

She tried pushing him away. She told him to stop. Please?

He squirmed his hand farther into her pants. Please what?

Leesha planned to say no. The phrase she needed was on a poster in her health class, an antidrug slogan: JUST SAY NO. It showed a clean-cut girl being egged on by a trio of scruffy-looking teens, the wrong crowd. But the poster didn't help when Gabriel came so close to her she could feel his hot breath against her neck and his hands now up her shirt too and all she ever wanted was to be loved by God with a dizziness that made you swallow your chewing gum and damp yourself just remembering it and when his mouth crushed rough and warm against hers his tongue a hot muscle inside somehow there was no moment in time to put their blood on pause and do as she had always been told as she was supposed to do instead she did what she was told in that instant dizzy and blind with Gabriel pulling off her blouse and telling her, We got time, baby. We got all the time we need. Don't you worry. Now don't you worry.

It was as if she had been hypnotized. Or as if she'd simply gone stupid on him. They shuffled into her bedroom and she kept blinking and looking to him with an imploring expression as if to say, Whatever you do, don't stop touching me or I will die of heartbreak right here and now. Witnessed by a menagerie of stuffed animals and amid the clutter of tenth grade biology and Spanish textbooks plus scattered clothes, Leesha stood weak-kneed in the center of the room with the white wool turtleneck pulled above her breasts but yet bunched around her neck and head as Gabriel put his mouth to her nipples with an urgency that made her sink sink sink with no strength left to stand until she was on her back and he was upon her possessing her like the devil she wanted, was ready to pray to sell her soul to as long as he didn't stop.

FALK HAD SPENT the afternoon ripping drywall off the studs of the Black Tooth Café with a claw hammer. It was godawful work and seemed endless as collecting tumbleweeds off a windswept prairie. The waterline of the great flood had reached about four feet up the walls of the Black Tooth. Everything below that was sodden, streaked, spotted green and black with mildew, seawater, and rot. The dining room smelled like a one-bedroom apartment with shag carpet and nineteen cats.

Gusef had already gutted the interior. He threw out the warped tables, waterlogged salt and pepper shakers, bottles of ketchup and mustard, napkin dispensers dotted with flowers of rust.

I should have unforeseen accident is what I should have, I should be so lucky, said Gusef. Perhaps great fire with suspicious origin. But insurance man know my mind and punish me. I do not wish rebuild but have no choice. This ugly redneck town needs place for drunken fishermen to hide from obese children eating two dozen tamales for breakfast.

Gusef showed Falk how to dig the hook end of a claw hammer into the drywall, tug hard, and rip the wall down in jigsaw pieces. Behind the drywall was a layer of pink insulation between two-by-four studs. The insulation was the worst. Still mushy from seawater, it was coated with a fur of mildew. After clearing each twenty-four-inch panel from floor to ceiling, Falk stuffed the mess into heavy-duty trash bags and hauled it to the Dumpster out back, roughly the size and shape of a hobo's boxcar.

It was miserable work but the money he made was going straight into the bank. Falk's arms were getting big in the process, putting a bit of construction-worker swagger into his walk.

Look at you, said Gusef. Soon you will get tattoo on shoulder and win hearts of big-bosomed dockside ladies of night. You will be useless as cook because with so much muscle you will crush food into tasteless paste like hush puppies hit by car.

While the café was in repair Falk seldom saw Una. She was studying for her college entrance exam and did not want to be both-

ered. He suspected she wanted to forget what had happened between them, but he did not voice this to her for fear of seeming too
mopey and hangdog. He called often but her trailer had no machine
to leave a message and he waited to hear her soft voice answer. It
never did. Since the fogs had arrived Una seemed to be swallowed
into the whiteness. As if she had never been, as if he had never felt
her thin rib cage against his body in the wind-howled motel room
of the Sea Horse in the storm.

Falk accepted this slow and quiet rejection like he had accepted
other loss: his mother's death by drowning, his expulsion from high
school, the destruction of Goodnight. Stoic and taciturn, expecting
the worst by now, anxious but doing his damnedest not to show it.

It was a chilly gray late afternoon by the time he left the Black
Tooth and headed for his aunt's house to shower the funk from his
skin. He drove Gusef's wreck of a Cadillac through the bends and
turns of Humosa Bay Road just to see the fog banks drift off the
dark-green waves topped with whitecaps as they broke frothy
against the cattails and saltgrass of the sandy shoreline.

At his aunt's driveway, marked from the coastal prairie by a
break in the oaks and a shrimpboat-shaped mailbox, Falk slowed to
turn but did not. In front of the two-car garage sat a tequilagold El
Camino.

He drove on. He didn't gun it. He didn't roar away in a cloud of
exhaust. He simply kept going. Same speed. For a hundred yards or
so, to the next intersection, where he took a left, another left after
that, then came to a stop in the middle of a cul-de-sac on a houseless
unnamed lane. This area was part of the subdivision that the devel-

opers had divided into lots, paved the streets, and installed fire hydrants and a sewer system. They had expected tourists and snowbirds to buy the lots and build bayside homes. Five years later, it was more or less abandoned. The rising waters of Humosa Bay and the destruction of Tanya made the whole idea seem a bit this side of greedy and foolish.

Falk parked in the cul-de-sac. He got out of the Caddy, looked right and left on the deserted street, as if someone could be following him, as if someone could be lying in wait. He saw nothing human. A bulldozer in a vacant lot, a scarecrow made of mop handles and burlap at the controls. Atop its basketball head sat a white hard hat. Beyond that, scraggly palm trees in the fog. Falk stared at the scarecrow for a moment. He half expected it to speak. A coyote trotted into an oak thicket on the other side of the road, like a spirit dog.

Falk left the keys in the Caddy and opened the back driver's-side door, rummaged in the junk that filled the floorboards. He came up with a tire iron. A four-way lug wrench it was, a black metal bar the shape of a cross. He held it for a moment as he stood beside the open door of the Caddy. The tool made him feel foolish, as if it were a steel crucifix for him to carry.

The cul-de-sac dead-ended right behind Falk's aunt's house. He cut across a marshy vacant lot, carrying the lug wrench behind his back. He felt as if he were masquerading as a thug. In the backyard he was tempted to drop it on the barbecue grill and go inside the house unarmed. But he didn't. He kept walking, his stomach floating up in his body like the globs of red goo in the lava lamp in the bedroom he shared with his bleached-haired cousin.

When he reached the back door, his hands were trembling. The wrench felt impossibly heavy. His body seemed disconnected, as if the strings tying it together had grown frayed. This did not have to end in violence and retribution.

His hands trembled now and were untrustworthy. He opened the screen door slowly, its springs creaking as it swung out. The whistle and palm-frond hiss of the north wind swallowed the sound. Falk could see nothing through the square of window in the back door. Only his reflection staring back at him, a green strip of yard over which hovered an inkwash of fog and white sky behind.

He leaned in close, seeing through the shadow he cast in the glass. In the house, a hallway darkened and motionless, a pair of rubber fisherman's boots leaned against the wall. He shifted the lug wrench into his left hand. He took the doorknob in his hand and turned it so as to make no sound.

The house quiet. Falk wiped his feet out of sheer good manners and fear of pissing off his aunt.

He stood and listened. The hum of a refrigerator compressor. The click of a wall clock in the hallway, an old-fashioned thing in the shape of Texas, decorated with bluebonnets and the silhouettes of longhorns. He could hear only the faintest of whisperings from the other end of the house. From the bedrooms. He shifted the lug wrench back to his right hand. He moved on.

He knew he might be in over his head. He had never hit a man before. Truth be told, he didn't really know the first thing about it. But he'd witnessed such crimes in movies and made his way through the quiet house, unprepared for the worst.

He reached the main hallway to turn left toward the bedrooms and what vague whispering scuffling sound he could hear but faintly. Out the picture window of the living room he had a clear view of the driveway.

The El Camino was gone. A wave of heat passed through his body as if he'd been injected with something wicked good. He walked more loosely now to the front door and opened it. The whoosh broke the tension and did much toward putting his psyche back together. The fog was even thicker now, like a flowing river of white cotton nightgowns. It cut the bay road from view.

A small plane flew invisible above, its engine muffled but distinct through the blank white sky. A flock of Canada geese passed low over the yard, honking. The driveway was empty as if it had always been and always would be. As if Gabriel Perez and his gold El Camino did not exist.

As Falk stood at the door, he realized night was coming. It was getting darker.

What are you doing? asked Leesha. Her eyes were pink and moist, her cheeks puffy, her blond hair disheveled. Why are you standing there?

I came home. That's all.

Then why are you holding that? She pointed to the lug wrench.

Falk started to lie, then stopped. He looked at the fog and told her he'd seen an El Camino in the drive. One that he didn't think belonged there.

What were you going to do with that? Hit him?

I don't know. I just thought. Well. Maybe.

Don't you learn anything? She took the lug wrench from his hand and held it, shook her head. He could tell then that she had been crying and was fighting back tears again. Her voice sounded funny.

I won't just stand there and let somebody hurt you.

She stared at him, her eyes shining. She remembered one of the last things Gabriel had said. It was after she had told him she was going to have his baby. He was buttoning his jeans, facing away, quiet. He tucked in his shirttail, sat down to pull on his boots. Finally he looked at her. You didn't tell nobody, did you?

What? You think I'm stupid?

I don't think you're stupid. I don't think you're anything, he said. All I know is we better keep this hush-hush. We'll take care of it. Later. Let me think. Right now I got to be someplace, about a new job, maybe. Better money. We're going to need it, right?

He had kissed her cheek. It was the only time he had ever kissed her cheek. Then he was gone.

GABRIEL DISAPPEARED. The tequilagold El Camino vanished from the streets of Goodnight. For good. Leesha called his phone number until the phone company cut it off. Her mother saw her in the hallway, with the phone in her hand.

Honey? she said. Who is it?

Nobody, said Leesha. Never mind.

So much went unspoken. Leesha sickened in the morning chill and moped at the window, watching the gray air for some relief from anguish. She could not find a place to put her disappointment. She carried it with her throughout the days and expressed it in everything she said.

What's got into you? asked her mother.

Leesha pressed buttons on the TV remote, shook her head, and wouldn't lift her face, her eyes downcast and glassy.

It's not drugs, is it?

Leesha did not reply, but her chin was trembling and tears ran down the sides of her nose.

Her mother shook her head and said, Good Lord. Then it must be a boy.

Leesha bit her lip. In a voice faint and cracking, she said, Everything is totally ruined.

What do you mean? What's ruined?

My life.

Eventually Leesha told her the truth. Or most of it. Her mother hugged her, squeezed tight her bones, smelled her hair. She kissed her forehead. Oh, my baby. She shook Leesha's shoulders softly. Oh, you stupid thing. She pulled her daughter close again and hugged her so tightly it hurt. She kissed her hard and whispered that she loved her, that everything would be fine. That she wasn't the first foolish girl in the world. That she would not be the last.

IN THE TIME after the flood mosquitoes filled the air like swarms of vampires the size of eyelashes. Everyone seemed to have the flu. The air itself seemed corrupt and infected. Mr. Buzzy dropped from sight. With the Black Tooth Café closed for repair and renovation, his absence from the streets and oyster-shell alleys, hobbling down the road on his bent cypress crutch, went unnoticed. One day in the fogs of late December, on lunch break from putting new Sheetrock on the café's walls, Gusef asked Falk, Where is old man Buzzy? I miss miserable son of bitch. When I see him I think, Thank God I have two legs.

After sandwiches, Gusef lit a cigarette and shuffled through the dusty bands of sunlight that illuminated the wrecked dining room. The tables were stacked atop one another and their spindly legs cast slanting shadows. Gusef returned with a bottle of cold Polish vodka from the freezer in back and two shot glasses. He poured one for Falk and one for himself, the clear liquid thick as syrup.

You are too young perhaps. But we do not care. He told Falk to lift his glass and down it in one gulp. To Old Man Buzzy, he called out, and tossed back the shot.

After swallowing the drink, Falk's eyes watered and he coughed.

Gusef frowned. Come on. What? You know how to drink, yes? I am not sure about you. Try another and we see.

They downed another shot. Falk wiped his eyes and tried to keep his face from scrunching up. Is that good vodka? he asked.

Gusef snorted. Is good vodka, he said. Is not good. Is best.

He lit another cigarette and stared at the stack of drywall sheets, four feet wide by eight feet long, gray against the exposed yellow pine of the two-by-four frame wall.

Fuck drywall, I say. We finish some other time.

He poured them another shot of vodka.

Maybe never, he added.

Oh, we're almost there, said Falk. Another couple weeks and you'll be open again.

Gusef shrugged. Does not matter. We now have unpleasant journey to drive.

He sighed and explained that he feared for Mr. Buzzy. Gusef had asked around and heard from Big Al at the liquor store that Buzzy had not bought a drop for a couple weeks. Bad sign, said Gusef. He may be home sick. That what I think. We must go see.

They drove down Shoreline to the Tombs. The wall of debris was still there beside Pirate's Lane, but had been pushed aside by bulldozers. The trailer park was in somewhat better shape now, though still weedy and woebegone.

Gusef was uneasy and vodka-flushed. He drove down the narrow lane into the trailer park.

America the beautiful, he said, shaking his head. Mosquito-infested swamp with view of ugly ocean. God bless U.S. fucking A.

Oh, come on, said Falk. It's not so bad.

No. Is not so bad. Is worse.

They parked beside Mr. Buzzy's trailer and got out. The neighbor's dog began barking. Gusef crouched to peer through a foggy glass pane. A cloth hanging inside obscured the view. He knocked, rattling the door. Falk tucked his hands in his back pockets and looked around.

The air smelled rank with rotting vegetation. Stacks of palm fronds and brown banana-tree leaves clogged the space between the drive and the trailer. A gang of purplesheened grackles croaked and gurgled in the limbs of the live-oak trees. After a moment Gusef banged again.

Mr. Buzzy! Old man! Are you there?

No answer came. The bodies of dead black crickets covered the concrete steps. Mosquitoes hovered in the air. One bit Falk on the forehead until he felt the sting and slapped it, leaving a smear of his blood like a benediction for Lent.

Gusef opened the door.

The smell that had been merely rank became sickening. Falk pinched his nose and coughed.

Jesus fucking son of bitch, said Gusef. This no good.

He was squinting, his wide forehead rippled with wrinkles.

You go inside, he told Falk. I too old for this.

I'm not, I mean, I think, you know. No way. I ain't going in there.

Gusef rubbed his forehead. Someday this happen to me, he said. With that he crouched low and stepped inside. Falk heard him coughing from where he stood, then a groan. Mumbled maledictions, rantings against a God uneared and eyeless.

Gusef emerged, holding his breath. He headed for the pickup. Falk climbed inside. Gusef started the truck and breathed deeply.

He was good man, he said. He was drunk, yes, but who of us is perfect? We all have such things. Weaknesses, yes. But he was good. He had one leg!

Gusef pulled out of the trailer park and headed toward town.

Imagine that, my young *amigo*. One leg. You be careful and keep both of yours, okay?

I'll try, said Falk.

If someone asks for your leg, you tell them, Go fuck yourself. I need both to get around, you tell them.

Falk nodded. Okay. I won't let it go.

Even if Una ask for your leg. You say, Fuck yourself. They are my legs!

Gusef was shouting now.

My legs and I need them!

On The Day of this fisherman's Viking burial, the sea was the bleached color of cataract eyes. In the chill and gloom they held a memorial service for the one-legged Mr. Buzzy who had died of West Nile. Gusef paid for his cremation, then cooked up a beach-side memorial service rather than keep the ashes in an urn.

Old Man Buzzy deserves better than box on shelf, he said.

They gathered on the white oyster-shell beach of Tin Can Point to honor him. Falk and Gusef carried Buzzy's skiff, the boat in which he'd fished the waters of Red Moon Bay for years until he'd lost his leg. They lifted it upside-down above their heads and lugged it to the shoreline. There they placed it with a gravelly crunch on the white ears of the oyster shells. It was a heavy old thing bleached and cracked by the sun and rain. The man and boy grunted with the effort. The rest, some twenty-odd souls, followed behind. Una was dressed in black. Her hair hid her face like a curtain of grief.

Leon the bartender lugged a jerry can of gasoline, wobbling as he walked through the egret marsh to the fishbone shoreline.

The sky wheeled with white and gray laughing gulls, a burst of shovelers beating the gray surface of Red Moon Bay as they hurried off, disturbed by this queer column of mourners. The air smelled of dank seaweed.

The mourners stood awkwardly about, waiting for some cue to begin. No dearly beloved we are gathered here, no priest to bring up the sacrifice of Jesus. A group of people cobbled together to take a moment for this man worth remembering as we all hope to be re-membered, no matter how quietly, when our time has run out and others live on.

Gusef unscrewed a vodka bottle, passed out white porcelain Chinese thimble cups decorated with a bamboo-and-panda pattern. He said, We all must drink. Buzzy would want this. I know this, yes.

Falk held his vodka-filled Chinese teacup awkwardly, as if it would spill. Dressed in black suit, white shirt, and wide tie, the bor-rowed jacket too short for his long arms, he resembled an appren-tice mortician.

Gusef waited for a moment, until all the ragtag group had a filled thimble of vodka. A bank of fog drifted across the water. Diaphanous, silvery white, palpable as a ship's crew of ghosts. Souls of the drowned and lost of Tanya come to join the chorus. The plank posts of the county fishing pier disappeared into the low white cloud. The mourners hunkered into their jackets, their noses and cheeks pink from the frosty air, sniffling.

Gusef raised high his shot glass. To Mr. Buzzy! He was good man. He was better man with one leg than many lousy sonsabitches with two!

He put the glass to his thin liver-colored lips below his bushy mustache and slowly drained it with a funeral-at-sea solemnity. The mourners followed him, raising arms and salutes to Mr. Buzzy and, in many hearts, to all the dead and lost of Goodnight.

He was a funny man, said Una. He always made me laugh. Even if he did usually smell pretty strong.

He was a man who liked his drink, said Leon. And from where I stand that's a minor sin at most. Man just tryin' to ease the pain. Ain't nothin' wrong with that.

Falk tried to speak, but no words came out of his mouth. He gave up. Gusef patted his back so forcefully he stumbled forward.

After a few moments Gusef told Falk to douse the skiff with gasoline. Falk crunched loudly across the oyster-shell beach as he emptied the five-gallon jerry can over the wooden boat, splashing gasoline across the gunwales and seat slats from bow to stern.

They placed the urn full of Mr. Buzzy's cremated remains on the middle slat with an intoxicated solemnity. The smell of gasoline tanged the air, overcoming the rank smell of beached catfish bloated at the shore.

Gusef brought forth a rolled sheet of newspaper and a butane lighter as Falk and Leon dragged the gasoline-soaked skiff into the waves.

The slowly drifting bank of fog enclosed them. Out of this whiteness flew a black skimmer, winging softly over the waves, its black wings and white body brilliant in the suddenness of its appearance, orange beak cutting a vee in the sluggish water until it vanished once again into the pale.

Gusef struggled to strike the butane lighter in the north breeze. When he did manage to get a flame, the wind sniffed it out before he could light the paper. Falk and Leon shivered in the cold waves, wet to their knees, keeping a hand on the skiff to prevent it from floating away.

The crowd shuffled, coughed.

Fucking piece-of-shit lighter good for nothing, said Gusef.

Let me try, said Falk.

Leon handed him a Zippo. The best there is, said Leon. Lights in the wind, I shit you not.

Falk cupped his hands and flicked it to flame. With a whoosh the skiff bloomed into flame. Leon shoved it, and the ebb tide pulled it into the fog of Red Moon Bay. The orange flames gushed, swirled, luffed, and crackled. They sent a plume of black smoke that mingled and merged with the white fog. The gray surface of the bay bloomed scarlet with the reflected fire. The mourners watched the flaming skiff dissolve into the fog and mist. For a moment the burning boat became an orange glow behind the veil of fog. As it disappeared, the sound of the crackling wood drifted out of the whiteness.

When all was completely quiet, save for the cries of gulls and the lap of water, they walked away. Sounds seemed amplified, detached from their visual signposts. The cries of unseen gulls gliding overhead, the clangs of bells on buoys, the bellow of foghorns.

Una rode with Gusef and Falk in Gusef's dented Cadillac, and on the ride home Gusef told Una he had a surprise for her. He did not look in her direction when he said this. He kept his eyes on the road. Falk also turned away and stared out the window.

What kind of surprise? she asked.

Do not worry pretty head, he said. Trust me.

I don't really have time for this.

He has something for you, said Falk.

Do not open big mouth, said Gusef. You will spoil moment.

I didn't tell her what it was.

You cannot keep mouth shut. I know this for sure.

What are you two talking about?

They pulled into the Sea Horse parking lot, taking a parking space beside a bright red VW Beetle. Falk stopped and turned to Una. He said, It was my idea originally. But you have to thank Gusef for actually doing it.

He and Gusef got out of the Caddy and stood there. Una kept her seat. She frowned at them through the windshield and held up her hands as if to ask what they were doing, and Falk waved at her to get out. He said, I told you, you have to thank Gusef.

Thank him for what?

Gusef opened the driver's-side door of the red VW and beckoned to Una.

Is yours, he said.

Una didn't move. What do you mean?

It's yours, said Falk. He explained how he had gone along when Gusef had bought Oscar Martinez's tow truck at the county salvage auction, and while they were there, they'd seen this VW for sale. He got it seriously cheap, said Falk. I mean, it's ridiculous, what you could buy there. I told him this would be perfect for you.

Gusef told Una he owed it to her. This is no charity. You work for me, is worth it, right? Take car. If you do not, I will dump it in bay. Is no use for me.

He placed the keys on the dashboard inside the car.

Falk smiled and added, He can't take it back.

Una stood beside the red car in the fog. Beneath its tires the oyster-shell gravel of the parking lot was piebald gray, speckled darker with barnacles encrusting the outer shells. She walked around the rear of the car, touched her fingers to the taillights, transparent red plastic revealing the bulbs inside. To her it seemed more of an idea of a car than the actual thing. Lacquered and unspotted. Her reflection shimmered in the curved sheen of the back window, stared back at her, mirror-image daughter of the lost.

I can't take this, she said. It's too much.

Bullshit, said Gusef. You must. I am offended if you do not.

Una made her way to the driver's side and leaned in to look at the instrument panel. I don't know, she said.

What don't you know? asked Falk. Take it for a spin. You need it. How else are you getting out of here?

Una wiggled herself into the bucket seat behind the steering wheel, checked her reflection in the mirror. As opposed to the witchy black figure with draping dark hair and distorted features in the back window's reflection, here in the rearview her features were complete and clear, a young woman with cinnamon-colored skin and dark brown eyes. An image of calm and quiet beauty.

Entranced and enchanted, for a moment she forgot about Gusef and Falk. And all the troubles of the months before. In the flower vase on the dash they had placed a handful of florist-bought daisies.

In The Beginning of the new year, the weather turned bitter cold. The sky was solid white, the mist turning to sleet, and flocks of ducks and curlews flew through the downtown streets of Goodnight, great blue herons and cormorants perched on the black pilings of the wrecked marina, mallards and pintails settling on the marshy vacant lot across from the soon-to-reopen café.

For several days the cold set records. The weatherman drew snowflakes with his Magic Marker. The pipes froze in the café and became one more thing to be replaced. Falk was also helping Gusef remodel the Sea Horse, and was painting there alone when he heard a banging at the office door.

He walked to the door, holding a paintbrush. His breath blew clouds. He passed the check-in counter and there she was, Una, smiling like she was glad to see him, her nose red from the cold.

Hey, stranger! She hopped inside the door and bussed him on the cheek, knocking him back a step, so he was barely able to keep his balance. Guess how I got here?

Let me see. You turned into a snow goose and flew.

I drove. She smiled. In my beautiful car.

He nodded. Look at you, he said. A complete person now, right?

She shrugged. Have you seen the bay? It's the strangest thing. Completely frozen.

Falk squinted. Oh, yeah. Right. I believe that.

She punched him lightly on the arm and insisted she was telling the truth. Honest. There's, like, icebergs out there. Una was wrapped in an ankle-length navy surplus coat with lapels and buttons on the sleeves, and she had the collar turned up, her black hair tucked inside a white wool scarf, mittens on her hands. Put on something warm and let's go skating.

They walked out on the Sea Horse's pier, climbed down the ladder at the end, and stepped onto the frozen surface of Red Moon Bay. It was mostly glaucous and gray, but parts of the frozen sheet were so clear you could see below the surface, like looking through the floor of a glass-bottomed boat.

I feel like Lady Jesus, said Una.

They held hands and skirted the perimeter of the pier, where the ice was thick around the black creosote pillars. Bubbles beneath the ice gurgled and slid. It was as if they had stumbled into another time and place, a dream of Newfoundland or Nova Scotia, seeing the bay frozen like that, the ski boats frozen in place.

Una found a sea trout in the shallows. What's all this nonsense about no fish? she cried. Here's a fish. Hey, buddy! We've been looking all over for you, she said, talking to the fish. She said a neighbor had told her that it wasn't just fish frozen in the shallows either, that there was something going on in the boat basin, the fish were running, and they were catching them like crazy.

They drove to the boat basin in her clean new car. The streets of Goodnight were apocalypse-empty, and Una drove through the red light, honking. At the café's parking lot they laughed to see the zebrafish had been returned to its place above the entrance. It had now become the centerpiece of the Swallowed Angel Café.

The papier-mâché horse legs and head were gone. In their place, extending out of the great fish's mouth, stood the wooden mermaid figure that had been the figurehead on Gusef's sunken sailboat. It had been brightly repainted, with a creamy white throat and rouge-red cheeks. From its shoulders rose two great wings. The mermaid's bosom was snow-white, full and pointed, nipples brown as toasted meringue.

Falk grinned. Rather buxom, isn't she?

Una shook her head. That Gusef, she said. He's the only man I know who could advertise a topless angel and get away with it.

Until Falk and Una reached the docks, the crowds were hidden. But there the parking lot was packed, and cars were lined up and jammed this way and that, all along the boat basin and the marina. People were getting out of their pickup trucks with rod-and-reel sets, bait buckets, tackle boxes, stringers, and plastic folding chairs. They carried their rods like delicate rifles, many of the rod tips arced and bent with the treble hooks on the ends of their lines dug into the cork handles. Snowbirds climbed down from their RVs, laughing and jubilant.

Falk and Una followed the crowds to the headwall of the boat basin, stepping carefully on the ice-slicked docks. Icicles hung from the booms of the shrimpboats, from the latticelike cords of the nets. They looked like a shipping fleet that had just crossed the Horn and had seen the shores of Patagonia. At the head wall that sheltered the basin from the choppy waves of Red Moon Bay, people congregated, packed into a vibrant line of bent and twitching fishing poles.

Some old-timers close to them were hauling in two at a time, using leaders so they could cast with two hooks. The bay wasn't frozen here because the water was too deep, but it was turgid and sloshy with chunks of ice that formed and broke off from the waves splashing against the head wall, and the orange marker buoys were draped with ice like wedding cakes.

The crowd cast their lines into the boat basin itself, whose calm waters were broken by the flash and thrashing of fins and gills as the people hauled in fish as fast they could reel in and cast back out. It was a running of red drum, a midsize game fish. The cold drove them into the calm waters of the boat basin, making them easy to catch.

Falk and Una saw Gusef in the middle of it all, wearing a comical fur-lined cap and blue-jean overalls. He looked like a booze-happy, well-fed Russian farmer. They made their way through the crowd to his side. He was pulling them in fast and said he didn't have time to chat. He knew this didn't happen every day, this moment of plenty, *este milagrito,* and he needed the fish.

ACKNOWLEDGMENTS

I'd like to offer much thanks and appreciation for the Texas Institute
of Letters and the University of Texas for their sponsorship of the J. Frank
Dobie-Paisano Fellowship, of which I was a grateful fellow in the spring of
2004, and at whose ranch near Austin much of this novel was written. Anne
Edelstein and Greg Michalson were enormously helpful. Y también,
muchas gracias a Joseph Obregon, para ayuda con el español.

And most importantly,
a simple thanks to Elizabeth,
who makes it all worthwhile.